First Debt
INDEBTED #2

PEPPER WINTERS

First Debt (Indebted #2)
Copyright © 2014 Pepper Winters
Published by Pepper Winters

All rights reserved. No part of this book may be reproduced or transmitted in any form, including electronic or mechanical, without written permission from the publisher, except in the case of brief quotations embodied in critical articles or reviews.

This is a work of fiction. Names, characters, businesses, places, events, and incidents are either the products of the author's imagination or used in a fictitious manner. Any resemblance to actual persons, living or dead, or actual events is purely coincidental.

This book is licensed for your personal enjoyment only. This book may not be re-sold or given away to other people. If you would like to share this book with another person, please purchase an additional copy for each person you share it with. If you are reading this book and did not purchase it, or it was not purchased for your use only, then you should return it to the seller and purchase your own copy. Thank you for respecting the author's work.

Published: Pepper Winters 2014: pepperwinters@gmail.com
Cover Design: by Ari at Cover it! Designs:
http://salon.io/#coveritdesigns
Proofreading by: Jenny Sims:
http://www.editing4indies.com
Proofreading by: Ericka: http://www.ericaedits.com
Images in Manuscript from Canstock Photos:
http://www.canstockphoto.com

This story isn't suitable for those who don't enjoy dark romance, uncomfortable situations, and dubious consent. It's sexy, it's twisty, there's colour as well as darkness, but it's a rollercoaster not a carrousel.

(As an additional warning please note, this is a cliffhanger. Answers will continue to be delivered as the storyline resolves, as will character motivations.)

Warning heeded…enter the world of debts and payments.

If you would like to read this book with like-minded readers, and be in to win advance copies of other books in the series, along with Q&A sessions with Pepper Winters, please join the Facebook group below:

Indebted Series Group Read

IF I HAD known my life would change so drastically, I might have planned a little better. Strategized a little smarter, researched a little deeper.

One moment I was the Darling of Milan, the next I was a Weaver Whore.

But despite my lack of skills and weapons, I wasn't ready to go down without a fight.

In fact, I prospered into a woman I'd always been too afraid to find.

I became more than Nila Weaver.

More than daughter, twin-sister, and seamstress.

I became the woman who would bring down a family's legacy.

I evolved into the woman who captured a Hawk.

Jethro

I STALKED TOWARD the stables and the very lodgings Nila had inhabited the night before.

The image of her bounding away—pristine naked skin glowing in the sunshine and long hair flowing like black silk—played on a loop inside my head.

Everything I'd been prepared for—every argument, every hardship I'd been drilled to expect—hadn't prepared me for the complication that was Nila Weaver. How could I understand and keep my bearings when the bloody woman had more personalities than a Picasso painting?

Sometimes naïve. Sometimes coy. Smart, fearful, proud, *gullible*.

And above all, evolving.

And rapidly.

I wasn't used to…mess. The chaos of a human psyche or the disgusting pull of emotions was not permitted in my world. In the short time I'd known her, she'd successfully made me feel something I had no fucking right to feel.

Don't admit it.

I balled my hands. No, I wouldn't admit it. I would never verbalize the slow burn of possession in my gut or the confusion in my mind when it came to understanding her.

Run, Nila. Run.

And she had.

Despite her nakedness, lack of sustenance, and the fact that my family had just finished abusing her, she'd glared into my eyes and bounded away like a deer bolting from a gun. A flash of vulnerability glowed on her face before she was swallowed by the forest.

I expected her to faint with her ridiculous condition—an experiment, as it were, to see what she would do when I pretended to give her what she wanted.

Run?

I never for a fucking moment thought she'd do it.

I expected her to cower. To beg. To cry for the men in her life who had let her down. But she'd done none of those things. I'd known her only briefly, yet she'd demanded more of me than any other woman ever had.

It wasn't permitted, and now that she'd run, she'd given away more of the disarray inside her. I'd glimpsed the perplexing woman who'd become my charge, prisoner, and plaything.

Someone who had successfully confused the shit out of me.

As much as you don't understand her, you want her. She came on your tongue, for fuck's sake.

I stopped in my tracks. She'd fought me on every turn, yet the moment I'd claimed her in front of my brothers, she'd given me ultimate control.

She'd spread her legs and forced her hips into my mouth, giving complete authority for me to lick and nibble and drive her high until she shattered, regardless if she meant to do it or not, she'd used me for pleasure.

She'd gotten off on me fingering her.

My cock stiffened.

The taste of her still lingered in my mouth—the phantom pressure of her cunt squeezing my tongue as she rocketed skyward and detonated. Her fingernails had scraped the table, hands spread thanks to the brothers holding her down. But she hadn't squirmed to get away from *me*.

No, she'd fought to get closer.

And I'd obliged.

Drowning myself in her scent, bruising my lips as I licked her harder and *harder*.

She'd squirmed and moaned and gasped. She'd delivered herself into my clutches, all because I knew how to make a woman come.

But she didn't just give me her pleasure.

Christ, no.

She'd given me the briefest taste of how divine it would be to own, not just her body, but her mind and soul, too.

It was fucking addicting.

It was fucking twisting with my head.

I growled under my breath, striding onward. The bloody hard-on I'd sported since she walked into my life poisoned me, turning me against everything I knew, everything I'd embraced since I learned the meaning of survival and discipline.

Hot lust tumbled through my veins.

How could I stay the cold beast I'd been groomed to be when my blood raged for another little taste? Another little indulgence of her tight, wet heat.

Shit, I was going to make myself come if I didn't stop thinking about her.

My cock rippled, totally agreeing.

I shook my head, breaking into a jog toward the stables.

You will remain everything you are.

You will.

There was no other choice in the matter.

I'd been taught to be the master of my emotions. I prided myself on embracing all that he taught me. One little Weaver bitch would not undermine me. This was the way of our world.

My world.

Her world.

No matter how she bewitched me, no matter how she turned my body and willpower against me, I wouldn't give in.

She'd learn that soon enough.

The moment I caught her, she'd learn her place. The moment I had her back in my arms, she'd never run again.

That was a fucking promise.

It's time to hunt.

The stables were empty apart from Kes's polo pony, my father's prized thoroughbred, Black Plague, and my ebony gelding, Fly Like The Wind. That was his show and hunting name. In private, I had another name for him.

Wings.

Because riding him allowed me to fly the fuck away from here and find a small sliver of freedom.

Nila wasn't the only one who wanted to run. Unlike my prey, I faced my demons and embraced them. I made them work for me, rather than control me, and forced them to submit by bowing at my fucking feet.

Just like I'd make her do the moment I found her.

The instant he saw me, Wings' velvet ears pricked, his metal shoes clicking against hay-strewn cobblestone.

A stable boy appeared from mucking out the stalls. "Sir?"

"Saddle him. I mean to leave in fifteen minutes."

You told her you'd give her forty-five.

I shrugged.

There was no point giving her any longer. Her feet would bleed from running barefoot. Her skin would bruise from whatever ludicrous illness she battled. And it would all be for nothing.

Contrary to what she thought of me, I wasn't a monster.

I needed her strong.

Plus, I could grant hours, days even for her to run—but she'd never make it to the boundary.

I knew that completely and utterly.

I knew, because I'd been in the exact same situation she was—only it hadn't been summer like it was now, but middle of winter. Training, he'd said. Masculine growth, he'd lectured.

Run in the snow, become the ice that drips from boughs and stems. Use the primal part of yourself to seek out the edge of our property, or pay the price.

Three days I'd run, jogged, and crawled. Three days I didn't find the boundary.

I was found the same way I would find Nila. Not through tracking or GPS or even the cameras dotted sparsely over the grounds.

No. I have much better means.

My lips twisted into a smile as I traversed the courtyard from stable to kennel. I whistled, listening to the scrabble of claws and excited yips inside. Then the hounds bounded from their home, bumping into each other, wriggling like they'd been electrocuted.

I stood tall, letting the sea of canines wash around my knees. Eleven in total, all with keen ears, sensitive smell, and the training of a hunter.

Leaving them to sniff manically around the yard, I headed into the tack room where supplies, medicines, and feed were stored for the horses.

My hands drifted over the blanket Nila had used.

My cock lurched, remembering how lost and young she'd looked with hay in her hair and eyes raw from tears. Yet she'd writhed on my fingers like a fucking minx. Her hips had tilted, seeking more as if she were born to be pleasured.

My balls ached for a release. Goddammit, I needed to come. Twice now she'd brought me to the edge, only to ruin the ending.

This wasn't me—I was never this sex-driven or clouded. I couldn't think straight.

The second I caught her, I was taking her. Rules be damned.

You think she wants you, knowing what you're going to do to her?

The question caught me in a trap with sharp teeth.

I froze.

What the hell sort of question was that?

One I'd never had before or even contemplated. My hands curled. I'd never considered someone else's wellbeing. Never been taught or shown how to be...compassionate. The closest thing I had to a friend was my younger brother, Kestrel. He somehow escaped the conditioning by Bryan Hawk. Kes took after our mother. God rest her soul.

And Daniel.

He took after the fucking psychopath who'd been our uncle until my father killed him for almost exposing us all those years ago.

Not for the first time, I wondered if my entire family tree was bat-shit crazy.

In the end, none of it mattered. Not heritage, or destinies, or debts.

The moment Nila came on my tongue, she owed me. Not my family. *Me*.

The least she could do was reciprocate.

Shaking my head, I gathered up a saddlebag and stuffed everything I would need inside. With each item I picked up, my heart thawed then refroze. A blanket of snow grew thicker with every heartbeat. As ice glittered and crept over my soul, the silence from my colliding thoughts deepened until all weakness, ideas of running, and traitorous concepts of betraying my family disappeared.

I sighed in relief as I slipped back into my icicle-barred cage.

You're tired, overworked, and dealing with a runaway. Keep your head in the game.

I knew what would happen if I lost control. I could *not* let that happen.

I checked my watch.

Twenty minutes.

Long enough. To her it would feel as if she'd run for miles. She would never know the difference.

Turning to go, I brushed past the shelf where my extra whips and spurs were stored. I grabbed one, sticking a whip through my belt.

It would come in handy if she disobeyed.

Taking a pair of sunglasses, I quickly traded my dress

shoes for knee-high riding boots, and checked inventory. Pity I didn't have time to change. Jeans were a bitch to ride in—terrible chafing on long excursions.

But this isn't going to be a long ride.

A smile stretched my lips. No, it wasn't going to be long. *But it will be fun.* And fun wasn't something I got to indulge in very often.

Exiting the gloomy tack room, I squinted in the bright sunlight and slipped the silver-tinted aviators over my eyes. Wings stood obediently by his hobbling post, his equine coat gleaming like the rare black diamonds we mined.

The foxhounds barked and threaded around each other like an organism, never taking their eyes off me as I gathered my reins and placed a foot into the stirrup. Swinging my leg over the massive animal, the rush of being on something so powerful whipped through my bones.

Wings was eighteen hands of pure fucking muscle. He was the fastest horse the Hawks' owned, excluding my father's race horse, Black Plague, and he hadn't been hunting in days.

He pranced in place, his large lungs huffing with anticipation.

The energy vibrating from his bulk infected me, reminding me who I was and the life of privilege I lived.

Twisting his head toward the open grounds of Hawksridge Hall, I dug my spurs into Wings' side.

An insane surge of power detonated through the animal's muscles. Wings went from stationary to flying, his hooves clattering with speed. With a sharp whistle, I summoned my canine companions.

The sharp scent of dug-up turf hit my nostrils as we tore across the grass.

I'm coming for you, Nila Weaver.

I'm coming.

Over the roar of galloping thunder, I commanded, "Chase her."

Nila

MY LUNGS BURNED.

My feet stung.

My legs ached.

Every inch of me screamed with fear.

Run. Run. *Run*.

I lowered my head, pushing harder, forcing my body to find non-existent energy and propel myself from hell toward salvation.

How long did I run? I didn't know. How far did I get? Probably not very.

But no matter the stitches in my side or the spasms in my lungs, I kept going. Kept running. I thanked God for my endless nights of pounding the treadmill, and for the first time in my life, was thankful for my small chest size.

Shadows chased my every step. The sun remained blocked by the tree canopy. The yellow glow was still light, still bright, coaxing me on, screaming at me to get up when I stumbled, and ordering my tears to stop as I gasped for breath.

I kept running—zigzagging as much as I could, cutting through a stream, and almost rolling my ankle on the slippery rocks below. I did everything I'd ever seen survivalists do when being hunted.

With my heart whizzing, I bypassed woodland trails,

avoided muddy paths, and obscured my scent as much as possible.

But I knew in my heart, it wouldn't be good enough.

He'll find you.

My body begged to stop and let the inevitable happen. To stop punishing myself for no purpose. My mind howled in frustration as lactic acid burned in my limbs.

It won't work. Give up.

Go on, just...stop.

I shook my head, driving myself harder.

He'll catch you.

It wasn't a matter of if, but when.

I could run for years, and he would still find me. How did I know? I didn't trust him.

I didn't believe he'd let me get away so easily. Everything about him was a carefully scripted lie. Why should his word be any different?

I had no doubt if he *didn't* find me, something else would—a snare, a trap—something just waiting to ambush its prey.

Every footfall I tensed, waiting for death—wondering if that last step would trigger a net or an arrow to my heart.

Stop running.

Just...stop, Nila.

My breathless inner voice was tired and hungry and completely worn out. My muscles cramped. My mind seized with too many questions.

At least it was summer, and I didn't have to combat the cold on top of everything else. My skin glistened with sweat from exercising so hard.

But I hated the defeat in my soul—the rapidly spilling courage and hope.

This wasn't about the chase. We all knew who would win. It was about defiance. The word that I never knew or put into practice until last night, but now I lived and breathed it. I would be the most defiant thorn, stabbing holes in Jethro's carefully made plans.

I would never be able to win. The only way I had a chance at surviving long enough to reap vengeance on the men who ruined my ancestors was to fight his ice with fire.

I had to burn.

I had to blaze.

I had to cinder his beliefs and control to the ground. And smear his soul with the ashes of his sins.

A loud howl came on the breeze.

My knees locked, slamming me to a standstill.

No. Please, no.

My heart squeezed. I should've guessed. He wouldn't run after me like a typical chase. Why would he waste his energy hunting in the wrong direction?

He was smarter than that. Colder than that. He'd use the tools he had to make sure this little inconvenience was over and dealt with. Of course, he would use the very animals who'd become my friends last night.

Teaching me not one but two lessons in quick succession. One, the animals currently tracking me, currently hunting me, were not my friends, no matter how warm and cosy they'd been last night. And two, everything here, no matter human or animal, would not hesitate to kill me.

The thought depressed then infected me with strength I'd only just become acquainted with. There was no hope at making Jethro feel. The only hope I had was to fight ruthlessness with ruthlessness.

I had to contest him on every step and ignite that spark buried deep within.

Another howl and a bark.

Energy shot through my body, hot and bullet-fierce.

I took off again, sprinting down a small hill, holding onto branches as a rush of vertigo threatened to spill me into nettles and brambles.

The collar on my throat was heavy, but at least it had warmed. The diamonds no longer felt alien but a part of me. The courage of my ancestors. The spirit-strength of women I'd never met, living in a piece of jewellery throbbing with their guidance and energy.

The hatred and repulsion I felt toward the collar disappeared. Yes, the Hawks had given it to me, sentencing me to death with an action I couldn't think about, but they'd given me a piece of my family. A piece of history I could use to my advantage.

Another bark, followed by a loud whistle.

You can't outrun him.

I scowled at my pessimism.

But you can hide.

I shook my head, fighting tears as a twig dug into the sole of my foot.

I wouldn't be able to hide. He came with foxhounds. Their noses were legendary.

Up high. Get up high.

I skidded to a stop. My neck craned as I peered up the length of a knobby-looking tree. The branches were symmetrically placed, the leaves not exactly thick but its trunk strong enough to take me from earth to sky.

I'd never climbed anything in my life. I could fall to my death. I could cripple myself when I suffered a vertigo wave. I'd never been stupid enough to try.

You've never had to run for survival either.

Shoving useless fears away, I moved toward the tree with out-stretched hands. It didn't matter I'd never climbed one. It didn't matter I'd avoided all gym games and apparatuses, because I only ended up getting hurt.

I would climb the damn thing and conquer it.

I have no choice.

Either stay on the ground and sit quietly for him to arrive, run blindly through woodland, or climb.

I'll climb.

My toes gripped the base of the tree as I reached for the first branch. I put my weight on it.

It snapped.

Shit!

Another bark—loud and clear, just over the ridge.

I moved.

Scrabbling at the tree, I hugged the rough bark and hurled myself up, reaching like a crazed, climb-retarded monkey for a branch just out of grabbing distance. I didn't think I'd make it. I closed my eyes in preparation for a painful fall, but by some miracle, my fingers latched around the bough, clinging harder than ever before.

Go. *Go!*

I gave myself over to a skill I'd never used but hoped remained dormant in some part of my human evolution. I placed my foot against the bark, pulling upward with my hands. I reached for the next.

And the next.

And the next.

My breath came hard and ragged, my heart an overworking drum.

I used the tree as my own personal stepladder to freedom, climbing higher and higher until I daren't look down in case I blacked out and tumbled from heaven to hell.

A large thundering came, overshadowing the yips and excited barks of dogs. The leaves around me shuddered as footfalls of a bigger beast came closer.

Had Jethro come with others? Would Daniel be with him? Or even his father?

My skin rippled with hatred. I meant what I'd said. I would find a way to kill them all before this was over. I wouldn't let them spill any more Weaver blood. It was the Hawks' turn.

I'll make them pay.

Turning slowly, cursing my shaking legs and suddenly nervous hands, I faced the forest floor from which I'd climbed. I was at least two and half stories up.

I closed my eyes, swallowing hard.

Don't fall. Don't even think about falling.

Faintness existed on my outer vision, teasing me with the awfulness of what could happen. I dug my fingernails into the bark, lowering myself slowly onto the branch. The minute I was sitting, with the roughness of the tree biting into my unprotected behind, I wrapped an arm around the trunk and sat wedged against the wood.

I looked around for weapons, but there were none. No pine cones. No easily snappable branches to stab him with. All I had was the element of disappearing. A naked girl vanishing into the green haze of the forest.

My heart lodged in my throat as the first dog appeared. I didn't recognise him from the night spent in the kennels. He whirled around and around, sniffing the spot where I'd stood.

Another dog appeared, then another and another, pouring from the woods like ants, growling in delight at the strength of my trail.

Distress gripped my stomach.

Go away, damn you.

Then, *he* arrived.

Sitting proudly astride a black horse, so big it looked like a beast from the underworld, he cantered into being. His polished boots soaked up the dappling sunlight; a whip with a diamond wedged on the handle glinted menacingly.

He looked in his element.

A gentleman out hunting with his faithful steed and gallant party of dogs. His silvering hair sparkled like tinsel in the sun. His ageless face the epitome of ferocity and winning.

In his late twenties, Jethro wore command like one would wear cologne. His strong jaw, pursed lips, and sculptured brow shouted power—*true* power. And there was nothing anyone could do about it.

Sitting with his back ramrod straight and hands fisted in the horse's reins, he was…majestic. It didn't matter if I hated him or wanted him. That fact would always be true.

Excitement blazed in his eyes as he scanned the undergrowth, a smile teasing his lips.

How long had this farce been going on? An hour? Maybe two? Had he kept his word and given me the full forty-five minutes? Somehow, I doubted it.

"Find her, goddammit," he snapped, losing his smile and

glaring at the dogs.

The canines wove around his horse's legs, sniffing, darting into bushes only to come back to try all over again.

Jethro spun in his saddle, planting a hand on the rump of his horse, glowering into the dense foliage. "Have you stopped running, Ms. Weaver, or have you somehow managed to trick my companions?" His voice caused the leaves to shiver, almost as if they wished to hide me further.

I held my breath, hoping to God he didn't look up.

A foxhound with a large black ear barked and took off down the path I would've continued on if I hadn't decided to prolong my freedom by hiding.

Jethro shook his head. "No. She's around here. Find her."

The dog licked its muzzle, baying in the direction its wriggling body wanted to go. The rest of the dogs, either brainwashed by their leader or picking up on the scent of rabbit, all joined in the urge to leave.

My heart galloped. *Please, let him go.*

I might have a chance after all.

The horse pranced—hyped up on the dogs' energy, wanting to chase after them.

Jethro stayed steadfast, his hand expertly holding the reins so tight the poor beast had no choice but to tread on the spot. His long legs wrapped hard around the animal, sticking glinting silver spurs into its sides. "Wait," he growled.

The horse huffed, tossing its head, fighting the tight possession of its mouth. It cantered in place, puffing hard through velvet nostrils.

The dogs disobeyed.

Their patience was done and with a loud howl, they took off in a cloud of tan, white, and black.

"Christ's sake," Jethro muttered. "Fine." Digging his heels hard, the horse broke into a gallop, disappearing in a whirl of black through the undergrowth.

Shakes. They attacked me hard and fast the second he'd disappeared.

Hope attacked me second.

Unbelievable hope hijacked my limbs turning me into shivering jelly until I was sure the entire tree vibrated. Did I actually stand a chance at making it to freedom? Could I make it to the boundary and escape their clutches?

I could save all of us—my father, brother, future daughters.

"Life is complicated, Threads. You don't know the half of it." My father's voice popped into my head. Anger filled me. Dreadful, terrible anger toward the man who was supposed to keep me safe. If he knew this would happen, why hadn't he protected me? I'd always trusted him. Always followed his rule explicitly. To see him as human who made a mistake—*many* mistakes—hurt.

A lot.

A wave of sickness had me clutching the tree; I swallowed back the misfortune of having vertigo along with the emotional upheaval of what I'd lived through.

The foreignness of dried saliva on my body made my skin crawl. The memory of shattering beneath Jethro's tongue totally blasphemous.

The sun glinted through the canopy—highlighting trails of where men had licked me.

My stomach threatened to evict the emptiness inside. I was hungry, dehydrated, and cracked out on adrenaline. But beneath it all, my soul ached with growing pains. My claws were forming, my tail twitching with annoyance.

It didn't escape my knowledge that, as a kitten, I'd stayed on the ground. But now I was in a tree—did that make me a panther? A feline predator that hunted from above, unseen?

I liked that idea.

Forcing myself to concentrate on the trees surrounding me, I strained my ears to hear.

Only insects and birds. No Jethro.

How far was it to the boundary? What direction should I go?

Time seemed to slow, braiding with the fluffy white clouds above as if there were no cares in the world.

It was hypnotic.

The lack of sustenance in my stomach made me tired; I needed a rest.

Just a little one.

The screech of a crow snapped me awake.

Shit!

How could I have faded out like that?

How long had passed? It could've been hours or just minutes.

I have no idea.

My heart rabbited, energy heating my limbs. *Move. Run again.*

Jethro was far away. I couldn't hear him or the howls of hounds.

Looking at the ground, my lungs crawled into my mouth. Down there, I didn't feel safe…up here, I did.

Move!

I couldn't move.

I would probably cling to my sanctuary until I died of hunger and became fossilized. To be found like a mosquito wrapped in amber a thousand years from now.

The thought made me smile.

Would they be able to bring me back to life like in *Jurassic Park*, outliving the Hawks by thousands of years to finally have the last laugh?

A twig snapped below, wrenching my attention back to the forest floor.

Oh, shit.

Squirrel stood below, looking directly into my eyes. His bristle tail wagged back and forth, his tongue lolling happily. He yipped, scrabbling at the tree.

Tears.

I couldn't hold them back.

The one dog that'd granted such comfort last night was

the one to ruin my future today.

How could you?

I wanted to scream at him for destroying me.

Jethro stepped silently from the shadows like a glacial ghost. His horse was hidden, along with the pack of dogs. In his hand, he held the whip and a saddlebag.

He touched the end of the whip to his temple in a salute. "Well played, Ms. Weaver. I didn't think you'd have the coordination to climb. I must admit, foolhardy of me not to think of all avenues." A smile crept across his lips. "I suppose desperation will make one do things they might not ordinarily be able to achieve."

Stepping forward, he nudged Squirrel out of the way. "What I would like to know is how did you manage to stay up there? Did you not have another one of your annoying fainting incidents?"

The oxygen in my lungs turned into spikes and spurs, digging painfully into my sides. I held tighter to the tree, wondering if I could kill him from up here.

When I didn't respond, he smirked. "You look positively wild up there. My own little forest creature, caught in my web."

My arms lashed tighter around the trunk.

Jethro shifted, his movements quiet even with the leaf matter littering the earth. The happiness from his victory dissolved. "Come down. It's over. I've won." He smiled, but it didn't reach his eyes. "Or do me a favour and fall out. That vertigo has to be useful for something." Spreading his arms, he muttered, "Go on, I'll catch you."

The strength that seemed to feed off Jethro's cruelty churned hot in my stomach. "You should know me by now. I won't obey you. You or the rest of your family."

He chuckled. "Found a backbone up there, did you?"

I bared my teeth. "I found it the moment you stole me from my family and showed me what a monster you are."

He held up the whip, a shadow falling over his features. "I didn't *steal* you—you belong to us. I only took what was rightfully mine. And I'm no monster."

My heart raced. "You don't know the meaning of the word, so how can you define yourself?"

He narrowed his eyes. "I think the height of the tree is giving you false confidence. I doubt you'd be talking to me that way if you were down here." He twitched the whip. "Where I could reach you, hit you, make you behave like you ought to."

He's testing you.

I tilted my chin, looking down my nose. "You're right. I probably wouldn't, but right now I have the advantage, and I mean to use it."

He laughed, absently stroking Squirrel's head as the dog plonked himself by Jethro's feet. "Advantage? I wouldn't go that far, Ms. Weaver."

My skin crawled at the use of my last name. He didn't use it out of consideration or even because the address was my identity—he used it to keep the barrier between us cold and impenetrable.

What is he so afraid of? That my first name will make him waver in his ludicrous family's goals?

"Why don't you call me Nila?" I leaned forward, not caring I was naked or stuck in a tree. I had the power for however long I kept him talking. "Are you afraid using my first name is too personal? That you'll start to feel something for me?"

He sneered. "You're doing it again."

"Doing what?"

"What you did at the stables. Showing me sides of you that you've kept hidden, in the hopes it will spark some sort of humanness in me." He shook his head. "I'm not someone you can manipulate."

A small smile stretched my lips. "I already did." Gathering my leaf-tangled hair, I draped it over my shoulder. The last dregs of sunshine disappeared behind a cloud, leaving us in green shadows.

"What?" His nostrils flared, his temper sparking like an uncontrolled blaze.

I smiled, enjoying his annoyance. He claimed he was cold-hearted and impervious. He lied.

I'll show him. I'll prove he's as ill-equipped to play this charade as I am.

"Do you want me to paint it out for you? To show you how hypocritical you are?"

He grabbed Squirrel's ear, making the dog flinch. Squirrel moved away, an angry reproof in his black eyes. "Careful, Ms. Weaver," Jethro whispered. "Everything you say up there will have consequences when you get down here."

I refused to let fear quiet me. Not when I had the freedom to speak—no matter how brief.

"Nila. My name is *Nila*. Say it. It seems we're going to be spending a lot of time together, so you might as well save yourself breath when you need to summon me. Or do you like reminding yourself that I'm a Weaver? Your so-called hated enemy. Do you need to reinforce that knowledge every time? How about that beloved silence you keep claiming you wield? You think you hide so well. Listen up. You don't."

Jethro backed away, crossing his arms. A dark, unreadable expression etched his face. "I call you by your last name out of *respect*." He spat the last word. "We aren't friends. We aren't even acquaintances. We've been thrown into this together, and it's up to me to make the fucking rules on how you'll be treated."

We both froze, breathing hard.

Oh, my God.

He's been thrown into this. My mind charged ahead with questions.

Did he not want this?

Was he forced, same as me?

Jethro hissed, "Get out of the fucking tree. I want to be home before dark."

Hoarding my questions and the small furl of hope, I pointed at the sky. "It's already dusk. How long did you hunt me, Jethro? How long did you search for a vulnerable, weak, little Weaver?"

He ignored my questions, focusing on the last part of my

sentence. "You think you're weak?"

"No, *you* think I'm weak."

"How so?"

I straightened my shoulders. There was a...genuineness in his tone. The animosity between us suddenly...disappeared. It took me a few seconds to answer. My voice was quieter, less abrasive. "You think I'll put up with what you plan to do with me—that I won't fight? That I won't do everything in my power to stop you from killing me?"

His face battled with a smirk and understanding. He settled on a frosty grimace. "Of course, I expect it. If you didn't, I'd say you were already dead inside. No one wants to die."

I had no reply to that. A chill darted over my skin. For the first time, we were talking. So much had happened since we met. There was so much between us that it felt as if we'd been fighting this war for years—which maybe we had, and we just didn't know it.

"What do you mean to do with me?" I whispered, dropping all pretence and opting for truth.

He jerked, his eyes tightening at the softness in my tone. "I've told you."

I shook my head. "No, you haven't." I looked away. "You've threatened me. You've made me come in a room full of men, and you've told me the method of my death. None of that—"

"You're saying that isn't being honest about your future?"

I glared. "I wasn't finished. I was going to say, before you rudely interrupted, what *else* is there?"

His mouth parted in surprise. "Else? You're asking what else there is to this debt?"

"Forget the debt. Tell me what to expect. Give me that at least, so I can prepare myself."

He cocked his hip, trailing the whip through the rotten leaves by his feet. "Why?"

"Why?"

He nodded. "Why should I give you what you want? This

isn't a power exchange, Ms. Weaver."

I bit my lip, wincing at the sudden hunger pains in my stomach. What did I have that he wanted? What could I hope to bribe him with or entice some feeling of protectiveness and kindness?

I have nothing.

I hung my head.

Silence existed, thick and heavy like the rolling dusk.

Amazingly, Jethro murmured, "Come down, and I'll answer three questions."

My head shot up. "Give me answers now, before I come down."

He planted his boots deeper into the mulch-covered dirt. "Don't push me, woman. You've already gotten more conversation out of me than my fucking family. Don't make me hate you for causing me to feel weak."

"*You* feel weak?"

"Ms. fucking Weaver. Climb down here right now." His temper exploded, smashing through his iceberg shell, giving me a hint at the man I knew existed.

A man with blood as hot as any other.

A man with so many unresolved issues, he'd tied himself into untieable knots.

My heartbeat clamoured as Jethro's ice fell back into place, blocking everything I just glimpsed.

I sucked in a breath. "Hypocrite."

He seethed. "*What* did you just say?"

"You heard me." Standing on awkward legs, I hugged the tree. "Three questions? I want five."

"Three."

"Five."

Jethro moved suddenly, stomping to the base of the tree, gripping the bottom branch. "If you make me climb up there to get you, you'll be fucking sorry."

"Fine!" I moved carefully, wondering how the hell I would climb down. "Call me Nila and I'll obey."

He growled under his breath. "Goddammit, you push

me."

Someone has to. Someone has to smash that hypocritical shell.

I waited, face pressed against knobbly bark, fighting against the weakness in my limbs from exhaustion and hunger.

The mere thought of climbing down terrified me.

Jethro paced, crunching the undergrowth beneath his black boots. He snapped, "I will *never* say your first name. I will never be controlled into doing something I don't want to do ever fucking again—*especially* by you. So, go ahead, stay in your tree. I'll just camp down here until you either fall or wither away. I don't revel in the thought of you dying in such a fashion. I don't relish the conversation I would have when I returned empty-handed with just a diamond collar sliced from your lifeless neck, but never think you can make me do something I don't want to do. You'll lose."

He smashed the whip against the tree trunk, making me jump. "Is that *quite* understood?"

His temper seethed from below, covering me like a horrible quilt of scorn. I pressed my forehead against the bark, cursing myself.

For a moment, he'd seemed normal.

For one fraction of time, I didn't fear him because I saw something in him that might, just might, be my salvation.

But he'd been pushed too far by others. He'd reached his limit and had nothing else to give. He'd shut down, and the brief glimpses I saw weren't hope—they were historic glints at the man he might've been before he'd been turned into…this.

I climbed.

It was a lot harder going down than going up. My eyesight danced with grey, my knees wobbled, and sweat broke out on my skin, even though I was freezing now the night had claimed the day.

I battled with him and lost.

Time to face my future.

The closer I came to the ground, the more fear swallowed me.

I cried out as Jethro's cold hands latched around my waist,

plucking me from the tree as if I were a dead flower, and spinning me to face him.

His beautiful face of sharp lines and five o'clock shadow was shaded with darkness. The hoots of owls and trills of roosting birds surrounded us.

"I have a good mind to whip you." His voice licked over me with frost.

I dropped my eyes. I had no more energy. It was depleted. Gone.

When I didn't retaliate, he shook me. "What? No reply from the famous Weaver who swore at my father and brotherhood and earned the right to run for her freedom?"

I looked up, stealing myself against his golden eyes. "Yes and what was the point?"

"There's a point to everything we do. If you've forgotten it, then you're blinded by self-pity."

A ball of fire rekindled in my belly. "Self-pity? You think I *pity* myself?"

He shook his head. "I don't think. I know." Letting me go, he grabbed the saddlebag resting against another tree and pulled out a blanket. Spreading it over roots and crinkly leaves, he ordered, "Sit, before you fall."

I blinked. "We're not—we're not leaving for the Hall?"

He glowered. "We'll leave when I'm damn well ready. Sit."

I sat.

Jethro

WHAT THE FUCK are you doing?

I couldn't answer that. I had no clue.

I should throw her over my shoulder and escort her back to Hawksridge. Instead, I made her sit. In the middle of a forest. At dusk.

What the fuck?

Nila sat by my feet smiling sadly as Bolly, the top foxhound, nuzzled into her naked side—his wet nose nudged against her breast as he whined for attention.

She sighed, hugging him close, pressing a kiss into the ruff of his neck. "You outted me, you rascal." Her voice wobbled, even though a tight smile stayed locked on her face. "I want to hate you for it, but I can't."

Bolly yipped, hanging his head, almost as if he understood exactly what she jabbered on about.

I stood staring at the odd woman—the woman who, even now, surprised me.

Something twisted deep inside. Something I had no fucking intention of analysing.

Everywhere I looked, she was scratched and bruised. New bruises on top of old bruises, shallow lacerations that'd scabbed over and deeper ones still oozing blood. My eyes fell to her feet. They were covered in cuts with a puncture on the fleshy part of her large toe.

I waited for a twinge of guilt—for that humanness I told her I didn't possess. The only emotion I got was annoyance at her hurting herself. She'd marred herself, and that reflected badly on me.

"You would rather slice yourself to pieces while running away from me, than suffer a few debts by my side?"

Her head snapped up, dark eyes arresting mine. "I would gladly hurt myself to gain my freedom."

"And why is that pain any different from the pain I might give you?"

So much feeling existed in her gaze as she whispered, "Because it's *my* choice." She let Bolly go, dropping her hands into her naked lap. "It's what I've been saying all along. You've stripped me of any rights. You've planted photographs ruining the only life I've ever known. You've destroyed—"

Something cold and angry slithered in my heart. "You talk of hurt and pain—as if I've treated you so unfairly." Leaning over her, I hissed, "Tell me one instance in which I've hurt you."

She frowned, her body neither flinching nor curling away from my encroachment. "Pain comes in many appearances, Jethro. Just because you haven't raised your hand to me—apart from a slap in the dining room—doesn't mean you haven't hurt me more than anyone else before. You degraded me."

"I've been nothing but civil. I wiped it all away for you. I did what I promised."

She shook her head, sadness glassing her eyes. "You think that by taking me at the end, everything that happened is forgotten?" She laughed; it was full of brittle anger. "You say I belong to you—that I'm yours—custom-made and born for your torment." A single tear fled her gaze. "Then why didn't you stop them? Why let them have me if I'm meant to be yours?"

I stumbled backward. "*That's* what hurt you the most? The fact that I let my father welcome you the way it's always been done? That I'm obeying *tradition*? You're hurt because I'm following the rules—the same rules which you don't seem to comprehend?"

My brain hurt. I'd never talked so much in my life. Never argued a subject or tried to understand another's point of view. That wasn't my world.

Shut her up.

I hated her questions and accusations. They didn't just stop at one but dragged a whole caravan of inquiry and slurs behind it. She made me second guess everything I knew and was.

I hated it. I hated *her.*

She said, "Those rules aren't mine. I'm not yours or theirs. I'm telling you how wrong all of this is, yet you shut down the minute I see something normal inside you."

Growling under my breath, I grabbed the saddlebag and turfed the supplies onto the blanket.

Bolly moved in front of Nila, sniffing at the items as if they were a danger to the woman he'd helped hunt down.

I was a hypocrite?

Look at the bloody dog.

Nila glanced at the packets strewn on the plaid. I shoved the damn dog out of the way, reaching for her.

She ducked, unable to disguise her flash of terror.

My stomach twisted. I bared my teeth. "What? You think I'm going to hurt you?" Breathing hard, I grabbed a blister packet and threw it at her. "I'm not going to hurt you, even though my whip would like to strike something more than just my horse after the issues you've caused."

Her dark eyes met mine, rebellion bright. Then her eyebrow rose as she glanced at what I'd tossed her. "You—"

I snatched the packet and popped out two high-strength painkillers. Stealing her hand, I placed both into her palm. She cupped them instantly.

"You're hurt. I told you I'm not a monster, Ms. Weaver. Would a beast give you something to mute your pain? The same pain, I might add, that you brought on by yourself?"

Her face went white, her fingers unlocking to peer at the

two white tablets. Her face twisted with a mixture of disbelief and utter confusion.

Another dagger to my gut. There was something about her injuries and vulnerabilities that were the perfect chisel to my iron-clad resolve.

The resolve that'd saved me from myself. The lifestyle that I'd been taught when nothing else had worked.

Fuck.

Looking away, I tossed a water bottle at her. She caught it clumsily. Unscrewing the lid, she placed the tablets on her tongue, and drained the contents in three seconds flat. She wiped her mouth, eyeing up the bag by my feet.

Silence existed for a heartbeat. Then two.

Her eyes met mine, granting me something I hadn't sought to gain. Her gratefulness. The fight and future was forgotten—her bodily needs overtaking everything else. And I was the one who could give her what she needed.

"If you're looking for food, I have some."

She swallowed hard.

I forced myself to shove aside my tangled emotions, grabbing my icy persona with both hands. "I need something from you first."

She grabbed the damn dog again.

I hated how her arms lashed around him, seeking something else she needed—something I couldn't give her.

I whistled.

Bolly instantly heeled, leaving Nila rejected on the tartan blanket.

She rolled her shoulders, looking longingly at the dog. Slowly, the strength I grew to recognise cloaked her; her eyes met mine. "Fine. What do you want?"

Everything.

The parts of myself I kept hidden, driven so far inside I'd forgotten they'd even existed, sparked with possession.

"You owe me something."

Her gaze popped wide. "Excuse me?"

I fell to my haunches, balancing myself with a fingertip

placed on the ground. My heart beat thickly. "I gave you something in that dining room...remember?"

Her lips curled in disgust. "You gave me to your father and twenty of your so-called brothers."

I shook my head. "More than that. I gave you freedom. I took their memory and made it mine..." I devoured her with my gaze, saliva filling my mouth remembering her taste.

Realization slammed into her. "You can't be serious. You expect me to repay the *favour*?"

I balled my hands.

She shook her head. "No way. You're insane."

Insane?

I couldn't do it.

I'd done my best to be civil. I'd spoken calmly, rationally. I'd been perfectly cordial and fought everything I was to become something I knew I had to be.

I was the exact opposite of insane.

"You really shouldn't have said that," I muttered.

She knew what I expected. I'd told her. It wasn't my fault she was totally stupid. I'd warned her never to question my mental state. And I wouldn't permit such ridicule from a girl who didn't recognise the entire world was fucking nuts.

Punish her.

I stood, towering over her. Moving forward, I grabbed the whip from the top of the bag, slapping it against my palm. "On your knees."

She scurried backward, slamming into a tree behind her. "Jethro. Please—"

I pinched the brow of my nose. "You insulted my mental state again, Ms. Weaver. I told you what would happen the next time you did." Bending over, I grabbed her shoulder. "On your damn knees." With a sharp push, I shoved her from sitting to kneeling.

Tears streaked her dirty face. "I didn't mean—I'm—"

I cocked my head.

If she apologised, I'd stop. Just one little word. A sign that she was permitting my power over her.

It wobbled unsaid between us. *Sorry. I'm sorry. Please forgive me.*

Her lips tasted the words, the syllables echoed silently in my ears.

But then she ruined it by sucking in a breath and clamping her lips together. With a glare that shot heat straight into my heart, she planted her hands on the blanket, and cocked her hips.

Fuck. Me.

My cock immediately sprang to attention. The perfect lines of her overly skinny body. The pert breasts and hard muscles of her back and thighs.

Shit.

I squeezed my eyes. *What the fuck is going on with me?*

Sure, I wanted her. Sure, I wanted to use her and come so deep inside her, she'd taste me for days. But lust had never made me see things like this. Never made me lose the fine frost of control. Every second spent with her undid all my hard work.

She was my pet. Her wellbeing and happiness hinged on me. Just like Bolly, Wings, and all the other hounds tethered in the forest just out of ear reach. I'd left them there so I could sneak upon her silently.

I'd known she was up there. I'd felt her eyes boring into me.

But this was all a game.

What was the fun in reaching the destination when the chase was the best part?

Nila looked over her shoulder, daring me with flames in her eyes. "I hate you."

Her words slammed me back to earth, her fire somehow giving me back my ice. I smiled. "You don't know the meaning of hate. Not yet."

Hair fell over her shoulder, hanging thick and enticing. "You're wrong again, Mr. Hawk. I know the meaning of it. It's becoming a favourite emotion of mine. I told you before you'll never own me. And you never will."

That reminds me.
"I caught you. You agreed you'd willingly sign that nonsense away."

"What nonsense?"

I fell to my knees, positioning myself behind her. Grasping her hips, I dragged her against my front. My jaw locked as my erection dug into her firm arse.

She cried out, trying to squirm away—not that it did any good.

I hissed between my teeth at the delicious friction she caused.

"You're mine. You ran and failed. I'll have the papers drawn up to ensure you know your place, and we can put this idiocy of you not believing this is your future behind us."

She gasped as I rocked into her, pressing punishingly hard.

Fuck, who was I kidding? She owned *me*. Her laughable rage, her stupid sense of fairness. Somehow, she'd ensorcelled me.

Fuck.

Forcing my terrifying thoughts away, I said, "I've made you come. I gave you a gift, which you took wholeheartedly. It's your turn to do the same for me."

The whip grew slippery in my grip as I pulled back. "You have three questions, and I have a point to make. You ask, and I'll make it. We both get what we want. Then, when it's all over, we'll go home and start our lives together."

"Until you kill me."

I sighed. Really? She was so repetitive. "Yes, until I kill you. Now, ask your first question."

She smashed her lips together, thoughts skittering over her face. Fine, if she needed prompting, I would oblige.

The whip was firm—plaited black leather and two supple ends made for shocking with noise rather than pain. Wings was so obedient, he didn't need it most of the time. It was fitting to use the equipment on something else that needed breaking in.

I stroked her lower back, ignoring her whimper. "You're green and unbroken, Ms. Weaver. Don't think I won't tame you before this game is through."

I struck.

The sound of the two leather ends snapping together ricocheted through the woods.

She cried out, rolling her hips.

"Question, Ms. Weaver. I'll keep striking until you ask."

To prove my point, I hit her again. "That's for your smart mouth undermining my control in front of my father and brothers."

Her skin pinked as I struck again. "That's for riding my hand like I'd given you everything you ever dreamed of, then looking at me as if I was a piece of shit."

"How long? How long will you keep me alive?" she screamed, staying my hand.

I paused. In all honesty, I didn't know. Her mother had been my father's charge for over two years. She'd known her place enough to permit a brief visit to her old family to sever ties once and for all.

I doubted Nila would ever be so well trained, but I didn't want to rush what we had. After all, once we reached the final debt, it would be over.

And that...didn't sit well in my gut.

"It depends," I murmured, stroking her burning skin.

I waited to see if she'd ask another question, but she remained silent. Pliant and listening. Her quietness soothed my nerves, and I allowed myself to give her a little of what she needed.

You're doing that far too often.

I shot the voice in my head.

"Years, Ms. Weaver. We have years ahead of us."

Her head sagged, lolling forward. Quietly, another question came. "And the debts? How bad are they? What do I need to prepare for?"

"Ah, ah, ah, I said you could have three questions in total. That was three in one breath. Pick one or forfeit anymore."

Nila sighed, a small hiccup jolted her frame. "How bad are they?"

I struck her. Short and fast. The noise was worse that the bite. I knew. I'd been on the receiving end myself.

"They start easy. Simple really."

She sucked in a breath, already knowing what I would add.

"Then they get worse."

I struck her again, loving the bloom of red and the way every muscle in her sinewy body twitched. Throwing the whip to the ground, I murmured, "One more. Don't be shy."

Her breath was ragged. "Will—will you ever be nice to me?"

The question hung between us, so at odds to the scene of her on her hands and knees and me positioned behind her. It wrapped around us with sadness, digging the newly placed dagger deeper into my heart.

"I am nice. Once you get to know me."

Her small laugh surprised both of us. "You're a lot of things, but nice is not one of them."

Anger boiled in my stomach. "You pissed me off before I had the opportunity to be nice. Didn't I say you deserved to be rewarded after this afternoon? I have many things to lavish you with, Ms. Weaver. You only have to give in. Grant me the power. Give up and stop fighting me." I stroked her spine, gritting my teeth against the ripple of pre-cum shooting up my cock. Goddammit, she was too delicious. Too strong. Too much.

She's a Weaver.

I shook my head, dispelling everything until only silence remained.

"You must know I can't do that. I've given up power to men all my life. I stupidly let my father control me, believing he knew what was best for me. And you know what that got me? A one-way ticket to hell to play with a devil I never knew existed." She looked over her shoulder, making eye contact. "Why should I give you that courtesy? Why should I let you rule the remaining shortness of my sad, little life?"

For once, I was speechless.

Nila murmured, "You can't reply, because you know this

is wrong. On some level, you know the only right thing to do is to let me go and forget about this madness, but you won't. Just like I won't give you the power you seek. Just like I will never stop fighting you."

She suddenly shot forward, breaking my hold on her hips.

My heart raced at the thought of her running again, but she turned to face me, kneeling upright so we were eye-to-eye. The muscles in her stomach shadowed in the rapidly gathering darkness, her white skin glowing with interspersed cuts and bruises.

"You said I owe you. I agree. You gave me something in that dining room. As much as you think you were only helping save my mental state, you showed me more than you probably wanted. I *see* you, Jethro Hawk. I see what you're trying to hide, so don't delude yourself into thinking I buy your hypocritical bullshit."

Crawling forward, her tiny hands landed on my belt, releasing the button and zipper in one short second. It was my turn to blink in shock.

She's a seamstress, idiot.

She dealt with buttons and zippers every day—they were her forte. Dealing with what lived behind them however was entirely another.

I hated, positively hated, that she'd stolen my power again. She'd drugged me with her witch potion, making me think only with my dick.

Fisting her hair, I growled, "You're on thin ground, Ms. Weaver."

Her temper exploded like a firework. She snarled, "Wrong. I'm on Hawk ground, and I'm still standing. You want me to pay you back? Fine. Tell me what to do, then feed me and take me back to your vile home. I'm ready for this day to end."

My mind went numb as her hand disappeared into my jeans, cupping me boldly.

"Or better yet, take what I damn well give you."

Nila

I HAD NO words for what I was doing.

Seriously, no words.

Part of me hated myself for being drawn to Jethro even now—especially after he'd hunted me down and punished me like some animal. But the other part—the bigger part—loved the woman I was becoming. I didn't have anyone to rely on. I had no one saying what was right or wrong. The rules of everyday life had no place in this new existence, and if Jethro thought I would play by *his* rules, he was a fucking idiot.

His erection leapt in my hands, hot and scalding—the only part of him warm.

His golden eyes were blank of all feeling, and for one blessed moment, he stared at me with lust. Only lust.

Then anger saturated him, his fingers latching around my invading wrist. "What the fuck do you think you're doing?"

I tugged the waistband of his boxer-briefs with my free hand, twisting my other from his grip, and sliding my fingers into the dark heat of his underwear. He locked his jaw as I traced the length of his cock.

"I'm paying you back. This is what you had in mind, right? An orgasm for an orgasm?"

He growled low in his chest, his eyes narrowing with hate and need.

Don't lie to me, you bastard.

He opened his mouth, but no words came out. I squeezed him hard—hard enough to cause shooting pains in my palm.

He jerked in my hold. "*Jesus.*"

That one word switched the rage splashing my insides into lust-blazing gasoline. The hardness of him sent electricity humming in my fingertips. The anger brimming below the surface turned my insides into hot liquid.

This.

This power.

This body-consuming connection.

It was pure.

Simple.

Intoxicating.

The whipping he'd given me hadn't made me wet. I'd never associated pain with pleasure. Sure, I'd read the books and heard rumours about how exciting a BDSM relationship could be with someone you trusted implicitly, but that was the key difference.

I didn't trust Jethro.

At all.

This was a battle.

Every time we touched, licked, and eventually fucked, it would be war.

And only one victor would come out alive.

I have every intention of winning.

Sex to me didn't come with past perceptions or notions. Sex wasn't wrapped up with love or sweetness in my brain. In a way, I had my father to thank for keeping me secluded and untouched. I'd uncovered an aptitude for delivering pleasure—an affinity for the basest of need.

I trembled, glowing so damn bright inside, I felt as if I'd swallowed the stars.

Jethro wanted me.

He couldn't deny it. He didn't want to deny it.

And I wasn't above using my body to make him *feel*. Make the cold-hearted, untouchable bastard come apart beneath my touch.

Holding a man by his most precious body part and making him bow to my commands.

That was true power.

This was true power.

Testing my theory, I jerked my hand up and down, thinking of every text Kite had sent me. Every dirty innuendo he'd replied.

I'm stroking my cock.

I'm jerking hard.

Stroking. Jerking. Made sense. In a way the motion would be the crude action of fucking. Jethro would be forced to make love to my palm all while my fingers squeezed him to death.

With determination strong in my heart, I stroked.

Jethro wobbled on his knees, his eyes snapping closed. "Fuuuck," he groaned as I squeezed hard, stroked even harder. There was no build up. No tease.

This is war.

Two sides. Two players. He'd made me come; now it was my turn to learn everything about him, so I could make him unravel.

Pushing his shoulder, I barely hid my victory smile as Jethro toppled backward. His eyes flared wide. "What the—"

I didn't speak. Instead, I clambered closer, never stopping the mind-crippling stroke of his cock. Up and down. Twist and around.

His sharp gaze turned hazy, his lips parting as his breath grew heavy.

His hips thrust, just once. Surprise battling for supremacy over his need. I didn't let him overthink it or realize I was winning. I crawled on top of him, spreading my legs, straddling his large, powerful bulk.

My heart strummed; my blood grew thick and cloying as every stroke I gave caused my inner muscles to clench. Giving him pleasure—*taking* his pleasure—was the headiest aphrodisiac.

I was a goddess. An accomplished geisha.

I lost track of lust versus vengeance. I didn't care about last names or futures. All I wanted, all I focused on, was the sweetly plaited emotion where the rush between my legs took control.

My touch turned frantic, jerking rather than stroking.

His icy hands clamped around my hips, grinding himself hard against my grip. Our eyes locked, our breathing synced, we became two animals in the forest.

More.

I wanted more.

Yanking at his boxer-briefs, I tried to push them down. Jethro raised his hips, taking my weight with him as he gave me room to wrench his jeans and boxer-briefs to mid-thigh.

The moment his cock sprung free, thudding against his muscular stomach, he lashed out, fisting my hair and dragging my mouth to his.

My tongue tingled to taste him—to indulge in a kiss. But he held me firm, millimetres away from his lips. "You're playing a dangerous game," he groaned as my fingers encircled the large girth of my enemy.

I didn't reply, my mouth watering for his so temptingly close.

Dropping my hand to the base of him, I cupped his balls in my palm.

His back bowed as I rolled the heavy, delicate flesh. "Christ!"

My tummy twisted, my heart thundered, and my nakedness couldn't hide how much his need turned me on.

His fingers went slack in my hair and I sprawled over him, unashamedly rubbing my throbbing core on his thigh. "You called me a disappointment. You said my hands were good for nothing but holding up my towel." I squashed my breasts against his chest, snapping at his lips with the threat of a kiss. "Do you still believe that?"

I jerked my wrist, stroking the velvety flesh of his erection.

His eyes rolled back, his entire body vibrating.

"I'm proving you wrong." I sat up, my gaze latching onto

his hot cock. Smiling sweetly, I murmured, "Isn't this what you wanted?"

His eyes stole mine. "There's nothing about this that I want."

I laughed—it sounded a little demented. "Who's the liar now, Mr. Hawk?"

His hand snaked up to cup my throat, the other captured my hip. His face darkened. "You want the truth? I'll give you the fucking truth." His muscles contracted as he braced himself against my touch. "I want you begging me. I want you so damn hot—you'll let me do anything to you."

His raspy voice tore away my past, throwing me headfirst into sex.

I squeezed harder, riding his cock with my fingers, driving blood to blaze in the tip.

He'd gotten what he wanted. By letting me touch him, he'd made me seduce myself. I'd never craved to be filled before. But now...every inch of me felt empty and greedy and needful.

I'm fucking your mouth. I want to blow down your throat.

The text from Kite suddenly popped into my head as if his ghost watched over me, giving me instructions on how to destroy the man glowering into my eyes with a mix of rage and lust.

Fear wrapped around my heart as I looked at the angry erection in my hand. I doubted my jaw would accommodate it, but I'd try. I would try my hardest and give it my all to make him come.

Not to please him. But to *ruin* him. To prove I could control him as easily as he could control me.

I moaned as a delicious throb worked its way from my womb. I was hungry for another orgasm. Instead of sucking him, I toyed with the idea of impaling myself on his huge size, wanting so much to chase my own pleasure.

My eyes couldn't look away from Jethro's parted lips. I would've given anything to kiss him. To be devoured the way my body craved.

You can't.

I shook my head, dispelling the connection. A kiss was too intimate. A kiss would destroy me.

Squirrel nuzzled closer, wondering what the hell we were doing, sniffing at the violent war taking place in the dark forest on a plaid blanket.

Jethro snarled, shoving him away.

In the same movement, he spread his legs, clenched his hands by his sides, and wordlessly gave himself to me.

My heart leapt, blazing with sunshine and happiness, before plummeting back into the tar pits my life had become.

"Suck me. Fucking suck me," he growled, thrusting his cock harder into my hand. The command sent a ripple through my core.

I didn't hesitate.

Bowing over his body, I straddled his knees and in one swift move, slid his silky, salty steel into my mouth.

He bucked, his entire body going rigid. "Fuck...me." His lips clamped shut as his eyes rolled back.

I moaned, adoring the power I wielded.

My nipples tightened. I stopped looking at him. Closing my eyes, I pictured another time, another place. I pictured my lonely existence in some repetitive hotel suite sewing tulle and silk. I pictured my life as it was—a slave to my craft with no peaks or valleys of living.

Then I pictured myself naked and spread over the man who meant to kill me, while my head bobbed furiously over his cock. I relished in how dirty and wrong and primal it was.

I preferred it.

Every inch of me screamed for a release. Every atom thirsted for blood and violence. My teeth ached to sever Jethro's body—horrible images of killing him in the worst pain imaginable consumed my mind. The other part of me wanted to give him the most pleasurable, erotic blowjob he'd ever experienced, with the hope I would smash his walls, liquefy his ice, and melt him into the man I *knew* was inside.

His hands fisted my hair, grunting low in his chest. He

drove into me, forcing himself deeper. "Take it."

I gagged; spit ran from my lips. I struggled to maintain the furious rhythm he set, but he didn't stop using me.

And more importantly, I didn't falter.

I forced him high. I forced him fast.

I stroked and licked and sucked and swirled until everything bellowed with pain. My jaw, my neck, my shoulder, my wrist.

All in the name of winning.

Jethro's stomach tensed, his balls tightened, and the musky smell of him shot up my nostrils, drenching my soul in his flavour.

His hands dug harder into my hair, fucking me just as surely as I fucked him. Our weapons were different, but we were duelling hard and fast.

Jethro groaned long and low as I cupped his balls and squeezed.

I'm winning.

I'm coming. I came down your throat. Kite's message burned my brain; I threw in every last reserve I had. My eyes swam, my brain swirled, and the world tipped upside down.

But still I sucked, and in some far off dimension, where sanity no longer existed, I tasted the first splash of cum on my tongue.

Jethro cried out, his body bowstring tight as his hips drove his erection past my gag reflex and emptied himself inside me.

I had no choice but to swallow. My stomach rolled as his salty release disappeared down my throat. I felt sick. I felt empowered.

He shivered as the last wave of his orgasm finished, a soft groan coming from his parted lips.

Despite the abhorrent dislike I felt toward him, something luminous dazzled in my heart as I sat up. I smiled, victory burning brilliant and sweet.

Jethro's light brown eyes met mine, wide with shock, pupils black with sated pleasure. He breathed hard and fast.

We didn't say a word.

We didn't have to.
We both knew who'd won.
And he was fucking pissed about it.

Jethro

FUCK.

Fuck her. Fuck me. Fuck everything.

For the first time in my life, I felt a stirring inside my frozen-over heart.

Not gratefulness or humaneness or tenderness.

No.

I felt...*undone*.

I should've known then that it was the beginning of the end.

I should've guessed how badly she would ruin me.

But all I could manage was dumbstruck desire.

I stared into the eyes of a worthy opponent.

I stared at Nila Weaver with awe.

Nila

CLIMBING TO MY wobbly feet, I ignored Jethro and beelined straight for the saddlebag. Inside, I found my running shorts, t-shirt, jumper, and summer sandals.

The instinct to turn around and make sure I was permitted to dress came sharp and strong. How had he worked his wizardry to make me second-guess my right to dress?

I would put a stop to that nonsense that very instant.

Slipping into the clothing, I winced as the shoes brushed against cuts and punctures. The painkillers he'd given me hadn't worked their magic just yet.

The second I was dressed, I snagged a waxpaper-wrapped sandwich from the almost empty bag.

Striding away a little, I inhaled the sandwich like an urchin or homeless vagabond. Food. Glorious food. I'd never been so grateful for something as simple as a sandwich before.

It tasted unbelievably good. Roast chicken, crisp salad, and creamy mayo on fresh white bread. I wanted another. Hell, I wanted ten.

"Here." Something landed by my feet. I ducked to pick it up, throwing a look over my shoulder. Jethro had stood and buckled his trousers. He ran a hand through his silvery hair, watching me with a livid expression.

I looked at the green apple in my hand then inhaled that,

too. I didn't care what I looked like. My body demanded I eat. I obliged as fast as humanly possible.

But no matter what I chewed, all I could taste was Jethro.

The apple core was the only thing left of my piranha-speed eating. It was gone too quickly and still I was starving.

Jethro prowled toward me.

My muscles moved, retreating from the anger wisping off him.

Don't move away. It's a weakness.
Stand up to him. Make him see you.

Tensing my muscles, I locked my knees. I'd won. If I backed down now, everything I had done would be for nothing.

Here and now—with no other Hawks or Weavers—it was just us; us in this game where the rules were unknown. The only way to win was to maintain the ground I'd gained.

If he wanted to control me with violence and softly spoken curses, fine. Then I would control him with sex.

The one thing I knew nothing about, but seemed to have a great aptitude for.

My lips twisted at the irony. I'd gone from untouched designer to depraved prisoner.

I only did it to prove a point—to extend my life by however long possible.

Liar. You're wet.
You enjoyed giving as much as you enjoyed his tongue between your legs.

I gritted my teeth.

Jethro didn't say a word, just stood there seething.

My body itched with need; I couldn't stop thinking of his mouth on my pussy or the exquisite sensation of exploding into pieces.

I wanted to come again. And soon.

Finally, he clicked his fingers. "Come. We're leaving."

Ducking, he scooped up the blanket and bag, before stalking to me and grabbing my wrist. He whistled for Squirrel to come galloping from the undergrowth and dragged me through the now almost pitch-black forest.

At least I had shoes, so twigs were no longer a painful foe. The food I'd eaten sat in my stomach like a gift, spreading its energy, while the clothing granted me warmth.

My eyes widened.

I'm...content.

Somehow, amongst the stress and fears, I'd found a small slither of serenity. How long it would last, I didn't know, but even Jethro couldn't take it from me.

We didn't walk far. My ears understood where we were going before my eyes did. The gentle snuffles of dogs drifted between the branches, followed by a soft huff of a horse.

Stepping into a small clearing, Jethro let me go, moving toward the huge black beast.

He murmured to the animal while securing the saddlebag to the pommel. His large hands were white flashes in the moon-starved night.

I stood silently as Jethro untied the foxhounds, patting them in greeting. The dogs couldn't contain their wriggling behinds, excitement sparking between them.

Squirrel joined his comrades, but he was never far from my side; his intelligent eyes always on mine no matter when I looked at him.

Jethro grabbed the reins of his horse, bringing the animal closer. He stopped in front of me. His body had shut down, face impassive. His chilly façade was back in place as if we were total strangers who happened to meet in the forest on some mystical night.

I've tasted you.

You've tasted me.

We weren't strangers anymore.

"Get on. I don't want you falling over."

I stepped back. "I've survived running through the woodland, climbing trees, and bringing you to an orgasm. I think I can manage walking back to Hawksridge."

"Don't, Ms. Weaver. Just don't." He ran a hand over his face, his mask slipping just a little, showing the strain around his eyes.

My heart clenched in joy. I was happy to see him tired. I was happy to see such an egotistical arsehole suffer from dealing with the girl who everyone thought was weak.

His gaze found mine. Something passed between us. This wasn't a challenge or threat. This was…softer.

"Get on the horse," Jethro ordered, but the unspoken word dangled behind his angry sentence.

Please.

I moved forward, eyeing up the giant beast. The horse swung its head to inspect me, its huge nostrils inhaling my scent.

Do I smell of your master?

Even though I'd eaten a sandwich and apple, Jethro's heady flavour still laced my tongue, saturating me with his essence.

In some horrible way, I felt as if I'd consumed a part of him—giving him power over me.

That's not possible. He didn't give you that willingly.

I'd taken pleasure from him. I'd forced him to give into me, even though his intention all along was to make me repay.

I couldn't stop my small smile this time.

Jethro muttered, "Smugness is not becoming on you, Ms. Weaver."

I shot back, "No, but vulnerability is such a fetching result on you, Mr. Hawk."

His eyes narrowed. In a whiplash, he grabbed my waist and hurled me up over his head. "Get on the fucking horse, before I lose my temper."

Not being given a choice, I grabbed the pommel and swung my leg over the saddle. The horse was a solid mass between my legs, the polished smoothness of the saddle sticking to my bare knees.

Jethro grabbed the reins, placed his foot in the stirrup, and swung up behind me. His hard body wedged against mine.

There wasn't enough room for both of us, but that didn't seem to matter. Digging his heels into the poor creature, we shot forward as his right arm lassoed around my waist, pressing me tight against his chest.

The night silence became awash with dogs and thundering hooves as he carted me back toward the torturous existence at Hawksridge Hall.

Morning.

The sun shone through the lead light windows, highlighting the embossed leather walls and maroon brocade of my four-poster bed.

All around me rested stuffed birds. Swans and swallows. Finches and thrushes. I knew Jethro had chosen this room for me because of the beautiful creatures all shot, murdered, and stuffed by fellow man. I knew because he'd told me.

He also told me I slept in the bed my mother had and her ancestors before her. All carefully designed to tear away my strength and send me hurtling back to the woman I'd been when we first met.

Pity for him, I had no intention of ever being that woman again.

It was early. The sunshine was still new and tentatively shooing away the night. I'd slept—deep and dreamless and awoken full of energy. A night alone. A night warm and unmolested.

There was something to be said for finding solace in one's company.

Shoving back the covers, I dashed to my suitcase that rested in the corner of the room. The bellhops of the Black Diamonds had been kind enough to deliver my belongings, including the maxi dress and jacket Jethro had confiscated from me in favour of the ridiculous maid's uniform I wore to serve the brotherhood's lunch.

I shivered, shoving away the memory of men and tongues.

Falling to my knees, I searched in the jacket pocket until my fingers found what I was after.

My phone.

I quickly located my charger in my suitcase and took both back to bed. Plugging the charger in, I allowed the wonder of electricity to grant new life to the dead machine.

As I waited for the phone to reboot, I smiled at the minor accomplishment I'd achieved last night.

The moment we'd arrived back at Hawksridge, Jethro had marched me to my room and thrown me inside.

Not a single word or lingering look.

The lock clicked into place, and he left me to shower in peace—to dress in a comfortable, baggy t-shirt and curl up beneath fine Egyptian cotton.

The time alone, coupled with the knowledge I'd stolen something from him in the forest, allowed me to relax for a few welcome hours.

Holding my phone—the link to the outside world—filled me with yet more strength. It was the key to finding a balance in this strange existence. My past wasn't gone, just hidden.

The moment the connection synced, the device went bonkers in my hands.

Messages flew into my inbox. Missed calls. Emails.

The emails I ignored: my assistant and designers. Requests for more patterns. Deposits from successful bidders on the collection from Milan.

None of that mattered—not anymore. The freedom I felt at ignoring the pressure of my career shouldn't please me so much.

Three messages from my father glowed on the screen.

My heart lurched, but I neglected them. I wasn't ready to deal with him. The mixture of despair and betrayal had yet to be unbraided and understood. For now, I needed some space.

I clicked on the latest message, sent early last night.

VtheMan: *Nila. Fucking call me.*

Vaughn's message reeked of desperation.

My heart hurt to think of him missing me. I couldn't stomach his loneliness or confusion. I shouldn't have rejected him. It was unfair, and I couldn't do it anymore.

Jethro could jump off a bridge, telling me not to contact my twin and best friend. V needed me.

Needle&Thread: *V, I'm fine. I'm so sorry I made you worry. I don't know how much Dad has told you, but I'm alive and doing everything I can to come home. Please know that I love you, and I wouldn't have gone if I didn't have reason to.*

I pressed send.

A reason like trying to keep you alive.

The melancholy from thinking about my brother threatened to sink my newfound hope. Quickly, I opened the messages I'd been eager to read since my battery died.

Kite007: *Had a pretty fantastic daydream about you, Needle. You let me tie you up and spank the living daylights out of you. Tell me...does that make you wet, 'cause it sure as fuck makes me hard.*

The familiar tug in my core was happiness on this bleak day. So much had changed but not this. Not him.

Careful, Nila.

I paused, tracing the keys with worry. Kite was the one constant in this mess. The only one not involved in some way or another. He wasn't a Hawk. He wasn't a Weaver. He was neutral territory where I wanted to camp and never leave.

You think he's not a Hawk.

The sudden thought stopped me, sucking up my oxygen with terror.

What?

My mind skipped back to the luncheon. To the strange connection I'd shared with the brother whose golden eyes weren't cold or full of malice but playful. My heart raced, recalling the inexplicable kinship we'd shared—no matter how brief.

He looked at me as if he *knew* me.

Kestrel.

I dropped the phone.

Could it be?

Shaking, I picked up the device and typed a response.

Needle&Thread: *I had a similar daydream. You spanked me in the woods with a whip. You kneeled behind me and struck just enough to* burn but not bite. I'd never been hit before, but you...you made it seem all right.

Send.

Only, it wasn't a daydream, and it was with my mortal enemy.

I settled back into the covers, breathing shallowly. I flip-flopped with fear, hope, and anger. If Kite *was* Kestrel, what did that mean? Why had he been so cruel to me yet considerate in the dining room? Why had he messaged me a month ago?

The text.

It was never a wrong number.

My hands fisted around my phone. Could I have been manipulated?

Angry tears shot up my spine. All my life, everyone I'd ever known had manipulated me behind the scenes, moving me around at their whim, tugging my skirts until I stood in the right place, while I smiled stupidly and so damn naïve.

I wanted to scream.

You're making something out of nothing.

It could very well be a wrong number and nothing sinister at all.

My anger was too hot—I couldn't reason with myself.

Kite007: *Fuck, that sounds hot. Did you come?*

I stared at the message with fire burning in my soul. I wanted to confront him. I needed to know the truth.

Needle&Thread: *Did you come after you licked me yesterday? Did you jerk off to the thought of me being tormented by your family, you sick bastard?*

My finger hovered on the send key, my breathing harsh in the silent room.

If I asked and I was right—what then? Where did that leave me? Was it better to play them at their own rules? Hide my tentative conclusion and finally learn how to play this secretive, devious game?

I deleted the message.

Needle&Thread: *No, but I made you come. You shot your release so deep down my throat, I can still taste you.*

I grinned, feeling a little psychotic.

If Kite was an innocent party in all of this, then he could

continue to be my escape. Meanwhile, Jethro would give me answers that I hadn't had before. Such as granting me knowledge to Kite's previous question. *What do I taste like?*

If he tasted anything like Jethro, it was an overpowering mix of no taste at all and too much taste all at once. An oyster mixed with caviar infused with the strongest shot of vodka. Not entirely pleasant, but not disgusting either.

I had experience now. Experience garnered by blowing a man who may or may not be related to my tormentor.

You might have it totally wrong. You're jumping to conclusions.

I paused, fingers stroking the screen. It was entirely possible I was clutching at straws, looking for connections to make sense of this catastrophe. But I couldn't ignore the tug inside—the sixth sense burning stronger with every second.

My lips twisted at how disgusting all of this was. How the unsaid lies made me endlessly suspicious.

Kite007: *Fuck, do you hear yourself? Something's changed. Again. I can't believe I'm asking this, but spill. I need to know how you've gone from shy little nun to confident tease.*

He wanted to know. As if he didn't know. As if the entire Hawk family weren't laughing behind my back.

You don't know it's him!

I knew I should calm down, seek out clues, and formulate the truth before tearing into the most-likely innocent Kite. But after being through a transformation from meek to fierce, I couldn't bottle myself up. I refused to corset my emotions any longer.

I would take back control message by message.

Needle&Thread: *You want to know? You want to hear personal details of my life? What happened to you, Kite? Someone drop you on your head?*

Kite007: *Careful. I'm one push away from deletion and walking away from this. You're the one who begged me to stay in contact. Remember?*

Needle&Thread: *You have a short temper.*
Kind of like someone else I know.

Kite007: *Want me to stay a fucking arsehole? Got it. Don't ever* say *I never tried to help you.*

My heart lurched.

If he *was* Kestrel, then he might be my only ally. I couldn't afford to piss him off—not while I lived in a nest of reptiles. If I could befriend him—make him care—he might be my ticket to freedom.

What better way for a Weaver to escape than for a Hawk to open her cage?

Back in the dining room, Kes had been the only one who'd looked at me with…compassion. He'd seen my struggle, and even though he'd treated me the same as all the rest, he'd been chivalrous in a strange, fucked-up way. Unlike his brother, who'd made me come—stripped me of my rights and privacy and given me a gift I'd never been given before.

Bloody Jethro.

Needle&Thread: *I'm sorry. I've been through a rather big change in the past few days. My temper is a little short.*

Kite007: *I've noticed. So…you going to tell me how you found a pair of balls?*

Needle&Thread: *No, I don't think so. You wanted no personal details…remember?*

I sat biting my lip, my fingers poised to cast my first web. How could I phrase a question to make him give away his identity: do you live in the country? Do you ride motorbikes? Did you happen to taste a woman yesterday along with twenty of your gang brothers?

Kite007: *Shoot me down, then. See if I fucking care. Enough talking. Let's get back to a subject we both enjoy. Touch yourself. Tell me how wet you are at the thought of me spanking you. Because you deserve a spanking. A fucking hard one.*

Needle&Thread: *I don't believe I've been anything but good. I don't deserve anything of the sort, seeing as you whipped me last night.*

Kite007: *What's with the whip fantasy? Why not my hand? I want to feel your skin burn while I punish you. I want equal pain in my palm as you scream and beg for my cock.*

I stopped.

My heart switched from burning to frozen. What sort of

response was that? Equal pain? Shared pain? Was that what pleasure-pain was all about? Equal measure of obedience and trust?

Kite007: *You've gone quiet. Fine. You want a whip. I'm hitting you with a whip.*

Needle&Thread: *No. Actually…I would prefer your hand. I want to feel you touch me. I want to be stroked, caressed by you, all while you do whatever you want to me.*

I swallowed the tiny thrill at the thought of Kes spanking me and quickly sent another message before he could reply.

Needle&Thread: *Where are we while you hit me? Bedroom? Forest? Countryside? Across your motorcycle?*

His response was instant.

Kite007: *How the fuck do you know I have a motorcycle?*

I threw my phone away as if it had electrocuted me.

I couldn't breathe.

Oh, God. It had to be. The strange connection. The glint and secretive smirk on Kestrel's face. Even the two words were similar. *They're both birds of prey.*

I'm so stupid!

All this time, I thought Kite stood for the winged paper craft decorated with bows and string, when in reality it was another bird of prey.

Don't believe it until you can prove it!

My internal dialogue went unheard.

I couldn't shake the overwhelming *knowing*.

My world ended again, and the one person who I trusted to be impartial and grant me strength to get through this was the vilest liar of them all.

Kite was Kestrel.

Kestrel was Kite.

He's a Hawk.

Jethro

I DIDN'T GO to Nila for two days.

Two long fucking days.

She'd successfully done what I'd sworn never to let happen again. She'd made me lose control. Bad things happened when I lost my ice. People got hurt. Possessions got broken.

Things did *not* go to plan when I stepped from the comfort of my arctic shell.

There was a reason people called me distinguished and shrewd—a carefully groomed perception. To be cruel but firm was the ultimate calmness—the persona that smoothed out my violent life.

I'd lived in the cold for so long, it'd become a part of who I was, yet all it'd taken was a silly little girl to burn cracks in my carefully designed control.

Those two days were a reprieve. Not for me, but for her. For my family. For every goddamn soul who had to live with me.

She thought I was a monster? Ice wasn't a monster—it was unyielding and inviolable—a perfect cage for something like me.

She thought she understood me?

I laughed.

She would *never* understand. I would never permit her to.

I made sure food was sent to her morning, noon, and night. I spied on her with the bedroom cameras to make sure she didn't do anything idiotic like break through a window or try to slit her wrists with a piece of crockery.

Two days I left her in the room of death, only to see the girl I'd taken evolve into a sexual creature who glowed like a beacon.

She spent most of the day on her phone—texting, reading, surfing God knows what. Sometimes, her face would fall. Sometimes, her lips would tilt into a smile. Sometimes, she'd pant, her small chest rising and falling. The flush of sex on her skin drove me fucking insane with jealousy.

Jealousy.

An emotion not permitted in my snowy world.

The second day I abandoned her, I went for a hunt. I let loose the hounds and thundered after a herd of deer. I stalked the poor creatures, and shot a quivering arrow through some feeble herbivore's heart. Some things still functioned correctly in my world, even if most of it had been bulldozed into ruins.

The bloodlust was sated. Calmed.

The cracks that'd formed froze over.

Rationality and tranquillity returned.

That night, my father and brothers had a family dinner—just the four of us. The deer I'd shot graced a stew, roulade, and roast.

Dinner talk was sparse, but an undercurrent of anger hummed between us. Daniel smirked with his insane arrogance. Kes smiled occasionally for no good goddamn reason, and my father...

Shit, my father.

I was a fucking twenty-nine-year old man. I had blood beneath my nails and ice around my heart, but still I wasn't good enough. Still, I *lacked*. I had something inside me that he'd tried to kill, but despite his best efforts, it survived.

I'd learned how to hide it.

But Nila...*fuck.*

She had the power to expose it.

I wanted to rage. To step into the truth and show my father who I truly was.

But I wouldn't. Not yet. That would be weak.

And I wasn't fucking weak.

I was one year away from inheriting it all. I had my own Weaver to play with. The power shift had begun—all the brothers of the Black Diamond knew it. My relatives knew it. The world fucking knew it, but my father...he wasn't happy with the change.

His gaze ensnared me; I glowered back.

The animosity between us was rife tonight, unable to be buried beneath the rotting veneer of respect and mutual alliance to never challenge each other again.

The last time we did, one of us walked away broken and the other almost didn't walk away at all.

Dessert was brought in, some raspberry soufflé affair. The matriarch of our family finally decided to show her face from her private wing at Hawksridge.

Bonnie Hawk might've looked bonny in her day, but she was well past her prime. At ninety-one, she moved painfully and with difficulty—the stubborn cow refusing to use a wheelchair or even a cane to get around.

"Hello, my son." She nodded at Bryan Hawk then looked to Kes, Dan, and me. "Hello, my grandbabies."

Daniel rolled his eyes, Kes shot up to help her into a chair, and I smiled the signature 'warm-but-not-too-warm' smile I'd perfected since I was ten. "Hello, Grandmamma," the three well-trained Hawk boys said in unison.

Bonnie sat, snapping her fingers for the unobtrusive staff to ladle her plate with the raspberry sweet. She placed an over-piled spoon into her mouth.

Her brown eyes landed on mine. "Tell me, Jet. How are things going with the latest Weaver?"

My back straightened as my cock twitched unbidden. That damn fucking witch had ruined me. I only had to hear the word *Weaver* and I became fucking hard.

That's why you're avoiding her.
Another reason, I admitted.
I scowled.

Swallowing my one and only mouthful of soufflé, I smiled tightly. "She's a work in progress, Grandmamma."

My father jumped in. "The little brat had the audacity to speak back after her welcome luncheon. The cheek of her. If she was mine to discipline, she would be missing a body part by now."

He spoke the truth. I'd seen what he'd done to Nila's mother, and I fucking *hated* him for it.

The venison in my stomach rolled as a wash of ferocious rage exploded through my blood. I stabbed my butter knife into the table. "Thank fuck she's not yours to torment, then. It so happens I like my women whole."

The moment the words were out of my mouth, I froze.
The table froze.
The fucking candles flickering on the sideboards froze.
Shit.

Bryan Hawk steepled his fingers, his eyes narrowed and dark. "That was a rather uncalled for outburst. Do you want to rephrase that, perhaps?" He never looked away.

My palms grew slick with sweat. I hadn't meant to show what I'd kept hidden successfully for years. My true nature was not tolerated in the Hawk family—even by my fucking grandmother, who by all rights should encourage us to be gentle and forgiving—not keeping alive a ridiculous debt over a family that made a few mistakes hundreds of years ago.

Fuck, I need time alone.

I needed to get myself under control, before I dug a grave worse than the one I just did.

When my jaw refused to unlock, my father muttered, "Maybe I've put too much responsibility on you, Jet. Are you taxed already? Maybe I overestimated you, and Kes or Daniel should share your workload?"

Something slithered across my soul.

Daniel snickered. "Give her to me, Pop. I'll make sure I

don't let you down." His eyes danced with evil. "Unlike some."

We glowered at each other; he tried to intimidate me but didn't succeed. He never succeeded. *Fucking twat.*

Tension crackled around the table. Kestrel stopped shovelling food into his mouth long enough to say, "You know Jet is the best man for the job. I've never seen him fail you yet, Pop. Give the bloke a chance." Giving me a conspiring look, he added, "She's highly strung and goddamn beautiful. Can't blame a man for wanting to enjoy the chance to break such a filly."

Goddammit, what the hell does that mean?

My temper raged beneath my thin exterior of ice. Lately, I was a fraud. A hypocrite, just like Nila said. The coldness inside was mysteriously missing. The blissful uncaring, the emotional detachment I'd been forced to live with since my father taught me how to behave was gone—almost as if someone had flicked a switch.

Before, I felt nothing. I permitted my senses to neither care, nor feel hate, nor feel happiness. I was blank, blessedly blank and strong. Now, I felt *everything*. I overthought *everything*. I wanted to murder every man I lived with purely because I wasn't what they'd groomed me to be.

I fucking hated it.

And I hated that Kestrel—my one ally who knew the truth about me—was pushing my damn buttons. "If you think a speech like that will get you near her, think again. Good try, brother, but I'm watching you."

Kes grinned. "We'll see. After all, she's *ours*. Not just yours. Our adoptive pet, if you will. Can't help it if the pet prefers someone else than the original owner."

My hand clenched around the butter knife.

"Enough," my father snapped. It echoed around the room, bouncing off the images of our forefathers.

"I expect you to do the First Debt before the week is out, Jet," my grandmother said, her lips covered in clotted cream.

I swallowed in disgust. "Yes, Grandmamma."

Cut, my father, muttered, "Do what you think you need to

do, Jethro. But mark my words…I'm judging your every move."

Judge me, you bastard. Watch me behave just as you've taught. Watch me be the perfect Hawk.

I would make sure to give him something to judge.

Tonight, I would 'fix' myself. Tonight, I would smooth away the chaos that Nila fucking Weaver had caused and find that saviour of snow.

Cut continued to watch me as he spooned dessert into his mouth. "Make me proud, son. You know what you need to show her and what needs to be done afterward."

Forcing my hand to uncurl around the knife, I placed it slowly on the table. Swallowing the overwhelming emotions that had no place in my world, I muttered, "I'll make you proud, father."

Cut relaxed into his chair.

Instantly, a wash of relief fell over me. It had always been the same. I lived with a family of devils. I was one year away from being emperor to them all, yet I still craved my elders' respect.

The kid inside never fully got over the need to impress—even though deep down he knew it was an impossibility.

"We'll be watching, Jethro. You don't want to disappoint your family."

My eyes snapped to Bonnie Hawk as she licked residual cream from her fingertip. Tilting her head, she quirked her lips into a secretive smile.

My muscles locked. Being the head of the family, she continued to hold the last say—the last piece of power over anything we did. She knew more about me than even my father. I might crave my father's respect, but I would never get over knowing I would never earn Bonnie's.

She would die and never grant me absolution of being satisfied with what I'd done.

I was the firstborn son.

I'd bowed to conformity and rules all my fucking life.

Yet, it was never enough.

Nodding stiffly, I muttered, "I won't let you down, Grandmamma. I won't let anyone down."

I'll make you see that your frailty only increases my power. I'll make you see that fire is better than ice, and I'll fucking show you how youth comes before wisdom.

I'll make you see.

Just you watch.

That night, I retreated to my wing at Hawksridge Hall.

I turned off the lights.

I sat in the dark and welcomed the shadows to claim me.

Before me rested my arsenal to 'fix' the things wrong inside me.

And just like my father had taught me—just like I'd done countless of times before—I found the frost deep inside and permitted it to chill me, calm me…

…

make me impenetrable.

Nila

I KNEW IT was too good to be true.

The last three nights and two days of being Jethro-free screeched to a bitter end when he came for me at daybreak.

I wasn't asleep but mid-text with Vaughn.

The early morning sun had a horrible habit of highlighting the stuffed birds around the room, sparkling on death and reminding me that my future only held carnage—no matter how alive I felt. No matter how strong I'd become from taking power from Jethro, in the end, it would all finish the same way.

With my head in a bloody basket.

I should've been petrified—wallowing in misery at the thought of how a successful career and life in the limelight had suddenly become so limited with options. But...strangely...I *wasn't*.

If anything, I was more focused now than I'd ever been. More aware of consequences of choice and the brutality of the world that'd been hidden from me. I'd been raised to believe in fairy tales—my father deliberately kept me naïve. Why? I hadn't figured that out yet, but now my eyes were open, and it was...refreshing to know the world wasn't pristine and taintless.

All my life, I'd pretended to be perfect. And all my life, I'd nursed the truth inside that I was far from it. The Hawks were crazy—there was no other explanation for their fixation on something so far in the past—but they were *passionate* about it.

Passion had trickled from my world as if every dress and collection had been vampiric—sucking my will to keep striving for greatness in my designs.

If you felt this strongly about it, maybe you should've gone on holiday. Had a break from being a Weaver.

But that was the thing. I would never have admitted it to myself, because I would never have recognised it. My vertigo spells, my lacklustre acquiescence of my father's wishes—I couldn't see how lost I was from my true self. I'd never been given the time to figure out who I was—only what was expected of a daughter born into the Weaver empire.

The beauty of distance meant I *saw* my life without being immersed in it. It all boiled down to the fact I'd never had anything of my own. I'd shared my life with a twin, who I positively adored, but who outshone me in every way. I'd been drowning with self-doubt and nervousness. I'd crippled my instincts and skills, terrified of letting others down.

Oh, my God.

I clutched the phone harder.

I'm a better person away from the people who love me most.

That meant I excelled while living with people who hated me.

It was fucked up.

It didn't make sense.

But how could I argue against something that was true?

VtheMan: *I know everything, Threads, and I'm coming for you. I'll bring the army. I'll kidnap the fucking Queen if it means I'll get you free. Just stay alive, sister. I'm coming.*

My attention reverted back to the current issue.

Vaughn.

Father must've told him what happened. I didn't know how much he shared—hell, I didn't really know how much he even knew himself—but I feared for my brother. I feared for myself.

Vaughn was volatile and likely to do anything to get me

back. Every day since I was born, I let him baby me, protect me from life experiences I really should've faced rather than hide from. That protectiveness sometimes came across as too much, and before, I secretly loved it. I loved being so significant to someone—their entire reason for living.

But everything had changed.

I'm not the same person I was a few days ago.

If I was bluntly honest, our relationship seemed a little much now. Blurring lines that had kept me firmly in my place as daughter and sister with no need to spread my wings and hurl myself from the nest.

"Get up." Jethro paced to the huge windows, wrenching open a sash pane letting the pretty English morning into the stuffy room. I breathed deeply as sunshine bounced around, merrily painting corpses of winged creatures.

Yesterday, I'd named some of the prettier ones. Snowdrop, Iceberg, and Glacier were all addressed in honour of their tormentor and mine.

I needed to reply to Vaughn, but I tucked the phone beneath the quilt, eyeing up my nemesis. "Nice to see you, too."

His nostrils flared. "Don't get uppity, Ms. Weaver. I don't have time for nonsense."

I stretched, deliberately taunting him. "Nonsense? You can't talk. All of this Weaver and Hawk charade is utter nonsense."

Jethro stomped over. Dressed in beige corduroys and black shirt, he looked as if he had a meeting with his local backgammon club. The requisite diamond pin glinted on his lapel. "Shut up and get out of bed. Now."

My heart thundered. His golden eyes were icy and steadfast.

The intensity and raw visceral desire I'd seen in the forest was gone. Hope fizzled into dirty bubbles in my chest. I'd thought we'd climbed to a new dimension with what happened in the woods. I thought I'd showed him that he couldn't undermine me without undermining himself.

How wrong I'd been.

Squinting in the sun, I whispered, "What did you do?"

He reared back as if I'd slapped him. "Excuse me?"

Shuffling in the covers, I eyed him closer, trying to figure out what had changed. Nothing outward looked different. He was the perfect resemblance of a country gentleman. But his tone was smooth as silk and just as unbreakable.

"You've done something. A few nights ago you looked human…now…"

"Now?"

I scowled. "Now you just look like the cold-hearted robot who came for me at my runway show."

Before he could answer, another vital question popped into my head. "Why now?"

"What?" His face twisted into a glower. "That doesn't even make sense. Your questions are really starting to grate on my nerves, Ms. Weaver." Running a hand through his hair, he said quietly, "If you rephrase that into a coherent sentence, I might answer, if it means you'll kindly get out of bed."

There he went all pomp and ceremony again. No curses. No snapping. No spikes of emotion of any kind.

He stayed away to distance himself, regroup.

I *had* affected him. So much so, he'd needed three nights to deal with it.

A hot douse of power shot through my veins.

"Why did you leave me on my own for days?" I held up a hand. "Don't get me wrong, I'm not complaining. The waitstaff did an impeccable job of keeping me fed, and the downtime was rather welcome after the manic few years I've had travelling and working non-stop, but it is a little odd."

He sedately placed his hands into his corduroy pockets. His eyes were completely unreadable—it was like trying to decipher a damn vault. "Please, tell me what you find so odd. Then perhaps I can help you."

If I hadn't seen the passionate man in the forest—if I hadn't wrapped my lips around his throbbing cock and swallowed his cum—I might've shrunk back in reprimand. I might've feared the silence more than his temper, because it heralded something terrible coming.

But now...now I saw it for what it was.

It's a coping mechanism.

We all had them. Mine was permitting my father and brother complete control over me. My only freedom from that was running until I passed out on my treadmill.

Jethro didn't run, but he did use something extremely effective to push aside the tangled emotions I knew he felt and embraced the glacier he pretended to be.

"Never mind," I whispered. "I understand."

Beneath the power in my veins, a small cloud of depression settled. I'd worked hard breaking his arctic exterior. I'd thrown my all into showing him pleasure that he could find by giving in to me. The fact he'd been so affected that he'd had to shut down and hide should've pleased me.

But really, it reset everything. I was back at the starting line.

For a second, I slouched in defeat. Did I have the energy to go through the arguing and battle of wills again?

Tilting my head, I stared at him. He clenched his jaw, not giving anything away.

My spine straightened as resolution fortified my defeat. So be it. I would do it all over again. And again. And again. Until he realized he couldn't win. Not against me.

I was strong enough to break him ten times, a hundred times. I was strong enough to kill him and his twisted family before he dispatched me. I meant to keep my vow that I was the last Weaver they would ever hurt.

Jethro crossed his arms. "Considering you no longer have any more frustrating questions, I presume you'll oblige and get up, like I ordered."

Without a word, I shoved back the covers and climbed from the warm sheets. "Where are we going?"

Jethro's eyes fell on my naked legs. I'd worn black and pink shorts with a matching camisole to bed.

"Did I say you could ask questions?" Moving smoothly, he

stepped away. Roaming sleek and sharp around the room, he gathered mismatched clothes that were draped on chairs and a sixteenth-century dressing table then came back toward me. Dumping them at the end of the bed, he said, "Get dressed. I'm going to count to ten. If you aren't decent, I don't care. I'm dragging you out of here naked or clothed—it's entirely your choice."

I wrinkled my nose at the attire. I had more of an understanding about my enemy, but I still feared him. I didn't want to go anywhere. I didn't want to be commanded or dragged—

"One." His eyes glittered.

He couldn't be serious.

"Two..."

Quickly, I reached for a peach t-shirt with Victorian lace on the collar and denim shorts.

"Three."

Shit, how could I get dressed with him standing there? I couldn't strip so blatantly.

He's seen you naked. You ran through a forest with nothing on. He's tasted you, for God's sake. Seriously, why are you suddenly precious about it?

"Four."

Biting my lip, welcoming my rational common sense, I hastily tore off the camisole and let it flutter through the air.

Jethro sucked in a breath at my exposed breasts. "Five."

Tugging the t-shirt over my head, I dropped my hands to my hips.

"Six."

Locking eyes with him, I shimmied out of the shorts, letting them puddle around my ankles. I had no underwear on.

I searched for the lust that'd burned in his gaze a few nights ago. I sought to witness just a hint of the Jethro who'd wrapped his fingers in my hair and driven his cock down my throat.

He merely cocked an eyebrow at my naked pussy and continued to count. "Seven."

Anger siphoned through my heart. Stepping into the shorts, I snatched them up and fastened the zipper.

"Eight."

Remembering Jethro's tendency to use my long hair as handle bars and worse, as a leash, I quickly smoothed the black thickness into a messy ponytail and secured it with a hair tie from my wrist.

"Nine."

The diamond collar sat around my neck—ridiculously expensive considering my understated outfit, making my breathing a little irregular. Slipping my feet into a pair of sparkly flip-flops on the floor, I was done.

I smirked. "Finished, oh impatient master."

Jethro stiffened. "Record speed, Ms. Weaver. I'm impressed." He held out his hand. "Give me your phone."

I blanched. "What? No!"

He leaned closer, his temper shimmering just beneath the surface of his cool exterior. "Yes. I won't ask again."

For a second, I wondered if I could hit him over the head and run. So many scenarios of running had entertained me these past few days. I'd tried to pry the diamond collar off. I'd tried to open the window. I'd tried to pick the lock on the door.

But nothing worked. Aside from death, I wasn't getting out of there.

I'm coming, Threads.

My heart seized at the thought of Vaughn charging in here trying to save me, only to be slaughtered by the men holding me captive. I couldn't let that happen.

Gritting my teeth, I turned and plucked my phone from the tangled sheets. Reluctantly, I passed it to his awaiting palm.

His fingers curled around the delicate device. "Thank you."

I couldn't tear my eyes from it. My only link to the outside world. My only avenue of freedom. I didn't realize until that moment how much I valued it and how stir-crazy I would go if deprived of the simple things, such as texting Kite.

Admit it, you're screwing yourself up over him.

The past few days Kite had been…different. The messages from the night before last came back to mind.

Kite007: *Have you ever noticed how things you've always been told were wrong are the only things that feel right?*

Needle&Thread: *That's rather deep coming from the man who only wants to sext and avoid personal subjects.*

Kite007: *If I said I wanted one night of blatant honesty, no douchebaggery, no bullshit of any kind, what would you say?*

Needle&Thread: *I'd say you'd completely lost it and wonder if someone with a heart had stolen your phone.*

Silence.

I'd been justified in not letting my guard down. After all, I'd tried many times to get him to be a little kinder, more human toward me, but he'd always shot me down. But as ten minutes turned into twenty and still no reply, I'd felt guilty for hurting someone who obviously needed to talk.

Why didn't he talk to others who knew him? Find solace in friends who would understand? My earlier conviction of him being Kestrel had faded a little after the initial panic attack. Since his vicious remark, asking how I knew about his owning a motorcycle, we'd both skirted the issue as if we were both afraid to pick at that particular wound.

It was best to let it scab over and not spew forth poison that wouldn't be able to heal.

This blindness—this naivety about our true agendas and names—was strangely hypnotic, and I didn't want it to change. I didn't want to let him go yet, and I would have to if I knew the truth.

Needle&Thread: *Kite, I'm sorry. No bullshit. No games. One night only to be ourselves and let the stark, painful truth come out. I'm here to listen if you want. If you've had second thoughts that's fine, too. Either way, I hope you have a great night.*

It'd taken a while, but finally he'd texted back.

Kite007: *Sometimes, it seems as if those who have nothing in life have everything, and those who have everything have nothing. Sometimes, I want to be the one who has nothing, so I can appreciate all the things I think I'd miss. But the scary thing is, I don't think I'd miss a single fucking thing.*

My heart fluttered. It was as if he'd pulled my fears straight from the darkness inside me.

Needle&Thread: *I understand completely. I love my family. I love their faults as well as their perfections, but I can't help being angry, too. By keeping me safe and sheltered, they made me become someone who was a lie. I now have the hardship of figuring out the truth.*

Kite007: *The truth of who you truly are?*

Needle&Thread: *Exactly.*

Kite007: *We're all a product of obligation. A carbon copy of what is permitted in the world we're born into. None of us are free—all raised with expectations to fulfil. And it fucking sucks when those expectations become a cage.*

I couldn't reply. Tears had spilled unbidden down my cheeks. I shook so much, I'd dropped the phone.

If Kite *was* Kestrel. He was hiding just as much as me. A man camouflaging everything real in order to protect himself in a family of monsters.

Jethro snapped his fingers in front of my nose, breaking my daydream.

My heart galloped at the thought of never being able to text Kite again, especially now we'd broken some barrier and admitted we had more in common than seeking sexual gratification.

"You're a thousand miles away. Pay attention."

I blinked, forcing myself to lock onto Jethro's golden gaze.

"I was giving you an idea of how today would go. You asked me to inform you, remember, back in the woods?"

Blinking again, I nodded. "Yes. Can you repeat?"

He chuckled coldly. "No, I will not repeat. I showed kindness in bracing you against today's events, yet you couldn't grant me the courtesy of listening. I refuse to reiterate myself."

Rolling my shoulders back, I tried not to worry about what my future held and only on what was important. "Please, I need my phone back."

Jethro shook his head. "No."

My heart sprinted. "But you said I could use it."

"I did." His lips twitched. "I also said you had to ask permission in order to do so. I want to check your history. Make sure you're not disobeying the rules."

Shit, why didn't I delete my inbox?

"The rules?"

His eyes narrowed. "Rules, Ms. Weaver. I don't have many, but I did request you didn't contact your brother. If you've obeyed, you have nothing to worry about, and I'll return the phone to you."

Shit.

Not only had I been texting V, I'd also shared more with Kite than I wanted Jethro to see.

If Kes was Kite, Jethro would know of the connection I had with his brother. He would use that knowledge. He would hurt me with it.

I can't let that happen.

I wanted to scream.

Standing as tall as I could, I said, "My brother knows."

Jethro went still, his face tightening. "I suppose I should thank you for your honesty. I thought he would by now. The Weaver men aren't ones for letting us take their women. Even with the correct paperwork."

I glared. "You knew he would come for me?"

Jethro nodded. "I suspected, and your father, too. It's been the case for hundreds of years. Do you really think your father didn't come and try to rescue your mother?" He laughed. "What sort of man do you think he is?"

A man I never knew.

Jethro smirked, seeing my answer flicker in my eyes. He reached out, tenderly tucking a stray strand of hair behind my ear. "To lose faith so soon in the ones you hold most dear is the worst crime of all, Ms. Weaver. I hope, for your sake, he never knows how you doubted him."

"Why are you telling me this? Isn't it better for you if I feel cut off and abandoned?"

He shook his head, his fingers dropping from my ear to cup the back of my neck. "No. Where's the fun in that? You were loved. You *are* loved. It's more bittersweet to know the men who tried to protect you are now on the outside trying to break in to free you. It's much more fun when there are more players in the game."

I whispered, "I don't understand you at all."

He grinned, looking positively light-hearted. "That's the nicest thing you've ever said to me."

"It wasn't a compliment."

He gripped my neck harder. "Regardless, I like it." His eyes drifted from mine to latch onto my mouth. The air between us went from sharp to lust-laden. His tongue came out, tracing his bottom lip.

My core warmed. I was too weak to ignore the masculine call of him, even while hating his guts.

His thumb caressed the column of my neck, both in a threat and a tease. "You won the other night. We both know that. But you won't win today. Today is mine. Today, you obey."

I couldn't breathe. His mouth came so close to mine, making me drunk on the anticipation of kissing.

He'd tormented me with the illusion of a kiss ever since we'd met: in the coffee shop, by the stables as I squirmed on his fingers, and now here. His lips were a fraction away from claiming mine. His breath smelled of mint and sin, and his fingers dug into my nape with everything he kept hidden.

A kiss could very well be the one thing that could shatter the icy wall he hid behind once and for all.

I swayed forward, trying to capture his mouth.

He reared back, clucking his tongue. "So eager, Ms. Weaver. If I didn't know any better, I'd say you like the taste of me." His brow lowered to darken his eyes. "You seemed to enjoy what I shot down your throat in the woods."

That was how he wanted to play? Fine. I would play dirty. I had nothing left but to tear away any illusion of being an innocent seamstress and embrace this nonsensical war. I wanted to roll in dirt and filth; I would meet him on the battlefield and never back down.

"I did enjoy it. But not as much as you enjoyed sticking your tongue inside me." Smiling coyly, I whispered, "Admit it, Jethro...admit that your mouth waters to have more of me. I bet your cock is hard right now, thinking of going where your lucky lips have been."

I quaked with an odd combination of fear and confidence. "You could do it, you know. I wouldn't stop you. In fact, if you want to know the truth—the deep, dark, bitter truth—I want you to fuck me. I want to feel you fill me, thrusting into me, stretching me to the point of pain. Want to know why?"

Somehow, I'd started this masquerade to get under his skin, but I'd successfully gotten under my own. My breath became a pant. My skin sparked with need. My core twisted with wetness.

Jethro's lips parted, his fingers clutching harder and harder around my nape. "I know what you're doing, and no, I don't want to know why."

The air throbbed thick and hot, threading around us with blatant need. "I don't care. I'll tell you anyway." Licking my lips, I murmured, "I want you to fuck me, Jethro Hawk, so you can see that you may own my body, but you will never own my soul. By taking me, you'll finally realize that I'm the strongest one here. That I can manipulate you into wanting me."

Taking a huge risk and gambling with my life, I reached up to cup his cheek.

He flinched but didn't move away. "The moment when you fill me, you'll see. That moment when you douse me in your cum, you'll be completely in my power. I'll own you. A Weaver owning a pet Hawk."

And when I'd collared and blinded him, I would use my bird of prey to hunt on my behalf. I would teach him to tear out the hearts of my enemies and obey my every whim. Because I was done being controlled. I was done being a girl.

I'm unconquerable.

Silence fell thick and cloying. We both didn't move, our breathing ragged and torn.

Then Jethro released me, stepping back with unmeasured

steps. "Confidence will only hurt you in the end."

The back of my neck tingled from where he'd held me. "I guess we'll see. Unless you plan never to sleep with me."

Ignoring that, he snatched my wrist and dragged me toward the door. "Enough. I'm done with your games."

I stumbled after him, following the muddy wake of his anger. "Where are we going?"

His voice dropped to a hiss. "First, you have a history lesson, and then…"

My heart fell into my toes as he wrenched open the door and tugged me into the corridor.

I couldn't help myself. I had to ask. "Then?"

Smiling cruelly, he said, "Then it's time for payment. Today is your First Debt, Ms. Weaver. The Debt Inheritance has begun."

Jethro

FUCK IT ALL to hell.

It'd taken the longest session of my life to claw back my chilly shell. It'd taken more out of me than even the first lesson taught by my father.

But within ten minutes, Nila fucking Weaver had found the smallest of cracks and used a crowbar of words to snap it wider.

Too bad for her, I wasn't giving in today. I had a job to do—a mandate to fulfil—and I would carry it out to the best of my ability. If I didn't, everyone would see. And everyone would know that the firstborn son was weak.

I'd been watching Kestrel and his sneaky smiles. I'd been stalking Daniel and his maddening glares. They both wanted what I had. And I wouldn't give my father any reason to think I couldn't tame Nila like any self-respecting Hawk. Cameras around the house would report how I treated Nila to Cut and the Black Diamond brotherhood. Spies would be on the lookout, judging my final test to ensure the Hawk fortune was going to the right brother.

This was the ultimate test. The Debt Inheritance was more than history and payments—it was an important sequence of events that every firstborn Hawk had to complete in order to inherit his legacy.

If I failed...who knew if my father would let me live. A firstborn son didn't necessarily inherit everything—not if death stole him too soon.

And judging by family records, there had been a few that hadn't passed the examination.

I can't afford to fuck it up.

Not if I wanted to keep Nila as mine.

Not if I wanted to keep my own life intact.

And not if I wanted to...*protect*...her from men who would undoubtedly be worse than me.

Protect.

What a strange, horrible word. It came layered with responsibility and commitment. Both were fucking vile on my tongue.

As I dragged Nila down the corridor, I gritted my teeth at the flashes of light on hidden camera lenses. What Nila didn't know was this was all a charade and we were the main attraction, playing it up for the audience behind the curtain.

In a way, we were both controlled—her by love, me by...

Clenching my jaw, I shook my head. *Get out. You found that silence. Time to find it again. The cameras are rolling, the puppeteers are tugging, and it's show-time.*

Stalking past the corridor that led to the bachelor wing—my bachelor wing—I kept tugging my unwilling Weaver toward the first part of the debt.

I was lucky that so much of the house was segmented just for my use. My brothers shared with the Diamonds. Their quarters far exceeded any other compound, but they still had strict rules to follow.

My stomach tensed, thinking of last night's business. We always conducted the bulk of our work at night. Ten of us had fulfilled the brief, and I'd cranked up my newest Harley that'd arrived from Milan, thanks to Flaw, and thundered through the darkness to ensure a new diamond shipment made it intact to the cutters and dealers.

Diamond smuggling was fucking dangerous. Not only was the law out to prosecute, but every sticky-fingered arsehole wanted a piece. Diamonds were the easiest, most convenient way to move wealth—small but worth a fortune. The Black Diamonds had formed, not for the love of riding and a brotherhood of like-minded bikers, but purely to kick the shit out of anyone who managed to get close enough to rob us.

Before, we'd moved merchandise with armoured vans and suits in broad daylight. But vans were such easy targets—so damn obvious.

So, we'd evolved.

Ten bikers...six with diamond cargo, four without. We rode in formation with guns armed and ready to defend. Police scanners kept us off roads where roadblocks were prevalent, and our fierce notoriety steadily grew.

Robberies were still attempted—shit, they always would be. Opportunists would give anything to intercept even a small shipment. Who wouldn't for an easy catchment of over three million pounds' worth of stones?

But we never chose the same route twice, we never let thieves walk away with their lives, and we earned the reputation of ruthless murderers.

After dealing with Nila and the mess she caused inside me, I'd craved an ambush. I'd wanted some motherfuckers to pounce, so I could give myself to mayhem and teach them a lesson. I'd wanted a fight.

But the night remained silent apart from our grumbling machines, and the delivery went smoothly.

By the time I crawled into bed at four a.m., I suffered a knot of tension in my gut and no amount of fantasising about fucking Nila could stop it. I'd laid in bed going over what happened in the forest. I gripped my cock and imagined sliding inside her and showing her once and for fucking all she couldn't win—no matter that she had. I'd never had an orgasm so intense, so draining. Her mouth had been alchemy. The release she'd given left me silent inside...but different to the icy silence I'd been taught to wield.

I'd been sated enough to permit my barriers to drop, to relax for the first time in my life.

And I wanted to hurt her for making me feel that. To glimpse an alternative to the one I'd been taught. But no matter how much I wanted to teach her a lesson, I also wanted to drive her insane with pleasure, so she felt what I did.

"I can walk on my own, you know." Nila tugged her wrist, trying to free herself from my grip.

Our feet—mine in dress shoes, hers in flip-flops—whispered down the plush red-carpeted corridor. "I like knowing you have no choice but to follow my every footstep, Ms. Weaver."

She growled under her breath.

Turning a corner, I took her down a different route. I had no reason other than to confuse her. She would have no idea where we were going until the final second.

"Wow." Nila lagged behind, her eyes fixated on the perimeter and the huge wall hangings. The beautiful tapestries hung from brass rods two stories high. Depictions of hunting mythical creatures—blood spurting from unicorns and griffons impaled on spikes—were the cheery décor.

"Who did all these? Was it your ancestors?"

I chuckled. "You think we're skilled at arts and crafts?" Shaking my head, I said, "We aren't weavers or sewers. We have much more important things to do."

"Like hunt?"

I nodded. "Amongst other pastimes."

"So who did them?"

I scowled. "Why do you think there has to be a link between something appealing to the eye and history? Diamonds buy a lot of things, Ms. Weaver. There comes a time when wealth transforms, and purchasing works of art is one of them."

She shuddered, looking away.

Why the fuck did she shudder? It was the way of the world. Everybody knew that the rich grew richer, and the poor sold their souls for a piece of it.

Silence fell awkwardly between us as we traversed the distance to the other wing of the house. I'd spent an entire lifetime in this monolithic prison and still managed to get lost.

Turning the last corner, Nila slammed to a halt.

My lips twitched at the corners. "Recognise something?"

Her dark eyes widened with horror. "You can't take me in there."

"I can and I will."

Before us rested the huge double doors of the dining room.

Nila squirmed in my hold. "You said I was to pay the First Debt. I've already paid the one where your foul associates licked me. You can't mean to repeat it."

I growled, "What time is it?"

Her face went blank. "Excuse me?"

I pointed down the hall, where the sun beamed through the French doors at the end. "It's morning. I was out late last night working up an appetite, and it's that time when people typically eat."

"Breakfast?" she squeaked. "You're making me eat in the same room where your awful family—"

"No need to repeat the facts, Ms. Weaver. I'm fully aware of what happened to you in there. Unfortunately for you, I don't care. I'm hungry. You're hungry. We have a big day ahead of us, and it's time for fucking breakfast."

Her head tilted as the curse fell from my mouth.

Goddammit to fucking hell.

Why did I have to end up with a Weaver who seemed to tap into a never-ending well of strength and intelligence? Her question before hadn't stopped ringing in my ears: *What did you do?*

How had she seen my transformation so clearly, so shrewdly? Even my own family didn't notice things like that—only if I went too far did they ever intervene. I had to keep her at arm's length if I had any hope of hiding my true self.

I leaned down to her level, my eyes disobeying my command not to stray to her lips. So pink and full, just the memory of having them wrapped around my cock made me ripple with need.

You want to kiss her.

I crucified that thought immediately. A kiss was connection—a kiss could never happen, because I wanted no connection with this woman. I *couldn't*.

"I agree it's morning and we should eat, but please, Jethro, take me somewhere else. Hell, give me a picnic in the kennels. Just don't take me into that room."

The plea in her voice disgusted me. I preferred her when she remained defiant, rather than begging. "No arguing. Gemstone is always held in this room. We won't break tradition for anyone, especially you."

Her eyes narrowed. "Gemstone?"

"Our biweekly meeting with the Diamond brothers. While you were relaxing the past few days, some of us were working. The meeting is a recap of dealings and revenue, and you're a Hawk now. You get to be privy to our inner empire. Lucky, wouldn't you say?"

She tried to jerk her wrist from my hold. It didn't work. "And if I don't want to be a part of it?"

I smirked. "Do you really think you have a choice?"

We glowered at each other.

Placing my palm on the doors, I pushed them open and pulled her into the room where her induction had taken place.

I looked over at Nila.

She sat wedged between Kestrel and Flaw. For the first twenty minutes of the meeting, she'd been jumpy, angry, and downright livid to be back in the room with the same men who'd seen and tasted every morsel of her.

Now, an hour into the meeting, she'd stopped hissing whenever a brother asked her a polite question, and had even eaten half of her salmon and poached eggs with hollandaise sauce. She'd refused coffee, which reminded me of how she didn't drink the one I bought her in Milan, and her body language was so fucking uptight, I expected her to pass out from muscle exhaustion any second.

For the past sixty minutes, we'd discussed the successful transaction last night, the rare delivery of a diamond over twenty-six carats next week, and the on-going politics in Sierra Leone. Boring stuff for an outsider.

She isn't an outsider. She's ours now.

More often than I wished, I caught myself watching her, my eyes seeming to land on her, regardless of who was speaking. She was the only splash of colour in the line-up of men on her side of the table—a peach fiesta smack in the middle of leather-jacketed bikers.

"Now that we've got the basics out of the way, Jethro, do you have anything to report?" Cut looked down the table, surveying his good disciples.

I stiffened in my chair as all eyes turned on me, including Nila's. Last night had been fucking boring. I had nothing to add. Now that I'd eaten, I just wanted to leave, get the debt over with, and go for a ride. I needed to get out of this place and away from these people.

"No, nothing to add. You've covered it."

Daniel snickered, his dark hair spiked with too much gel. "Yeah, Pop, you've gone over the boring shit. Let's get to the good part."

Nila froze; her dark eyes glared, shooting hatred across the table toward my younger brother.

Couldn't say I blamed her; the feeling was mutual.

Daniel sneered at Nila, licking his lips and blowing her a kiss. "I want to see how our guest reacts."

My fists clenched on the table.

Kestrel shifted beside her, nudging her shoulder with his. Loud enough for his voice to carry, he said, "It's okay, Nila. You're on the sane side of the table. I won't let him touch you."

Nila tensed as her head swivelled to look at him. Her eyes searched his, her chin cocked in a strange mixture of defiance and curiosity.

The second turned into a drawn-out moment, and still

they stared.

What the fuck?

Finally, Nila nodded, her black ponytail draping over her shoulder. Never tearing her gaze from Kes, she said softly, "Thank you."

Kes beamed, his golden eyes, the trait all Hawk men carried, glowed. "You're welcome." Something passed between them. Something I fucking hated.

Running a hand through his dark, silver-flecked hair, Kes tore his eyes from Nila's to look directly into mine. "You only have to come to me if you ever feel overwhelmed."

That lowlife bastard.

My hands balled in my lap. "Enough."

Kes reclined in his chair, dropping his forearm—the one tattooed with a bird of prey—beneath the table.

Nila jumped a mile.

He'd touched her! That goddamn arsehole touched what was mine.

The instant Nila jolted, Kes pulled away, a smug smile on his lips. "Sorry."

"Don't touch me," Nila hissed.

Something warm sprang from nowhere in my chest. Warm? How was that possible when my heart was full of snow?

My lips twitched, smugness of my own unable to be hidden. Nila might be intrigued or even drawn to Kes, but it was my cock that'd been in her mouth, *my* tongue that'd been in that pretty cunt of hers.

Kestrel's suave smile dropped. He always did think too highly of himself. Just because the club whores preferred him, it didn't mean he was better than the rest of us. He was my favourite person; however, I would not tolerate him poaching my prey.

Kes hung his head, turning on the charm and magic puppy-dog eyes that twisted the knickers off many women. "I only meant to offer comfort. I'm sorry if I offended you."

Nila crossed her arms, breathing shallowly. Before she

could respond, a Diamond brother muttered from across the table, "Yes, I'm sorry if we offended you the other day."

Nila's head shot up.

Daniel thumped him in the arm. "What the fuck, man?"

Stupid Daniel.

He didn't understand how unravelling a person's psyche went. First came cruelty—a stripping of every high and mighty concept that they were untouchable. Then came tenderness—an acknowledgement of going too far and promises of safety.

This was the second stage.

I'd seen it happen with Nila's mother. I'd witnessed the bewitchment as she fell under my father's spell.

That's going to happen to Nila.

My heart froze at the thought of her looking at me the way her mother looked at my father. Not with fear or panic or loathing but with trust and happiness and...affection.

"Excuse me?" she whispered, almost mute with shock.

The brother who'd spoken, an older man with a goatee, smiled gently. "You have to understand, it was our way of welcoming you into our midst. You do not need to be afraid of us."

She squared her shoulders. "I'm not afraid."

I swallowed hard as a foreign emotion crawled into my chest. Goddammit. *Jealousy.* Again. I was fucking jealous of the men around this table. I wanted to rip their heads off for tasting what was mine.

Don't go there, Jet.

My father was right to give her to the brotherhood the moment she arrived. If he demanded I strip and deliver her for a round of service again, I would draw a sword from the armoury on the walls and strike him down.

I would never be able to stand behind his chair now. Even though only a few days had passed, so much had happened. Nila had evolved into someone who drove me past rationality and straight into the chaos she wielded so well.

While Nila had been licked and tasted, I'd fought an unwinnable battle of possession. I'd said the words—I went along with the act of sharing her—but that was fucking bullshit now…

Now, I would never be able to share.

Never.

She was mine.

Not my brothers', not my father's, and definitely not the conclave of bikers, who by rights were my minions.

Mine.

Another brother broke through my tormenting thoughts, saying to Nila, "It was a special circumstance to welcome you into our family. We were all honoured to have you become a part of us."

Nila's face twisted in disgust. "A *part* of you?"

I jumped in before anyone else could. Ingrates. There was a way of delivering this so it made sense, not repulsed. "We all tasted you. We all licked a part of you and absorbed your sweat, your tears, your fears. No other initiation could've broken the barriers between newcomers and old-timers better than stripping you bare."

Nila's mouth fell onto the table. The same table I'd spread her over and driven my tongue deep inside.

Fuck, shouldn't have thought about that.

My cock went from soft to hard in an instant. I shifted in my chair as memories of her blowing me in the forest came thick and fast. *I'd* come thick and fast. All down that beautiful throat.

I felt Cut watching me, the intensity of his gaze searing into my skin.

"*What* did you just say?" Nila whispered, her features strained.

Cut sat taller in his chair at the head of the table, steepling his hands in front of him. "Jethro's right, Nila."

Nila.

I hated that everyone called her Nila. They had no right to her first name. If and when anyone addressed her by it, it should be me.

Why don't you then? She wants you to. She asked strongly enough in the woods.

I didn't have an answer to that. And I didn't have the guts to search for one.

Nila shook her head, looking at my father. "Is this another one of your mind games?"

Cut smiled reservedly. "No games. I told you, you're a part of this family now. You'll be treated kindly and respectfully. You will come to care for us, just like you care for your own flesh and blood."

"Never," she spat.

Cut chuckled. "Your mother said the same thing, but by the end, she willingly paid the last debt. A pet can only hate its owner for so long. But ply it with warmth, safety, kindness, and good food, and soon…you'll have no choice but to let go of that hatred in your heart and embrace the life we're giving you."

"The life you mean to steal."

He nodded. "The life we mean to steal. But also the life we will continue to nurture as long as we have your strict obedience." His eyes landed on me. "Give me an update, Jet. How are things progressing? Have you followed my instructions?"

Not one.

Not a single fucking rule had I followed. And yet…what had happened in the woods after I'd hunted her down had taken something from her. We'd shared something. Something I never wanted to share with another human being, because it made me feel so damn weak.

Ignoring the question, I sat taller. "The First Debt will be paid this afternoon."

Nila sucked in a breath. Her fear of the unknown did a much better job than I ever could.

Cut relaxed into his chair. "Good."

A second passed.

Another ticked silently before Nila snapped, "Have you forgotten my promise so soon, Mr. Hawk?"

The table froze; men looked from the skinny seamstress to

their leather-jacketed leader.

Cut tensed. "No, I haven't forgotten."

"I meant what I said," Nila growled. "I *will* kill you. You can pretend you're kind and keep me in good health, but I will never forget what you've done."

I stood up, slapping my palms loudly on the table. "Ms. Weaver!"

Her head snapped in my direction, her dark eyes blazing. "Was I talking to you? You're as bad as he is. I have a good mind to kill you, too."

My heart raced, shedding the glacier in favour of excitement.

Excitement? How the hell did she confuse me and draw out such lubricous reactions? "Oh, you can try. We'll see who wins. A seasoned hunter or a fumbling dressmaker? I know who I'd place money on."

Nila shoved her chair back, standing in one swift move. She looked as if she would hurl herself over the table to slap me.

Cut shouted, "Out! All of you."

Shit.

Tearing my eyes from the trembling, angry woman before me, I muttered, "Cut, let me—"

Punish her.

Fuck her.

Ruin her in my own way.

Anything to stop you from touching what's mine.

My father pursed his lips, pointing at the doors. "Out. I won't ask again."

The Diamond brothers stood up, their chairs sliding over thick carpet, before disappearing out the door in creaking leather and boots.

Daniel, Kes, and I didn't move.

Nila stood locked in place.

Cut raised his eyebrow. "I believe I just gave an order?"

"What? All of us?" Kestrel asked, disbelief in his voice.

Cut didn't reply, only glowered until the power of his rank, and the fact he was not only our father but our president, overrode our rebellion.

My brothers stood.

I gritted my teeth as Kes placed a hand on Nila's shoulder, sharing a look with her that made my stomach fucking shake off any pretence of ice and go nuclear with fury.

Nila smiled softly, standing and moving toward the exit.

"Not you, Ms. Weaver. You and I are going to have a little chat," Cut said quietly.

Nila closed her eyes briefly, blocking her panic. When she opened them again, all that remained was reckless confidence.

I wanted to say something, but my tongue tied into a useless piece of meat.

"Out, Jethro. I won't ask again."

Nodding once at my father, I moved stiffly. Nila refused to meet my eyes as I stalked out of the room, following my two siblings.

The last thing I heard as the doors closed was my father's voice. "Now that we're alone, my dear, I have something I want to share with you."

I COULDN'T MOVE.

My knees locked against buckling. My heart thundered from fighting with Jethro. I hated myself for *missing* him. The instant the door closed behind him, I couldn't stop the overwhelming urge to follow.

It's because you think you understand him enough to predict his next atrocity.

I supposed that was right. Locked in a room with the man who killed my mother was a lot worse than being with the son I began to see as more than just a cold piece of ice.

"Sit, Nila." Mr. Hawk smiled from the head of the table. I was grateful he didn't come toward me or request that I go to him. But it did nothing to stop fear, repulsion, and rage from saturating my heart.

Pouring himself some orange juice from the carafe beside him, he muttered, "You have such a low opinion of us."

Slowly, I sank back into my chair. Gripping the lip of the table, I forced myself to stay calm and ready to fight. "What do you expect? You stole me then let your men *lick* me."

"Did they hurt you?"

His question hung heavy between us.

I wanted to lie and say yes they'd hurt me. Mentally scarred me. But that wouldn't be the truth. If anything, they'd been the first step into finally embracing the strength I'd always been afraid of. Hurt me? Yes, they'd transformed me into a stranger.

I tilted my chin, looking down my nose. "It was wrong."

"Was it? You seemed to find it pleasurable."

I refused to let my cheeks pink.

"To give an unwilling woman to a room of men is wrong. Gross. Against the law."

He chuckled, sounding way too much like his son. "Let me lay this out for you, seeing as Jethro currently seems to be struggling with following orders and discipline." He placed his elbows on the table. "Obey, and you will have free reign of my home, go where you please, direct my staff as you see fit, and truly become one of us. I don't have the time nor the inclination to keep you trapped in a tower with only the occasional scraps to keep you alive. That, my dear, in my experience doesn't make a good pet, nor does it make a willing Weaver to pay back the debts owed."

There was so much information in that small speech, I grasped at each word with eager fingers.

Jethro struggled with discipline?

Free reign?

Willing?

I wanted answers to all my questions, but I focused on the one I needed most. Twisting the truth a little, I asked, "Why do you say that about Jethro? He's been nothing but freezing cold since we met."

Mr. Hawk smiled. "Yes, he's been doing well with that. I'm rather proud of him."

My heart seized. What did that mean?

He added, "You seem to think these debts will be monstrous. Shall I put your mind at rest, so you may relax and enjoy our hospitality?"

There's nothing you can say to make me relax while under your heinous roof.

"No. I'll never enjoy anything you offer me."

He scowled. "The First Debt will be the easiest. The

simplest extraction of payment for something your ancestors did. The next will be slightly more taxing and so on and so forth, until all debts are accounted for."

I know that, arsehole. Your son told me.

Smirking, he added, "The timeframe for each debt will be decided by Jethro and myself, depending on your acceptance of your new life. And rewards will be given when you fully cooperate." Taking a sip of juice, he finished, "Don't worry about your future; we have it completely under control."

Ugh, I couldn't stand his egotistical attitude. "You do realise none of this is legal. The Human Rights Act abolished selling people into slavery. You can't keep me forever."

Mr. Hawk went deathly still. "I see you've been researching while cooped up in your room." Wiping his mouth, he muttered, "No amount of laws or rules will save you, Ms. Weaver. The debts between our two families trump all that."

Only in your sick, twisted mind.

Changing the subject, I crossed my arms and snapped, "Jethro already told me how the debts would be laid out. Tell me something new."

Mr. Hawk froze. "He did *what?*"

Oh, God. Jethro's weakness around me was to my advantage. Why did I say that? Why tip off his tyrannical father to his son's hidden softness?

Backtracking, I muttered, "He told me while dragging me back after hunting me down." Holding up my scratched arms from tree branches, I hoped the evidence of being mistreated at Jethro's hands would mollify him. "He hunted me with the same dogs he made me sleep with. You should be proud of your son, sir. He's a monster."

A monster with a heart buried deep beneath that snow you make him embrace.

Mr. Hawk smiled coldly. "I'm rather surprised and impressed by his initiative. That wasn't discussed, nor part of the planned activities, but perhaps I underestimated him."

Standing, he threw his napkin from his lap onto the table. "Now, if you'll excuse me. I'm late to another meeting. I'm sure

Jethro will come collect you."

Bowing, as if I were the Lady of the Manor all set for a day of cross-stitch and sedate relaxation, he pressed his fingertips to his mouth and blew a gentle kiss. "Good day, Ms. Weaver."

My ingrained manners almost repeated the polite parting; I bit my tongue.

Don't you dare. He's the devil, not some kind-hearted father figure.

Keeping my lips glued together, I remained silent.

Mr. Hawk passed my chair, stopping briefly to run his hand through my ponytail.

I shivered as the soft tug of his fingers whispered through the black strands.

"Such a pretty thing. I can see I'll have to step up my lessons with my son to ensure you both behave."

My heart lurched, speeding around my chest.

What the hell did that mean?

Staying stiff and unyielding, I didn't mutter a sound as he tugged once on my ponytail, then disappeared from the room.

I was left alone in the cavernous space with the beady eyes of past Hawks watching my every move. The glittering chandeliers above twinkled with sunlight spilling in from leadlight windows.

Little rainbows danced across my knuckles, reminding me of the design that'd come to me when I stood naked and about to run for my life. Fractals from the diamond collar around my neck had inspired rather than repulsed.

That seemed like an age ago.

My old life had faded so fast; it seemed almost dreamlike. Had I really been heralded as the next star of London couture?

It seemed surreal and something I didn't even crave. I hated the limelight. So how did I think I could walk headfirst into a career where I would forever have to sell myself in order to peddle my creations? I would no longer be holed up in a room full of calico and satin with assistants. I would be the face of *Nila*—my brand.

The show in Milan had taken every reserve I had. And that had been the first one.

I would never have survived.

Yet another part of my life where the Hawks had meddled and granted me a reprieve. I hated that they'd shown me a different way of existing—one I was better suited to than my own heritage.

The longer I sat there, the more my mind skipped from subject to subject. My fingers itched to text my brother and Kite, but bloody Jethro had my phone.

I have to get it back.

I didn't know what I waited for. Someone to come and claim me? Jethro to ensnare me and cart me off to do whatever horrible things he planned next? But no one came to fetch me or demand I follow.

Staff, a mixture of men and women in smart black and white uniforms, entered the room to clear away breakfast.

They smiled kindly, going about their business as if life was normal. Completely fucking normal.

I deliberated staying in the dining room where it was moderately peaceful with the bustle of staff and gentle clinking of crockery, but I couldn't look at the table without flushing and suffering a dreadfully unwanted spasm of lust at the memory of Jethro's tongue.

My skin crawled to think that I found comfort in the very same room men had stripped me bare—not just my body, but my sanity, too—and delivered me into this new fate.

I have to leave.

Standing, I stumbled forward as the room went blank.

I groaned as I clutched frantically at the table, only just managing to stay on my feet as a heavy black wave of vertigo stole my vision and hijacked my limbs.

"Miss, are you okay?" a sweet maid asked. I couldn't see her as my vision remained blocked.

"Yes, I'm fine. Just stood up too fast, that's all."

I began counting down from ten silently. By the time I hit three, my vision suddenly shed the blackness, splashing colour and images onto my retinas.

I sighed in relief.

Swallowing back the small wash of sickness, I smiled at the maid and made my way to the double doors. I pushed them open, heading into the corridor.

The attack had been the first one today.

I didn't want to admit it, but the last two days of peace locked in my room had done me a world of good. I would never tell the truth to Jethro, but my episodes seemed to have relaxed their lunatic need to torture me. Either a mixture of my new strength or just the vacation from overworking…my body had found a sustainable equilibrium.

For now.

Looking around, I frowned.

No one.

The corridor was empty with only glittering polished weapons and immaculate tapestries for company.

Where is everyone?

Mr. Hawk did say I could roam free. Should I see if that was true?

Hesitantly, as if I expected someone to jump out from behind a suit of armour and attack me, I drifted left—the same direction where Jethro had dragged me toward the exit and given me my one and only chance for freedom.

Peculiarly, knowing that I'd had my shot and failed granted a sense of indulgent serenity. I lacked that drive to run, because I knew there would be no point. As much as I wanted to escape, it took away the obligation of *trying* to get free by knowing it was impossible.

I couldn't get it balanced in my head. But there it was.

Another truth I'd been made to face—another facet of myself I had to come to terms with.

Deciding not to go outside, despite the pleasant sunlight, I turned right down another corridor. Following the ribbons of pathways, I moved toward the bowels of the house.

After a few minutes, the rumble of voices came from an ajar door.

I froze.

I didn't want to get caught doing something I wasn't

supposed to, but I couldn't stop my abhorrent curiosity.

Tiptoeing closer, I peeked inside.

There were two men in leather jackets, laughing as they packed guns into a satchel. I leaned forward for a better vantage. *Guns?*

The floorboards creaked beneath my toes, whipping their heads up.

My heart sank. Kestrel and Flaw.

"Nila," Kes said, dropping the bag on a wingback chair. Striding quickly to the door, he dragged me into the room.

The décor was best described as old-world comfort. A saloon of sorts with glass cases full of antiquities and soaring shelves of leather-bound literature. The huge windows permitted sunshine to illuminate dust motes and drench the slightly faded geometric carpet.

My skin tingled beneath his touch.

I backpedalled, tugging on his hold. "Let me go."

Kes grinned. His broad jaw, dimple in one cheek, and muscular frame was so different to Jethro. Jethro was sleek, refined—a true diamond. Kes was more of a diamond in the rough.

His fingers squeezed mine in welcome. "A pleasure to see you again." He poked his head back into the corridor. "And wait...no brother to fight for your affections?"

I couldn't untwist my tongue to reply; my mind was otherwise occupied with all things deception. *Kite. Is he Kite?*

When I didn't reply, Kes let me go and moved deeper into the room. Smiling, he asked, "Exploring the place?"

My heart raced at the way he watched me. Eager, interested, and...inquisitively kind. The crude text messages and short temper of Kite all tripped and tangled in my mind. He was such an arrogant arse via text messaging, but he seemed open and...understanding in person.

Of course, he understands. He's been talking to you for a month. Having phone sex with you. Masturbating to the messages you sent.

I shuddered in disgust and embarrassment.

It'd been fun when we'd had the power of anonymity.

Now, faced with what I'd said, it was downright mortifying.

How can I get you to admit what I know? Correct that—what I think I know.

How could I be so sure that the tall, strong Hawk before me was Kite?

"Cat got your tongue?" Kes cocked his head.

"I think she's bowled over by your welcoming charm," Flaw chuckled.

My attention diverted to him. To the biker who ruptured my life by planting false photographs and standing by as I fell prey to a heartless hellion.

I wanted to tell them what I really thought. I wanted to ask why they were being so nice to me all of a sudden, but the only word I could catch hold of was Kite.

Kite.

Kes.

Kite.

Get it together. Until you know for sure, don't let on.

Straightening my shoulders, I inched forward. "No one has caught my tongue, and I wouldn't kid yourself that I'm speechless thanks to a welcome from either of you."

"Oh, she has a backbone," Flaw said, grinning.

Kes's golden eyes, so like Jethro, Daniel, and Mr. Hawk, searched mine. "She has more than that. Her entire body is made up of steel."

My knees locked into place. I wanted to scream at him to speak the truth, then strike him down for lying to me.

What did that mean? Some cryptic clue that he knew I knew along with some vague acknowledgement that we weren't strangers? That he was my...*friend?*

No, he's not my friend.

He's my enemy in disguise.

I couldn't let myself be swayed by anyone's motives.

Sticking my nose in the air, fully embracing an uppity heiress, I said, "You're just like the rest of them."

Kes blinked. "Pardon?"

"Don't 'pardon' me. You know exactly what I'm talking

about."

The messages, you idiot.

Flaw stepped forward, looking at both of us. Standing just outside my personal space, he extended his hand. "I think we got off on the wrong foot. I'm Flaw. Real name's Rhys, but we never go by birth names in this place."

I couldn't stop anger heating my cheeks. "You think I wish to shake your hand? The same hand that went into my room, packed up my belongings, and wrote a note to my father explaining my disappearance?"

Flaw held up a finger. "Technically, that wasn't for your father but for the paparazzi who followed you around. But I will take responsibility for breaking into your room and packing."

The way he talked and moved reminded me a little of my brother. Both were black-haired with lanky frames. A crippling pang of homesickness filled me. "Were you there?"

Flaw frowned. "There? Where there?"

I balled my hands. I didn't remember him being there, but then again my attention at that welcome luncheon was skewed. I'd been more focused on the pieces of parchment rather than tongues. "Were you one of the ones who...*licked* me?"

Flaw had the decency to blanch. "No. I was overseeing a shipment for Jet. I heard about it, though."

I laughed coldly. "*Heard* about it?" I shot a glower at Kes. His arms were crossed, looking pensive.

My voice ached with defiance. "If you've been told details of what happened, what is your opinion, from an outsider's perspective?"

What are you doing?

The whole conversation had no point. I didn't know why I pushed it. I just knew I couldn't breathe properly ensconced in a room with Kestrel. I was argumentative, jumpy, and completely on edge.

Flaw looked at Kes, shrugging as if asking for guidance. Kes nodded, chewing on the inside of his cheek, obviously just as lost as I was with where I was going with this.

Taking a deep breath, Flaw muttered, "I was told why they did it—it was an icebreaker. To remove barriers between you and the brotherhood. I was told it was a onetime thing and from now on to treat you as one of us."

"Better than one of us," Kes murmured. "You're our guest, first and foremost, and we're responsible for your wellbeing."

There were so many inconsistencies in that sentence; I didn't know where to begin.

Didn't he get it that I wasn't a guest but a woman destined to die? I was their captive!

Ignoring Kes for now, I glared at Flaw. "That was the reason you were told. What about what *you* believe? Tell me if you found it acceptable. Tell me how you would feel if all of this happened to your sister or wife."

Kes sucked in a breath beside me. "I see what you're doing, Nila."

I shuddered at the use of my first name. I'd been trying so long for Jethro to use it, yet his younger brother needed no such encouragement.

Abandoning my witch-hunt on Flaw, I turned to the man who made me itch with annoyance, intrigue, and temper. "What do you see, *Kestrel*?"

Kes's eyes tightened; something harsh and hot flowed between us. Some resemblance of the kinky, sexual man from our text messages flashed, then was hidden. "I know you're searching for validation of being debased in such a way. Regardless of what you think, it wasn't sexual. Those men weren't there to get off on tasting you. They were there to strip you."

I laughed. "Well, they certainly succeeded."

I was naked and had my first orgasm in front of them. *If that isn't the bare essentials of any human, I don't know what is.*

Kes continued, "What if I told you that whole thing wasn't just about you? What if I told you the men who witnessed your nakedness and were privileged enough to taste you were now indebted to you?"

"Don't talk to me about debts," I snarled.

Kes inched closer, encroaching on my mental safety. "By seeing you struggle, by witnessing the power that grew in you with each round of the table, you earned their respect. You earned their devotion. And you were welcomed into our world with no barriers. *That's* what the lunch was about. A power play where you gave up your power and gained theirs in return."

I couldn't stand his crisp, accented voice delivering something that shouldn't make sense, only for it to resonate perfectly inside.

Murmuring, he said, "You can't deny you feel different. Stronger. Braver. You were at your most vulnerable, but you survived." Reaching up, he captured the ends of my ponytail cascading over my shoulder. "We showed you your true worth, Nila Weaver, and now you'll have the strength to face the future intact and not break until it's time."

My heart stuttered then died. "You gave me all of that, just so I wouldn't be broken for the final debt?"

The cruelty. The *brutality*.

Locking eyes with me, Kes whispered, "I give you my word. You are strong enough to get through this."

The room faded until the only thing that existed was Kes and I. I didn't know if it was the possibility of him being Kite that drew me to him or the empathy deep in his gaze but *something* was undeniable. The longer we stared, the more he drained me of fight and fortified me with courage.

"Forgive me?" he whispered.

"*Forgive* you?"

My mind skipped. Was he asking for forgiveness for licking me like his brothers or for deceiving me with text messages?

Either way, I had no willpower to offer him absolution.

Did I take a wrong turn somewhere? Had I entered an alternate universe where I was no longer a prisoner, destined to be a plaything for bastards, and somehow became an...*equal?*

Kes moved closer, his body heat making me quiver. "I understand why you can't. I was selfish for asking something you can't give."

A crashing headache squeezed my temples. "I—I don't understand what's going on." I flinched as the words spilled from my mouth, raining confusion and vulnerability.

Kes didn't twitch or move away, only twirled his fingers in my hair. "You'll understand, soon enough." Closing his eyes briefly, he released my ponytail and took a step back.

Instantly, the real world swamped into being: sunlight, the feel of luxurious carpet beneath my flip-flops, and the crackle of wood burning in the large fireplace behind Flaw.

If this was another game orchestrated by the hellish Mr. Hawk, then he'd just won because Kestrel had drained me more successfully than anyone. He'd made me pliant and submissive. He'd done what no amount of fear or arguing with Jethro could achieve.

And that made Kestrel deadly.

My heart thrummed with true fear.

Another huge difference between the brothers: one used softness to control me; the other wielded frost and fury.

How naïve was I to believe Kes could ever be on my side. He was the polar opposite—the snake in the proverbial grass—just waiting for Jethro to fail, so he could sink his fangs of pity into me and bring me under his spell.

I knew without a doubt I had to understand my enemies, and quickly, before they manipulated my mind with falsities.

Taking a deep breath, I crossed my arms across my chest, wishing I had a jacket. The chill of my conclusions stole into my blood, making me shiver with trepidation.

What had just happened, and why did I feel as if I'd lost?

At least with Jethro, I *saw* him. We were evenly matched in will and temper. And we both conceded defeat with yet another challenge met head on.

Kestrel was dangerous.

Treacherous.

Skilled in manipulation so clever, my thoughts were enamoured and I had no hope of deciphering what truly occurred.

Flaw clapped his hands, completely dispelling the tense mood. "I'm glad that's all resolved."

Moving toward the wingback where a saddlebag revealed the muzzles of weapons, he plucked it off and patted the buttoned leather. "Sit. Hang out with us, if you don't have anything else to do." Shooting a look at Kes, he said to me, "Can I get a maid to bring you something? Coffee, tea, a snack?"

I looked into his dark eyes, utterly gobsmacked. "Is this a new strategy? Commiserate with the indebted girl—give her the illusion she has *friends*?"

Flaw shook his head. "Uh…"

"Everyone is to treat you with utmost civility, Nila. It isn't a trick," Kes's deep voice rumbled.

Trick?

This was beyond a trick. It was an entire *production* of tricks.

But what could I do? Nothing. I just had to play along and hope I could see the truth through the lies.

Flaw nodded at the door. "You found us—remember? We have nothing to gain by inviting you in here and talking."

Kes said, "He's right. We're not going to hurt you."

But you did if you're Kite. You hurt me by pretending.

I glared hard, hoping he'd get my unspoken message.

Kes looked away, hiding any hint he might've picked up on my temper. Stalking toward the groaning bookshelves lining the walls of the saloon, he cupped his chin, searching for something.

"Ah, ha." Snagging an oversized tome with tatty bindings, he brought it back toward me with a twinkle in his eyes. "I think this might interest you."

Beckoning me to take a seat, he pulled up an ottoman and sat beside the empty wingback. Quirking his eyebrow, he waited for me to deliberate.

Should I leave or stay? Should I continue to play whatever this was or go and hunt for the man who made me wet and terrified me?

Slowly, my feet moved toward the chair. Sinking down onto the firm leather, Kes placed the heavy book into my lap. "Relax and forget about this world for a while."

I couldn't take my eyes off the literature. A large gold filigree 'W' embossed the cover with what looked like an oak tree sprouting countless limbs of foliage.

"What is it?" I asked, tracing the majestic old-wealth of such a book.

Kes grinned, inching closer to open the first page. "It's your history."

My heart thrummed as his bulk seared my left side. My eyes devoured the beautifully scripted calligraphy.

"Every Weaver woman who's stayed with us has made notes and shared her journey, along with patterns and fashions created while living with us." He gently flipped a page, where faint sketches decorated along with the signature of one of my ancestors. Notes scribbled about what sort of fabric to source, along with diary-like entries of what life was like living in the nest of Hawks.

My hands shook. Leaning over, I couldn't read fast enough.

Today was a good day. Bonnie had the chiffon I requested delivered, and I spent the afternoon in her chambers, creating a new crinoline evening gown. She's a surly old bat, but when you get to know her...

The next paragraph had been scribbled out, so dark and determined, I had no hope of reading what was written. It continued:

The passion to create had disappeared. I lived in a void with no urge to sketch or pin or sew. I hate that I've found that passion here of all places, but at least...

As much as I do not wish to admit—I'm happy.

My eyes shot up to Kestrel's. "You're trying to prove that my family were *content* with their imprisonment?" My heart froze over at such atrocities. But how could I deny it when it was in black and white?

Kes smiled softly. "Happiness comes in many forms: sex, freedom, control. I think everyone has the capacity to find happiness in even the darkest of places."

Grabbing the majority of the pages, he flipped them over, revealing unmarred parchment.

Chills scattered down my back.

It's for me.

It's been waiting for me to fill with my journey.

"This is yours, Nila. If there aren't enough blank pages, we'll have a book binder add more." With gentle fingertips, he tucked a loose piece of hair behind my ear.

I jolted from his touch, my emotions going haywire.

"This is the first gift of many. You'll see."

My eyes locked with his; a ball lodged in my throat.

Awareness sparked between us; my lips parted as I sucked in a breath. Kes looked at me the exact same way Jethro had after our fight in the forest, after he'd blown down my throat, after I'd won. That same awe, same secretive amazement, now blazed in his brother's gaze.

Words deserted me as I fell into his soul, allowing him to spellbind me, despite everything that he was.

I gasped as his fingers clasped mine, squeezing hard. Dropping his voice to a soft whisper, he said, "Whatever you think of my family, don't let it taint what you think of me." Waving with his free hand, he continued, "These are my quarters. My bedroom is off this saloon. If it ever gets to be too much, if my brother ever goes too far, you're welcome to find sanctuary here."

Bowing his head, energy and connection poured from him. "You're *always* welcome."

My heart hurled itself against my ribcage, bruising itself in its urge to flee or perhaps surrender to the perfectly delivered offer of kinship.

I froze as he cupped my chin. My skin twinged as he held me firm. "Now, Nila Weaver, read. Forget us, and spend time with your true family."

Jethro

THREE FUCKING HOURS, I looked for her.

I hunted through Hawksridge Hall, opened doors into rooms I never wanted to step foot into ever again, and stalked down corridors I'd long since forgotten about as I never explored that part of the house.

I bumped into Diamond Brothers and got caught up in a strategy meeting for the next shipment arriving in three days, but no matter how many bedrooms, bathrooms, and lounges I searched, I found nothing.

Nothing!

Had she run again? Could she be that fucking stupid to try and escape after I'd proven how useless that was?

Damn my father for dismissing us.

The moment I'd stepped outside the dining room, Kes had requested my help on a matter. Seeing as he was the only person I had time for, I reluctantly followed, even though I wanted to wait till Cut had finished with Nila. I fucking *hated* her being alone with him. My knuckles ached from fisting so hard, and I didn't know how I would survive when the time came to share.

I'd go fucking insane.

I'd have to make sure all loaded ammunition was barred from the house, so I didn't end up slaughtering my entire family.

Nila Weaver was mine, goddammit. I didn't want anyone talking, touching, or twisting her thoughts without my permission.

Calm the fuck down.

I slammed to a stop in the middle of a corridor. If I bumped into Cut in this state, he'd know I wasn't coping. He'd take me so damn low, I wouldn't stand a chance of climbing out of the glacier so fast.

You shouldn't be thawing so quickly.

I agreed with my internal logic. I shouldn't be feeling this type of emotion. I shouldn't be letting my feelings get the better of me.

Breathing hard through my nose, I locked my jaw and recited the same thing I did every day, ten times a day, twenty even—all to remind myself of who I was meant to be and hide who I truly was.

My lips moved as I let the words trickle silently in my mind.

I'm a shadow lurking in plain sight.
A predator in sheep's clothing.
I prey on the weak with no apology.
I hide my true temper beneath a veil of decorum.
I've mastered the art of suave.
I'm a gentleman. Distinguished, accomplished, and shrewd.
I'm all of those things but none of them.
Rules and laws don't apply to me.
I'm a rule-breaker, curse-maker, life-stealer.

The minute I'd finished, my hands balled, and the devil's advocate whispered in my ear.

You're lying. It's a farce.

Clenching my jaw, I forced my heart rate to calm and for the ice to take me hostage. Repeating the mantra, I slowly fell under its hypnosis. My back relaxed, the knots in my muscles unthreading. My sweaty palms went paper dry and cold, while my face turned slack with uncaring.

Finally.

The calmness siphoning through my veins was welcome, turning everything frigid and controllable in its path.

Everything about my life since I was fifteen fucking years old was a carefully designed and executed illusion.

Up till now, I'd survived.

I'd buried the true me beneath a man so cold and perfect—even I believed—most of the time.

But every now and again, a hairline fracture would show in my glacier shell.

And my father would notice.

And he would…'fix' me.

Until I was old enough to fix myself, of course.

Which I'd done only the night before, so why was I having such difficulty now?

The thawing had happened too fast. Normally, I could pass a few weeks, sometimes more, before I ever needed to be fixed. But Nila Weaver was the sun upon my ice, turning me into a river that wanted to flow and change and *grow*. Not freeze and remain forever unmovable.

There was only one course of action to get through her invasion into my senses and survive her stay with us. I just didn't know if I had the strength to do it.

Shaking away that terrible thought, I prowled forward.

The sounds of men came and went as I passed rooms, and scents of fresh baking from the kitchens made my mouth water.

I almost walked right past her as I moved through the house lost in my thoughts. The sounds of conversation muted my attention, and if it hadn't have been for the strangest sound imaginable, I would've strode right by.

I slammed to a halt outside my brother's room.

Outside my *brother's* room.

The abominable sound came again.

Laughter.

Feminine laughter.

Nila's laughter.

And it wasn't cynical or full of contempt—it was light-hearted and relaxed.

The lyrical sound twisted my heart, turning my self-pity into fucking rage. I barged into Kestrel's apartment wing with no knock, no request, and slammed to a halt.

Flaw, Kes, and Nila sat in a grouping of wingbacks, smiling and sharing a good old fucking laugh.

What. The. Fuck?

Kes looked up, his mouth spread into a broad smile. "Jet! Nice of you to join us." His tone was a direct contradiction to his welcome.

I narrowed my eyes, trying to understand how my brother—my one ally who knew the truth about me—was antagonising me to the point of ruining everything. What was his deal?

I stupidly felt betrayed—worse than betrayed—*provoked*.

Nila's laugh cut off as she sat straighter in her chair. Her cheeks were flushed, annoyance at my interruption bright in her dark eyes.

She had the gall to be annoyed at me? When she *belonged* to me?

Flaw had the decency to stand. "Eh, I think I better go check on the..." Clearing his throat, he moved away from the small group. "Catch you guys later."

With a sideways look at me, he disappeared through the door, shutting it behind him.

The moment he'd gone, I seethed, "Care to explain what's going on?"

Kes stood up. "Calm down and no, I don't. You don't have to understand everything, Jet." Throwing a quick grin at Nila, he asked, "Unless you'd care to tell my brother what's so funny?"

Nila stared at me coldly. A second ticked past, then another, her temper shooting me cleanly through the chest.

"Well?" My heart pounded, once again shrugging out of the frosty shield in favour of rage.

Finally, she shook her head. "No. I don't think he deserves to know."

Okay...that was just plain rude.

Kes snickered. "Fair enough."

My teeth almost cracked from clenching. Why had I been worried about what I was about to do to her? She made me believe she cared—just a little—about me. She'd sucked me off for Christ's sake. She'd asked me to *fuck* her. She was attracted to me. I *knew* that.

Just like I was attracted to her.

So much.

Too much.

I was beyond fucking ready to slam inside her wet heat and finally show her the truth. That no matter her birth-right or mine, we were equals. And I'd never met anyone as challenging or intriguing.

But she'd manipulated me.

She'd used me, not once, but more times than I knew. All along I'd been fighting for the right to gain her trust, only for her to give it to my bloody brother.

Damn woman. Damn Weaver Whore.

Snapping my fingers, I hissed, "You've had your fun. Congratulations on winning once again, Ms. Weaver." Pointing at the ground by my shoes, I ordered coldly, "Come. It's time. You've wasted my day hiding. Now it's time to get this over with."

Nila tilted her chin insolently. "I didn't know we were fighting for something. Why exactly did I win?"

Goddammit.

Ignoring her question, I repeated. "Come. Now."

Kes crossed his arms, watching us as if we were his favourite volleyball match.

Nila rose gracefully from her seat. In her hands, she held the Weaver journal, which she stroked reverently, before transferring it from her lap and onto the chair she'd just vacated. Her actions were stiff, back ramrod straight.

"Whatever you believe, I wasn't hiding, Jethro. Merely finding friends in the unlikely of places."

I froze as she moved toward Kestrel.

He opened his arms.

She walked into his embrace.

She walked into his *fucking* embrace.

I couldn't understand.

I didn't *want* to understand.

She prefers him over you, idiot. She can see you're different. She can sense you're screwed up.

The hug lasted far longer than my tolerance level. Who was I kidding—I *had* no tolerance level.

Kes was mine, and Nila was mine. They both belonged to me. They had no right to gang up against me.

"Kes..." I immediately snapped my lips together. I refused to be weak and ask him what the hell this meant. Instead, I embraced vulgarity. "I wouldn't get close to her, brother. Never know where her mouth has been." My tone was a viper ready to strike.

Kestrel let Nila go, eyeing me coldly. "If it's been anywhere on you, then I can guess. But you're forgetting, *brother*, I'm not the one with sharing issues. Am I?"

My mouth fell open. A pain shot deep inside my heart. In our entire lifetime together, he'd never provoked me that way. Never brought up something so painful or the crux of my whole issue.

"Fuck you," I growled.

Kes's eyes tightened, finally showing some sign of regret. Bastard.

Nila looked between us silently, crackling with energy. No doubt this family drama was hugely amusing to her. I never wanted her to see me like this. What was this? Had Kestrel finally had enough of being second best to the firstborn son, or had he seen something he truly wanted in Nila?

Either way, it didn't matter. He couldn't have her. No one could.

"Jet, let's forget it, okay?" Holding up his hands, he added, "Bygones, yeah?"

"Bygones? What the hell are you doing?"

Kes shook his head. "We'll talk about it later. Right now,

you have things to do."

"Things like extract a debt from me?" Nila snapped.

My attention flew to her, just in time to see her topple sideways as one of her stupid episodes rendered her incompetent.

"Shit." Kes ducked at inhuman speed, catching her before she hit the ground.

My stomach twisted with jealousy.

Moaning, Nila crumbled into Kes's arms.

"You all right?" Kes slowly guided her onto her feet.

That—right there. *That* was the true difference between my brother and me. He caught those who needed to be caught, while I stood by and watched. The memory of Nila falling to the parking garage floor at the Milan airport showed me just how true that statement was.

I have no choice.

Empathy and softness weren't permitted. They were the root of all evil for a person like me.

Taking a deep breath, Nila pushed Kes gently. "I'm fine. Thanks for your help."

Kes nodded, shoving his hands into his jeans pockets. "You're welcome. You should probably have that looked at."

"It's not a disease," I jumped in. "Besides, she's better than when I first collected her."

Nila's cheeks blazed with colour. She wobbled a little as another wave hit her. "Do you know why that is? I was thinking about it before actually."

No one spoke, waiting for her to continue.

"I get them when I'm stressed. I probably suffered five or six a day when I was working so hard and presenting my new season to buyers and reporters. And yet, here...I only seem to suffer them around *you*." Cocking her head, she placed her fists on her hips. "What does that tell you, Jethro?"

What did it tell me? Apart from the fact she was weak-minded and needed professional help for a counter imbalance? "That I stress you out."

"Exactly."

Another wave crippled her. Kes was the convenient arsehole who captured her elbow giving her an anchor. "There you go again. You okay?"

She nodded, rubbing her temples. "Sorry. Damn vertigo. Can't control it."

Kes smiled, his body curved into hers. "Don't apologise. We all have flaws, and sometimes they're not something we have the power to change."

He's talking about me again. Fuckwit.

Nila's lips popped open, her eyes searching his. "You're nothing like your phone messages."

My muscles instantly locked.

Her voice was barely a whisper. I wouldn't have caught it unless my ears weren't already straining for every nuance in her tone.

She knows.

Kes cocked his head, his eyes blocking all clues and answers. Laughing self-consciously, he quickly pressed a kiss on her cheek and released her. "If that's a good thing, I'll take the credit."

That's it.

I was fucking done.

Stalking forward, I plucked Nila from the carpet and threw her over my shoulder. Kes's mouth fell open. "Um…"

"Don't say another word, *brother.*" I transmitted everything I couldn't say with one glare. "Stay out of this. All of it."

Nila squealed, hitting my back with tiny fists. "Put me down, you arsehole."

"No chance," I growled. "I'm not letting you go until I have you exactly where I want you."

Preferably naked with my cock driving between your legs.

But because I was the perfect son, I would have to save that for another day.

There was a small matter of a debt. A debt that had to be repaid before the day turned into dusk—for no other reason but tradition. We'd run out of time.

Kes stared at me, his eyes waging with an apology and

confrontation. If Nila wasn't here, I had no doubt we'd either pummel each other or have the deepest, longest conversation of our lives. This one incident had brought everything we'd avoided to a head.

Kes and I were friends—more than I could say for the rest of the people inside this house—but despite our friendship, there was still a thick rivalry between us. Not just because of primogeniture and the fact I would inherit everything, but because we'd both been hurt by the same incident in our pasts.

We just dealt with it differently.

He'd played a good game where Nila was concerned. A game I'd never been able to master—the art of wielding kindness. My kindness came with too many conditions and more pain than if I remained cruel. But Kes, he was...better than me.

I knew the real him. And despite my agony at him wanting Nila's attention, he was a good guy.

Silently, he raised a finger, pointing it in my face. Nila couldn't see him as he mouthed, "I know it's not working. We need to find other methods."

Shit, if he could see, Cut wouldn't be too far behind.

"Dammit, Jethro, put me down." Nila hammered on my lower back.

Ignoring her, I shifted her higher over my shoulder and nodded once.

Then I put every worry and thought in the vault deep inside me and lashed the chains tight. I had work to do.

Not giving Kes the satisfaction of seeing me ruffled, I spun around and left without a word with my prize slung over my shoulder.

"Let me go!" Nila continued to pummel my back with every step.

"I won't put you down until we get there. I've wasted three hours of my life wondering where you were. I'm not going to release you just so you can escape again."

"We've already solved the 'what if I ran game.' I know you'd hunt me down. I wouldn't waste the energy trying to escape."

I grunted. "At least you've learned one thing that's valuable."

"I've learned a lot more than that," she muttered quietly. *Yes, like who Kite007 is.*

My arm squeezed tighter around her. Bloody brother. The minute I had time, I would confront him with all the shit he'd caused.

Swallowing hard, I forced myself to slip back into the ice and embrace everything that I ought to be.

I had a debt to extract.

This was what was expected of me.

And I meant to do it fucking well.

It didn't take long to arrive in the room where the First Debt would take place.

Tradition dictated where each one was to be carried out. And this one was the nicest location of them all.

As the debts progressed, witnesses would be called, but as this was the first, it was just me and Nila. Blessed silence and no critical eyes on my deliverance. Only the hidden video camera would document everything and go on file.

Entering the solarium, I locked the large glass doors and pocketed the key before gripping Nila's waist and placing her on the ground. She immediately stepped backward, her chest heaving with fear.

If she passed out again, my brother wasn't there to catch her. She'd fall, and I'd use her unconsciousness to place her exactly where she was needed.

"Where have you brought me?" She glanced around the space, taking in the palm trees, exotic ferns, orchids, and soaring three-story glass roof. The room was big, shaped like an octagon, made entirely from glass. It was hot, humid, and stuffy.

Perfect for being naked and encouraging skin to flush. To react to something painful and bloom.

"Be grateful it's not the dungeon or the ballroom—both of those will be used, and both will be a far sight worse than this."

Nila swallowed, the column of muscle of her throat contracting with nervousness. "You really are insane."

I stepped forward, secretly pleased when she reeled backward. After spending time in my brother's company, she had to remember who she truly liked. As much as she'd vehemently deny it, she enjoyed sparring with me.

And fuck, I enjoyed it, too.

"Mental health, Ms. Weaver. Need I remind you I'm in perfect capacity?"

Her head swivelled to a large post in the centre of the room. It was used mainly for fern seedlings and vines, before being replanted once their root system was strong enough. I wasn't a gardener, but my grandmother often brought me and my sister in here to teach us about decorum and what was expected of us. She'd prattle on, all while tending to her beloved greenery.

Nila drifted forward, noticing what was hidden amongst the cleaned post and silk flowers that were there purely for morbid decoration.

Cuffs were chained to the top of the post, dangling down the sides. There was a winch and pulley so as to tighten the length of chain. It was simple, entirely in keeping with how they would've used a whipping post six-hundred-years ago.

She shook her head, swivelling to face me. "Whatever you're about to do, stop."

"Stop?" *As if I have a choice. Smile for the cameras. We're both on show.*

"Yes. Just—find that morality I know is inside you. Show some compassion, for God's sake." She staggered to the side, another small vertigo spell.

I'd hated her weakness before, but now it could be used as an aid. Whenever she stumbled or fell, it meant I was getting to her. It meant I'd made my way beneath her skin and stressed her just enough for her mind to try and flee.

It was a symbol of power over her.

I liked it more than I should.

"Compassion isn't in my repertoire, Ms. Weaver. I have no remorse, no pity. The unnecessary emotion of affinity for victims is the worst kind of betrayal." My father's words came out smoothly, stroking my raw nerves, granting a strange kind of peace.

"You can sprout bullshit all you want, but no matter your lies, you *feel*, Jethro. You felt something for me in the forest. You felt something for me when your brother held me in his arms. And if you can't see that, then I feel sorry for you."

I prowled forward, chasing her slowly around the post like a hawk chases a sparrow. "You're mistaken. I've told you on numerous occasions—please me, and you'll be rewarded. You pleased me by making me come, and you pleased me by showing how affected and scared of me you truly are by seeking comfort from my brother. Both will be rewarded."

I hoped to God she didn't hear my lies.

She stopped moving, holding her ground. "Fine. Have it your way. Your father repeated what you told me about the varying degree of each debt. This whole thing is completely ludicrous, but I'm done playing your game."

I cocked my head. "This isn't a game."

She sneered. "It's the worst game of all, don't kid yourself." Spreading her stance and opening her arms wide, she murmured, "Do your worst, Jethro Hawk. I'm ready to pay your First Debt."

Nila

I WANTED TO hyperventilate; my heart winged with such terror.

But I wouldn't give him the satisfaction. He already knew he affected me by my stupid vertigo spells. He didn't need to know the complex fear and fascination bubbling in my blood.

Why hadn't I seen it sooner? Why hadn't I seen past what he projected and looked deeper into his golden eyes? He was so tangled up in what he *thought* he was, he had no clue what he might be.

And that was a pitiful shame, not to mention dangerous for all involved. I could predict how he would react, based on what values he pretended to follow, but he could easily snap and do something completely the opposite.

Damn man.

Damn Hawk.

Jethro lowered his chin, glaring at me from beneath his brow. His hands opened and closed by his thighs. "You're ready to pay the First Debt? Just like that?"

I nodded. "No point in dragging it out. I want it over with."

Something flashed over his face, but he didn't retaliate. Instead, he gritted his teeth and moved toward the post in the centre of the octagonal greenhouse.

My vision wouldn't stop hazing in and out, tugging on the strings of my brain, threatening to throw me into the wall or shove me to the ground.

This is the First Debt.

Mr. Hawk's and Jethro's words echoed in my head. *The debts start off easy.* It was the later ones I had to worry about. The ones I didn't know of. The ones that would ultimately deliver my head.

Don't think about that.

I turned my mind to Kestrel and the surprising kinship I'd begun to feel, before Jethro rudely stole me away. For almost three hours, I'd found something I didn't think I'd ever find—in my old life or new.

A friend.

Kes had been witty and kind, sharing anecdotes of his childhood, Jethro's childhood, and even some details he remembered of my mother. For some reason, having him talk about her didn't upset me nearly as much as hearing it from Jethro or his father.

I knew I had to stay on my guard after what Cut had said: *I'm to be treated with kindness and compassion.* I could easily fall into the trap of thinking their concern was genuine. But...if Kes *was* Kite, we had a connection that went past family obligations.

Don't we?

Regardless, we'd spent a couple of hours sharing things that'd transported me away from Hawksridge Hall and to a place filled with softness. A connection formed, dusting my tummy with tentative bubbles of attraction.

He was nice...despite my healthy suspicion of his motives.

But one thing niggled me.

One thing I hadn't been able to figure out.

He was completely different from the man who cursed and acted so crude via text messages. His arrogant way of demanding sexual gratification when not face-to-face was a direct contradiction to his kindness in person.

It didn't make sense—almost as if he had split personas—once again proving my theory that all Hawks were daft.

"What did my father tell you?" Jethro asked.

I blinked, forcing myself to pay attention to the mad man currently circling me like a vulture. "What?"

Jethro balled his hands. "When he kept you back, what did he say?"

I shrugged. "Same thing as you. I learned nothing new." The way he watched me hinted that he had secrets he didn't want spilled. Narrowing my eyes, I asked, "Why?"

He shook his head. "No reason." Clearing his throat, he added, "So, you were told you're now the obedient family dog, correct? To be treated kindly and receive everything you want."

My heart squeezed. Anger flowed thick and cloying. "Something like that." *And just like a mistreated pet, I'll shred the fingers that feed me.*

Jethro huffed, returning to the post again. With competent hands, he tugged on the hanging cuffs and kicked something covered by a towel at the foot of the wooden structure.

His eyes locked on mine. "Tell me, Ms. Weaver. Are you sure you're ready?"

My heart bucked into panic mode. I'd taunted him and said I was, but now faced with willingly handing myself over and letting him do whatever he wanted, it was entirely different.

When I didn't move, he murmured, "No tears. No screams. Own this just like my ancestors did when it was done to them."

The Debt Inheritance came back to mind. What had my family done that was so heinous that it called for such horrendous payback?

Swallowing hard, I inched closer to the post. "I need to understand why."

"Why?" His forehead furrowed. "Where exactly is the fun in that?"

"Fun?" Oh, my God, he would enjoy this? *What did you expect?* I supposed I kept seeing the man who was human beneath the icy robot. It led me to false conclusions, which Jethro seemed to love to smash.

"I suppose that is the wrong word." Jethro stilled, his eyes filling with things I couldn't decipher. He stood still for a long moment, before visibly shaking off whatever held him hostage. "Come here. Let's begin."

My stomach fell into my toes. Making me come on my own made all of this worse. I was the sacrificial lamb willingly walking toward the pyre.

Goosebumps broke out over my body as my feet whispered slowly toward Jethro.

He sucked in a breath.

The air went from humid to sharp with awareness. I hated that he had the power to tingle my skin and twist my belly. It wasn't fair. It wasn't right that I found him so attractive when I ought to be abhorred.

My eyes fell on the cuffs dangling between fake flowers. I didn't need to ask what he had planned. It was obvious, and I wouldn't give him the enjoyment of dragging out the suspense and toying with me.

Gritting my jaw, I pressed closer, holding my wrists up to the leather cuffs.

Jethro quirked an eyebrow, his tongue darting out to lick his bottom lip. "What are you doing?"

Gathering as much courage as I had, and hoping to God my vertigo would stay away, I smiled diabeticly sweet. "The cuffs are obviously there for a reason; I'm just saving you the trouble of instructing me."

Silence fell, rippling around us.

His jaw worked. "Just like smugness, cockiness is not becoming on you, Ms. Weaver." Leaning forward, his torso turned the already sharp awareness into biting attraction. His scent of woods and leather enveloped me. Against my wishes, my stomach clenched, and I breathed deeply.

His nostrils flared, but he didn't say another word as his strong, cold fingers latched around my wrist, tugging it higher to wrap the supple cuff around me.

The chemistry between us—or was it just blind hate—crackled and fizzed, sending the hair on the back of my neck bristling.

I couldn't deny I was drawn to Kes—partly because I thought he was Kite and partly because he had an ease about him, a generosity that made me want to know more—but it was nothing, *nothing*, compared to the fierce hunger I felt when Jethro touched me.

His lips parted as he buckled the cuff. Refusing to make eye contact, he remained focused as he cinched it tight.

Moving stiffly, he captured my other wrist.

A small gasp fell from my lips as his fingers kissed the paper-thin skin. His eyes held me hostage. The golden brown was now a swirling bronze, raging with the same demanding hunger I knew reflected in mine.

"This sort of reminds me of the forest," I whispered. "The trees around us—no one else." My words fell like petals, waiting for Jethro to crush them beneath his glossy shoe.

But...he didn't.

Tracing one hand from my wrist, along the inside of my arm, and right to my throat, he fisted my ponytail. With intensity that stripped my soul to the very essence of who I was, he pulled my head back slowly, sensually, full of sexual power.

His eyes dropped to my mouth. "I'll let you in on a little secret, Ms. Weaver."

I panted, my neck straining against his hold, but I made no move to break the poignant awareness.

"You won that night, but I lied when I said it pissed me off." His mouth dropped, his tongue licked my bottom lip with the barest of grazes. "I've never enjoyed coming in someone's mouth as much as I did in yours." He licked me again, quaking my frame. "In fact, I would willingly let you win again, if I received the same ball-shattering release."

My lips begged to connect with his. This single-minded lust between us was sacred. The only place where we were both equal, and heritage had no authority. I'd made a promise to use sex against him, but now I added to my promise.

I will use him to make me stronger, better—invincible.

I wanted to become a woman whose arsenal included lust

and sensuality, regardless of my slight frame and inexperience.

"Kiss me," I murmured, tugging my hair gently in his hold.

Jethro shook his head, his fingers tightening around my ponytail. Tracing the tip of his tongue once more on my bottom lip, he whispered, "I don't kiss my enemies."

My heart became an inferno, sending flames blazing with every beat. "You just fuck them?"

His mouth twitched into a roguish smile. "Only if they beg."

His body pressed against mine, his thigh going purposely between my legs.

My eyes snapped closed as he rocked against my throbbing clit. "Would you beg, Ms. Weaver? How hot and frustrated do I have to make you before you'll beg me to drive my cock inside you?"

My brain spasmed at the thought. The answer? Not long. I would beg right now if it meant he would forget about the debt and take me back to his room. I wanted to see where he slept. I wanted to infiltrate the home ground of my opponent and undermine him right at the source.

"You're all talk. You won't even kiss me, let alone fuck me."

Jethro yanked my head back. Pain shot down my spine. "How wrong you are, Ms. Weaver." Then a vindictive smile replaced the black desire. "Very clever, though, I must admit."

I blinked, trying to dispel the fog of lust and keep up with him. "Why?"

His thigh slid out from between my legs; his fingers untwined from my hair. "Very clever to make me focus on other things than the true reason of why we're here." Stepping back and sucking in a deep breath, he dragged a hand through his hair. "You keep on surprising me, and I keep on despising what you show me."

I laughed tightly. "Doesn't look like you despise me." I cocked my chin at the straining erection in his trousers. "I think you like me, and despite what you're going to do and who you are, I still find you attractive."

And believe me, if I had a cure for that insanity, I'd take it without hesitation.

Cruelly, he snatched my free wrist, wrapping the remaining cuff tightly. Quickly securing the buckle, he muttered, "The way you threw yourself into my brother's arms hints you might have a desire for all Hawks." His breath was hot in my ear as he spun me to face the post. "You're just a conniving manipulator."

I cried out as he disappeared behind the post and hoisted my arms high with the aid of a hidden winch. Another jerk and my wrists burned in the supple leather. My torso smashed against the damp wood as my body weight transferred from my toes to my arms.

"How does that feel?" Jethro asked, coming back around.

My shoulders screamed; my blood throbbed with effort to reach my raised fingertips. I dangled with no chance at escape.

How does it feel?

It fucking hurt! It made my previous thoughts of lust seem ridiculous.

All concepts of seducing him disappeared. I only wanted this over fast, so I could admit defeat and lick my wounds in private.

"I asked you a question," Jethro growled, his hand stroking my spine.

I flinched at his touch. It was sacrilegious, because even now it *still* made my core clench with want. "It hurts. Is that what you want to hear?"

Jethro's torso pressed against my back, squashing my cheek against the damp wood of the post. The crispness of plants and the musky scent of earth overpowered his smell, giving me a welcome reprieve from the man who drove me mad.

"You look rather tempting like this, Ms. Weaver. Perhaps it will be *me* begging before this is done."

I couldn't stop my skin shivering with awareness or my heart seizing with anxiety and desire.

"Don't touch me," I hissed.

With a small laugh, he pushed away, ceasing contact.

I twisted my neck, never letting him from my sight. I hated having him so close. I hated that I had no power to stop him. I hated how he stood there, wrapped in silence, watching me like some mystery he had yet to solve.

We didn't speak, waiting to see who would break first.

Finally, after a minute, he said softly, "I'm going to give you a history lesson, Ms. Weaver. You'll listen closely and understand why you're repaying this certain debt." Pacing, he added, "Every debt will begin this way. The history will be told, then the debt repaid. You'll be informed of what your ancestors did to mine. You will apologise and repent for their past sins, and only then will the extraction take place."

Coming close, his body heat burned me. His words were tiny whips lashing my ear. "If you do not repent and permit the debt to be paid, you will be beaten. If you do not accept why a debt has to be paid, the extraction will be taken twice. Do you understand?"

Twice?

Double horror.

Double terror.

Then...I laughed. Morbid, yes, but the image in my head was comical.

"You mean to tell me, you'll behead me twice?" I smiled. "Are you necromancers as well as lunatics? Please, inform me on how that will work."

His hand lashed out, spanking my denim-clad behind.

I groaned, jolting in the binds. I couldn't unravel the painful smarting from his strike and the throbbing in my nipples and clit.

Shit. Don't let him see that he's broken my mind already. If he touched me, felt how drenched I was, I would never live with myself again.

"I've had enough of your mouth, Ms. Weaver."

"Are you sure? Didn't seem that way in the forest with my lips around you. Did you know that was my first ever blowjob?"

He sucked in a breath. His hand landed in my hair, fisting the thickness and burning my scalp. His lips tickled my ear as he whispered, "You keep taunting me with what happened in the forest. Do you think just because you swallowed that I'm what...*grateful?* Sentimental? In *love?*" He shook me. "What, Ms. Weaver? Shall I not remind you it was *you* who clenched around my tongue so hard you almost fucking bruised me? Every lick and fucking taste I had of your pussy, I drove you wild." He trailed the tip of his tongue from my ear to my cheek.

I trembled, every part of me tightening.

"We're on even ground. Orgasm for an orgasm. Don't think it gives you power, because it doesn't."

I breathed hard, trying to find some resemblance of the hatred I'd nursed. But he pressed his body flush against mine, grinding his erection into the small of my back.

He groaned under his breath. "What I wouldn't give to fuck you. To stop your teasing and use you like you want me to."

Everything inside me charged, ignited, spindled out of control.

The thought of having him inside me both repulsed and enticed. The mental image of us fighting this unknown battle while our naked bodies fought for domination sent scorching thrills through me.

My breathing turned to pants. "Why haven't you?"

Damn, the words fell from my lips before I had time to censor them.

Jethro's hips twitched harder against me. He didn't reply.

The question hung like a flag fluttering in the lust-thick breeze. I couldn't take it back, and Jethro wouldn't answer it.

Pulling his body heat away, he shoved his hands through his hair and paced the room. "Time for your history lesson."

I wriggled against the pole, dreadfully uncomfortable and vibrating with anger and desire.

I hated the wetness between my legs. I hated that whenever he touched me, I would rather kiss *then* kill him, rather than flat-out destroy him.

My body was hot and confused. Desperate for freedom. Ravenous for lust.

"In 1460, the Hawks were nobodies. We had no land, no titles, no money of any kind. We were the lowest of the low and survived on the generosity of others. Luckily, after years of begging and living on the streets, my ancestor and his family managed to find employment in a household who were the opposite of everything they were.

"At the beginning, it seemed like luck had finally shone upon them, and their days of thievery and struggles were at an end. What they didn't know was it marked the end of their freedom, and, ultimately, their lives. They became slaves—available at the Weavers' every beck and call for every frivolous demand. Not only did my ancestor work for the family, but his wife became their kitchen maid, his son their stable boy, and his daughter their scullery underling. A family of Hawks working for a family of Weavers."

Jethro's voice was hypnotic, whisking me away from the greenhouse to a time where sewage flowed in busy streets and rat meat was as common as chicken in the slums of London.

Jethro never stopped his tale. "They worked every hour—cooking, cleaning, fetching—ensuring the Weavers lived a life of well-tended luxury. Nothing was too much for them—they were the cogs that made the household run."

"So they were employees," I butted in. "They were hired to look after my forefathers and no doubt given room and board as well as food and clothing."

Jethro stalked toward me. Fisting my hair, he snarled, "You'd think that, wouldn't you? A fair trade for the amount of hours they slaved. But no. The Weavers didn't believe in fairness of employment. They didn't pay a cent—not to those who came from the gutter. But you're right—they did provide board and lodging, but they taxed it so heavily, my family existed in the Weavers' cellar with scraps from their table. Every year their unpayable taxes grew higher."

Sickness swirled in my stomach. "How do you mean?"

Jethro let me go, continuing his stroll around the room. "I mean that every year they were worse off, not only working but *paying* their employers for the chance. Every year at Christmas, they were ordered to pay back their taxes of being privileged enough to live in the graces of the Weavers, and every year they couldn't pay it back."

That's awful.

My heart hurt for such unfairness, of such unnecessary brutality. *It can't be true. No one could be that horrid.* Then again, it happened so long ago. It was still insanity to make me pay for it.

I gritted my teeth, fortifying myself against Jethro's brainwashing. I couldn't believe my forefathers were tyrannical employers. There would've been rules—even then. Surely?

It's sad, but it's also hundreds and hundreds of years ago. Get over it.

I said with half-hearted conviction, "They could've left and found other work. They didn't have to put up with that treatment, even if it was true."

Jethro laughed coldly. "Seems so simple to you, doesn't it, Ms. Weaver? Inhumane treatment, so leave." He glowered. "Not so easy when *your* ancestor was raping *my* ancestor's wife every night, and the mistress of the house had turned every law enforcer in the county against them. She spun such an elegant tale of espionage and thievery; no one would listen to the truth. Everyone believed the Hawks were cold-hearted criminals who were unappreciative of the generosity of the upstanding Weavers."

Jethro crossed his arms. "Can you believe the Weavers even managed to coerce the police to issue a standing warrant, stating if ever a Hawk stopped working for the Weavers, they would be punished? The law said they'd be thrown into the keep and tortured for their crimes, then murdered as an example to other misbehaving working class."

My stomach twisted into knots. I wished my hands were untied so I could clamp them over my ears and not listen to Jethro's lies.

This was sick. Terrible. Woefully unjust.

Jethro moved closer, no sound, just like his beloved silence. "Needless to say, they were very unhappy. The wife tried to commit suicide, only for her daughter to find her and the Weavers' best physician to bring her back from the dead. She couldn't escape the nightly exploits of the man of the house, and day by day, her children starved from lack of proper care and nutrition.

"So, one day Frank Hawk waited until the Weaver bastard had raped his wife for the second time that night and put her to bed with her ailing offspring. He waited until the house was quiet and everyone rested, before sneaking from the cellar and into the kitchens."

The image Jethro painted drove needles deep and painful into my heart. I couldn't think of such horrible people or such a sorry existence. How could my ancestors have done such a thing?

"He should've snuck up the stairs and slaughtered his employer while he slept, but his inner fire had been well and truly beaten out after years of abuse. He had no other drive but to stay alive in the hope redemption would save him.

"That night, he only took enough to keep them alive, because no matter their rancid living conditions, he wasn't ready to die. He wasn't ready to permit his children to fade away. He was ready to find his self-worth again and fight. To find the rage to commit murder. And to do that, he needed strength.

"Tiptoeing back to the basement, he and his family had their first good meal in years. Scotch eggs, crusty bread, and anything else he managed to pillage." Jethro smiled, before continuing, "Of course, their meal didn't go unnoticed."

I gulped, completely wrapped up in his tale.

"The next day, the cook announced someone had been in her kitchen and stole. Mr. Weaver immediately turfed my family from their beds, finding evidence of misdeeds in the way of crumbs and hastily devoured food. He announced a crime had been committed; therefore, punishment must be paid.

"He dragged Frank Hawk to the village square where he strung him up on the whipping post and left him to hang by his wrists for a day and a night in the dead of winter." Jethro's hands suddenly clasped mine, straining above me to thread his fingers through my digits—his touch cold and threatening.

I shivered, biting my cheek.

His lips brushed against my ear as his cock twitched against my lower back. "Do you know what they did to thieves back in the 1400s, Ms. Weaver?"

I closed my eyes, bile scalding my throat.

Yes, I knew. The methods of law enforcement were a hot subject at school. The Tower of London had extreme inventions for dishing out pain to those who didn't deserve it.

"Yes," I breathed.

Jethro tugged my fingers. "Care to share?"

Swallowing, I whispered, "The usual punishment for stealing was hands being cut off, ears nailed to spikes, flogging...all manner of beastly things."

My fingers ached beneath his as he squeezed hard.

Then he stepped back, letting me go. "Can you empathize with my ancestor? Can you tap into the panic he must've felt to lose a hand or other body part?"

I squeezed my eyes, nodding. It would've been awful and even worse for the wife as she stood by and watched the love of her life—the same man who had no power to protect her—accept punishment, all for just keeping her alive. A life she probably didn't even want with rape and destitution as the highlights.

Jethro said, "This is the easiest debt to endure, Ms. Weaver. But back then, it was one of the worst." Moving behind me again, his fingers fumbled at the hem of my t-shirt. Pulling it from my skin, he tore it in half with one vicious tug. The crack of the material ripping echoed in the octagonal space.

I jerked as humid air kissed my naked spine.

A moan escaped my lips as I finally understood what he would do.

I wanted to beg for mercy. For him to stop this ridiculous ancient tally and let bygones be bygones, but no sound came as he shoved my tattered t-shirt to my shoulders, exposing my back. His fingers were firm and unyielding as he reached in front and undid the button on my shorts.

"Please," I moaned as he undid them and shoved them to my ankles.

Jethro didn't reply, nor did he ask me to kick the discarded shorts away. I let them stay—imprisoning my ankles, just like the cuffs imprisoned my wrists.

Leaving me naked and quivering with fear, Jethro disappeared.

I didn't try to follow him with my eyes. I kept them squeezed tight, shivering and trembling, wishing I was anywhere but here.

Jethro tapped me on the shoulder a few moments later, his touch harsh and demanding. "Open your eyes."

I reluctantly obeyed, focusing on his flawless face and cold, unforgiving gaze.

He dangled a flogger in front of my vision. It held a multitude of leather strips with knots in regular intervals down the strands. "Have you seen one of these?"

I nodded.

I was a designer. I garnered inspiration from everything and anything, including different lifestyle choices, eras, and kinks. However, there was nothing sexually playful about this one. It was mean and meant to hurt.

I balled my hands, cursing the pins and needles in my fingertips as blood rushed faster. "Yes."

"And do you think it was a just punishment for stealing something, all to keep his family alive?"

I shook my head. "No."

Jethro agreed, "No. Especially in the dead of winter where his body was frozen and brittle, and the slightest touch would've been agony." He ran his finger down my shoulder blades. "You're warm, in a humid room. Your skin is supple and flushed. Pain won't register as badly as if I'd placed you inside a freezer or dumped you in ice water before we started."

He dropped his voice. "Want to know another secret, Ms. Weaver? Want to know something that could potentially get me into a lot of trouble?"

My eyes flared. The way he asked…he was serious. I twisted, trying to catch his eye, but he remained just out of looking distance. "What?" I breathed.

Jethro pressed his body against mine again, digging his belt buckle painfully into my lower back, sandwiching my naked skin harder against the post. "I was supposed to do that. Supposed to make you so cold, I could snap your arm with one touch. You were supposed to be numb and chattering with chill so that every lash would make you scream in endless agony."

I swallowed hard, fear lacing my blood. "Why—why didn't you?" Even my heart stopped beating in fear of missing his answer. I needed to find a way to understand this man, before it was too late.

He dropped his voice to barely a whisper, "Because no one should have to be as cold as I've been taught." He suddenly stepped back, letting the flogger hang down in his grip.

He snapped, "I suggest you hug the post, Ms. Weaver. This is going to hurt."

Jethro

NILA IMMEDIATELY DID as I said.

With no hesitation, she pressed her body harder against the post, doing her best to hold on despite the restricting cuffs.

Every muscle in her back stood out: every ridge and valley from her trim arse to her taut shoulders. Bruises from vertigo stained the flawless white. Scratches from trees and nature marred her with violence. Every rib stood out as she stopped breathing and locked her knees.

I couldn't have her passing out from lack of oxygen. She had to stay with me. We were in this together.

Gathering the knotted torture device, I murmured, "Do you repent? Do you take ownership of your family's sins and agree to pay the debt?"

Nila pressed even harder against the post, as if she could morph into the wood and disappear.

When she didn't reply, I coaxed, "I asked you a question, Ms. Weaver." Running the flogger through my hands, I stepped closer. "Do you?"

She sucked in a breath, her ribcage straining against her blemished skin. "Ye—yes." Her head bowed, and her lips went white.

I nodded. It was on record. I'd asked and she'd agreed—that was all I needed.

Taking my place for deliverance, I murmured, "I want you to count."

Her eyes shot wide, her cheek squished against the bark of the post. "Count?"

I smiled. "I want to hear you acknowledge every lash."

With my heart in my chest, I spread my thighs and jerked my arm back. I told her the truth about disobeying the order to lock her in the chiller. If my father found out, I could be in serious shit.

We both could.

I hadn't found the balls to delve into the reasons why I hadn't obeyed the procedure. All I could focus on was delivering the First Debt. Then I could get out of here. Then I could get some peace.

"Don't stop counting," I grunted. My arm sailed forward, sending the four-stranded flogger whistling through the air.

For a split second, I suffered an out-of-body experience. I *saw* myself. I witnessed the anger and power on my face. I watched as if I wasn't the one wielding pain but an outsider. And I wondered what it would be like to belong to a different family. To have a different upbringing.

But then the experience stopped, slamming me back into my body.

The flogger sliced through the thick silence.

Nila screamed.

I jolted.

Raw redness bloomed as the lash licked across flesh.

Her skin was so delicate; blood welled instantly.

I stumbled at the sight. My heart shot from my chest and lay beating and mangled on the floor. Images of hunting and killing flurried in my mind. Drawing blood was not new to me. But drawing it from a woman I'd developed feelings for was.

It felt...

...

Fuck, I don't know.

Strange. Exotic. Not entirely distasteful but not fully delectable either.

A realm of uncertainty.

Nila slouched against the post as pain washed through her system. She panted, moans ragged in her chest.

I'd done my part, but she'd yet to do hers.

"Count!" I roared.

Flinching, she stood taller. Sniffing back unshed tears, she yelled, "One!"

Her voice hijacked my body; my cock throbbed.

I'd been prepared to do everything that I'd been ordered. After all, I *wanted* to. I'd been taught to crave this control. To hurt others.

But in that second, I craved something entirely different. I wanted to feel the heat of her whipped back against my front as I slid into her tightness and fucked her. I wanted her to scream for an entirely different reason.

Goddammit, what the hell is happening to me?

I struck again, sending the flogger flying. The soft leather bit into her back. "Count!" I snapped. Causing her pain helped ease a little of mine. This woman had the power to ruin me. That would never be permitted. *I have to ruin her first.*

She screamed again. "Two!"

My muscles already ached from being tense and on edge. My balls disappeared inside my body with the urge to come.

How the fuck will I get through this?

Two down.

Nineteen to go.

The number was written in the logbook of the county enforcer. Twenty-one lashings for Frank Hawk on account of thievery. His son, Bennett Hawk, was the stable boy who wrote up the Debt Inheritance.

Frank had been bleeding and left to freeze. Twenty-one oozing cuts turning to red frost before being deemed repentant for providing for his family.

Like for like.

Debt for debt.

That was my purpose.

That was the madness of my family. Not so much for

principle or honouring our ancestor's hardships—but to embrace the power we once lacked. Power we now wielded in perfect precision. The Weavers weren't our agenda—it was the convenience of having an exclusive family tree destined to let us torment and torture, to keep our fangs dripping and claws sharp.

I raised my arm, sailing the knotted strands, tearing across Nila's skin.

"Ah!" Her body shuddered with agony.

My cock stabbed painfully against my belt as Nila writhed on the pole. Dropping my hand, I grabbed the rock hard piece of flesh, rearranging its position so it didn't snap itself in two in my trousers. "I don't hear counting," I growled.

"Three," she cried.

Another lash.

"Four."

Another.

"Five!"

With each one her back blistered, turning from unwhipped perfection to weeping rawness. The humidity of the conservatory drenched my shirt until liquid salt covered my skin. Every lash, savage hunger built inside, feeding off Nila's pain and my own for wanting her.

My mouth watered to kiss her spine, to lick at the mess I'd caused.

I wanted to nuzzle her tears and whisper the truth of who I was.

You never can.

Just the mere thought of being honest petrified me. If I spoke it, how would I keep it hidden?

I should never have done this in such a hot place. I should never have attempted something so barbaric without shielding my mind properly. Every strike hurt Nila externally, but she couldn't see what it did to my soul.

I struck again, breathing hard through my nose.

"Six," Nila moaned.

The heat of the room seeped through my pores, twisting

my heart, melting any frost I might've conjured. Every cold shard melted, turning into a cascade of warmth.

I swallowed as I drank in Nila's exquisite form. The way she trembled but refused to let her knees buckle. The way her cheeks flushed and dark eyes sucked power from the room.

She was...magnificent.

I cocked my arm, sending the flogger to claw at her lower back.

Nila groaned loudly. "Seven."

My arm ached as I struck again.

"Eight."

And again.

"Nine."

Nine down.

Twelve to go.

Shit, I was ready to collapse. I was ready to crawl to her feet and beg for her to forgive me.

Forgive me?

There was nothing to forgive. She deserved this!

I struck hard, forcing myself to stay ruthless.

"Ten!" she screeched.

My ears rang with her pain.

I gave up trying to control my emotions and surrendered. The sooner I delivered her penance, the sooner I could undo the wrong I'd done.

Gritting my teeth, I picked up my pace. Delivering blow after blow, quicker and quicker.

"Eleven," Nila sobbed.

"Twelve."

"Thirteen." Her voice broke and a glistening tear slicked down her cheek.

It cleaved my fucking heart.

"Fourteen!"

Sweat poured down my face as I hit again and again. My breathing matched hers. I'd never been so turned on in all my life or so fucking disgusted.

It made me face things I'd hidden deep, deep inside. It

drew ghosts and terrors all into confrontation. I needed to run. Before I lost myself.

But I couldn't leave. I knew in my heart, I wouldn't be able to walk away from this without fucking her. There was nothing on this earth that would stop me from taking her the moment I'd finished the last lash. I didn't care I wasn't supposed to touch her until the Third Debt.

I don't fucking care.

Everything was on the line. Everything that before had been enough to keep me subservient and in my father's pocket, now wasn't.

I'd been obedient. Loyal. Done everything he ever asked of me.

But that was before I found something I wanted more than what my future held.

My cock rippled with pre-cum as I struck.

"Fifteen!"

Nila was mine.

I wanted her.

I'd take her.

I grunted as I swung again, throwing my body weight into the strike.

"Sixteen." She shifted, pressing her forehead against the post. Her hair stuck to the blood oozing on her shoulders. She gasped, dragging in air as if she drowned.

"Seventeen!" she screamed as I drew forth more crimson agony. Her abused, glowing skin split, sprinkling rusty droplets down her ribcage.

My eyes glazed; I stumbled closer.

I'm sorry.

You're not sorry.

I needed to touch her. Heal her. Fuck her.

My arm bellowed as I delivered three in quick succession.

"Eighteen."

"Nineteen."

"Twenty!" Nila collapsed, her knees buckling. Her weight transferred entirely to the cuffs.

My arm fell by my side. I could barely stand. My lungs sucked in air as if I were dying; my heartbeat existed everywhere, vibrating in the plants around us, roaring in my ears.

One more.

Do it.

I looked to the camera hidden in the ferns. My father would watch this later and reprimand me for being affected. He would see the glaze in my eyes, the desire on my face. He would make me pay for not freezing her first. He would destroy all the warmth that now existed in my heart and take me back to the person I hated.

That was my future.

But this was our present.

This was *ours*.

I struck. Hard. Too hard. Too fucking hard. My mind couldn't free itself from things Nila would never understand. Her world was black and white. Betrayal versus love. Truth versus deception.

My world was different. So very, very different.

"Twenty-one!" Nila let go of her frayed self-control. Sobs broke through her lips, tears cascading down ghost-white cheeks. "Please—no more. Stop." She tried to stand but couldn't find the strength. "Please! No—I can't—"

Twenty-one.

The lucky number.

Her tears dragged dangerous compassion from my arctic soul, hauling me into humanness.

Bad things happened when I let myself get this way.

Terrible things that I couldn't control.

But Nila was my undoing.

I think I'd known that the moment I tore her dress off in Milan. I had no strength to pretend—not after this. Not now.

I needed to take her. To fully claim her, so I could give in completely to the one thing I'd run from all my life.

If I took her now, there would be no turning back for me. Damn the fucking consequences.

Groaning, I threw away the flogger. "It's over."

Nila sobbed harder, gratefulness a sharp tang in the air.

With shaky fingers, I unbuttoned my jeans, moving forward into destruction and disrepair.

She was my prize.

Nothing would stop me from taking it.

Nila

I COULDN'T MOVE.

I couldn't stand up, breathe, think, or feel without being bombarded by agony. I'd never hurt so much. Not even after a tortuous fifteen-hour day huddled over a sewing machine, or twelve hours on my feet in stilettos.

I'd never been subjected to pain such as this.

To a *beating* such as this.

And this was the easiest of the debts?

Terror clogged my throat at the thought of what the others entailed.

Movement caught my attention. I forced my tear-stained vision to focus on Jethro as he prowled to the ferns and reached into the foliage. What was he doing?

A second later he moved toward me, every step full of temper and thick, thick lust.

Shit.

I squirmed, tugging on the cuffs. Before the whipping, I would've willingly let him take me. I *wanted* him to.

But not like this.

Not like this!

Not when my brain wept with agony and my emotions were completely screwed up.

"No," I groaned.

Jethro gritted his jaw, his hand disappearing into his jeans. A keening wail clawed up my throat. I couldn't let him fuck me. I hurt. So damn much. I wasn't turned on or interested in the slightest. I couldn't stomach being molested further.

You don't have a choice.

My heart cracked at the thought. No, I didn't have a choice. He would take me. There was nothing I could do about it.

Apart from...

Appeal to the warmth you know is inside him. Make him listen. Make him see.

Jethro's hands landed on my hips, yanking me away from the post. My body was jelly, my skin slick with sweat and blood.

Shaking my head, I moaned, "Please don't touch me."

Jethro's only response was rubbing his thumbs in slippery circles on my damp hips.

Clamping my thighs together, I forced my depleted body to obey. My ankles crossed awkwardly, my breathing tattered. "Jethro—please...don't do this."

He froze, panting harshly in my ear. "You want me. You've toyed with me and offered yourself up every time we fight." His forehead rested against my nape, his breath scattering down my spine. "Yet, now that I'm willing to throw away the fucking rule book, you decide you don't want me?" His voice dripped with venom. "Make up your damn mind, woman."

His knee tried to wedge between my legs, working its way to widen my thighs. I used every ounce of remaining strength to lock my knees tighter.

"Let me give it to you. Don't take it. Not by force. Don't make me ha—hate you more than I already do." Tears torrented from the corners of my eyes.

Jethro sucked in a breath. "Goddammit." His voice was alive and full of need. More alive than I'd ever heard him. Gone was the cold precision and careful calculation. He was hot-blooded and raging, and some part of me was flattered by his desire.

He wanted me.

A lot.

That power turned the burning fire on my back into something twisty and wrong. But I didn't succumb. I couldn't.

If I did, there would be no hope for me. No chance at ever redeeming myself if I let him take me like this.

I wanted to seduce him.

I wanted the power of winning.

This...this would be rape, and it would reinforce in his head that he could take whatever he damn well wanted and suffer no repercussions.

"Stop it!" I screamed as his hands drifted down my front. The fight inside intensified, blotting out the awful radiating pain in my back.

Something hot and silky nudged against the small of my spine. "Christ's sake, woman. You have no idea what you're doing to me."

What is that?

All senses shot to where he stroked me with a hard throbbing...

It's his erection.

My heart leapt into my throat.

Jethro rocked harder, his body heat scalding every inch. His naked cock lurched against my bloody back.

I hissed as pain intensified.

He grunted as I jolted in the bindings. "Please—" I begged.

The tips of my fingers scrabbled at the post as I tried to keep my balance. His knee worked harder to unlock my thighs.

"You can't stop this. Neither of us can."

The truth in his voice daggered my heart.

If we did this, we would slip from humanity and turn over our souls. We'd become animals, forever fighting and cursing each other.

My back flared with flames as his arm wrapped around my waist, pulling me from the post and into his twisted embrace. I wriggled against him, blocking out the agony. "Jethro!"

His cock nudged me again, bruising me with his need.

"Shit, let me—"

"I won't! Not like this."

He groaned, a savage mixture of a growl of frustration and grunt of regret.

My vision blacked out then returned, masking the pain and encouraging me to drift. I expected a longer war. In complete truthfulness, I expected to lose and be taken like a common slave against the whipping post with my blood smearing between us.

It was better to give in—get it over with.

Then I could rest.

Yes, rest. Sleep...

Fight siphoned from my limbs, succumbing to the inevitable.

But Jethro...the moment I submitted, he stiffened.

He...he let me go.

His body heat stayed blistering and all-consuming behind, but he didn't touch me.

Neither of us moved. I was too shocked to ask why.

Then, a noise hit my ears. A noise I wasn't familiar with yet knew *exactly* what it was. Some primal part of me needed no confirmation, painting a vivid scene in my head of what Jethro was doing.

My heart sped up as the rhythmic sound grew louder. His breathing came short and sharp, sending my skin prickling with knowledge.

My mind filled with images of him. I pictured his head tossed back, his chest rising and falling, and legs spread for balance. I bit my lip as I let my imagination wander, bringing into focus his strong fingers wrapped around his cock, punishing himself with a grip that worked up and down, up and down. Faster and faster.

His breathing matched my sick daydream. My tummy clenched at the thought of him masturbating while I stood there prone, bleeding, and silent.

A soft groan decorated his harsh breathing as something hot and stinging splashed across my lower back.

Did he just—?

He moaned louder as another stream lacerated the cuts on my spine.

He grunted one last time as a torrid spurt marked my skin, seeping into my wounds like acid.

My eyes shot wide as my lips thinned in repugnance. Like some crazed beast, he'd marked me with his cum. He'd respected my plea and not taken me, but he'd had to service himself.

I shuddered in the cuffs as Jethro's forehead landed on the base of my skull. "Fuck, you're ruining me."

The atmosphere changed instantaneously. It switched from abuse and debt payments to fragile and perplexed.

I couldn't calm my heart or ignore the fiery sting of his cum on my wounds.

Wordlessly, Jethro stepped away. The faint sound of a zipper being refastened was the only sound apart from our tattered breathing.

Awareness slowly came back—I wished it wouldn't.

Inch by inch, pain on top of pain made itself known. My muscles bellowed; my back hummed like a hundred bee stings. And the questions that bombarded me made nausea swirl with confusion.

Tears stole my vision as everything became too much.

The whipping.

Jethro's desecration and confession.

It felt as if my skeleton had been ripped into view, hanging bony and stripped bare with every colliding thought on display. The licking flames of whiplashes stole the remainder of my energy.

I buckled, giving up all control to the cuffs.

I didn't want to cry again.

I didn't want to seem weak in front of the monster who'd not only hurt me but gotten off on it. He'd been turned on so much, he had to mark me with ownership. Like I was his territory—his possession.

No matter how much I wished I were stronger, I wasn't. I couldn't stop the tears rivering from my eyes or the hiccupping sobs building in my chest.

Softly, silently, the winch released, dropping my arms so I only remained standing by leaning against the post.

The buckles on my wrists were removed, cuffs no longer imprisoning.

Jethro's touch was infinitely gentle and kind.

My legs gave a second warning before they collapsed from beneath me.

I braced myself for the fall. I gritted my teeth against more agony.

But I didn't tumble to the travertine floor.

I landed in strong arms.

And the only thing that registered was shock.

The arms weren't cold.

But hot.

I came to being placed gently on my stomach.

Whatever I lay upon was soft as a cloud and smelled just as fresh.

I snuggled deeper into the fluffiness, wishing for oblivion once again, but the agonizing pain from my shredded back wouldn't let me fade.

My hands balled the sheets beneath me as I struggled to stay still and not squirm.

It hurts. Crap, it hurts.

I would've murdered for a painkiller—something to dull the mind-numbing agony.

A cool hand pressed against my naked behind, holding me against the mattress.

My mattress?

Where am I?

I couldn't tell without raising my eyes. I would have to

tense my spine to look, and no way in hell was I moving.

"Stay still," Jethro ordered, his voice calm but lacking the usual icy edge.

I froze, just waiting for more torture or horrible mind games. I was at my weakest, most vulnerable. I had no defence—mental or physical—if he decided to hurt me more.

His touch drifted over a particularly violent lash mark.

I hissed, biting my lip.

I wanted to moan—to see if vocalizing the agony would help release it. Coupled with the cuts on my feet from running and my bruises from vertigo, I'd never been so banged up.

Vaughn would kill him for this. My brother could never stand to see me hurt.

The bed shifted as Jethro disappeared. Vaguely, the sound of a tap being turned on and the groan of old pipes expanding with water drifted to my ears.

I didn't know how much time passed; I drifted in and out of pain, wishing I could transplant a pair of wings from the stuffed birds around the room and fly away.

Then the mattress dipped again, my skin crackling with awareness as Jethro hovered beside me.

Something clanked onto the bedside table, smelling sharply of antiseptic.

I flinched, turning my head to see what it was.

At least we have drugs to stop infection. Back in the 1400s they wouldn't have been so lucky.

Jethro's fingers landed on my hair, stroking softly. "I'm going to fix you. Don't move."

"Fix me?" My voice came out scratching and sore from previous screaming. "You can't fix me."

He didn't reply.

Instead, he dipped a soft white cloth into the bowl of clear brown liquid and wrung it out.

His eyes met mine then locked onto the mess that was my back. The moment he pressed the warm dampness against a cut, I burst into tears. The lashes roared with everlasting brimstone. "Stop! Ah, it hurts."

His other hand held me down, petting my head as if I would endanger myself further. "I know it hurts, but I have to clean your wounds before I can bandage them."

My mind twisted, trying to make sense of this. "Why—why are you the one tending to me?"

He took a while to reply, dipping the now hated rag into the disinfectant concoction and once again searing my skin with purgatory.

"Because you're mine."

I hated that reason. "I'm not yours."

His voice came softly. "There are a lot worse things than being mine, Ms. Weaver. Being under my control means I'll do anything to keep you safe. Keep you from other's cruelty. Don't throw my offer in my face without fully realising what I'm giving you."

His touch dropped lower, gently dabbing my open sores.

My hands fisted the sheet, breathing hard through my nose. My head ached from tensing, and tears leaked unbidden from my eyes.

"I do know what you're offering, and I don't want it."

The moment I said it, I wanted to snatch the words back.

I *wanted* him on my side.

I wanted him to care for me, so I could use him to exterminate his family like vermin.

"Are you sure?" he murmured. "Are you sure you want to throw away whatever's building between us?"

I flinched, bracing myself to deny it. *There's nothing building between us.*

You always were a hopeless liar, Nila.

How could I admit to an emerging connection between hunter and prey?

Jethro caressed my hair again. "I know what you're thinking—I know you feel it, too." He dropped his voice, whispering, "Don't lie, Ms. Weaver. Not when we both know the truth. Do you deny we're drawn to each other? Fighting more with ourselves than what we know we shouldn't feel?"

Silence.

I had no reply. Nothing that wouldn't give me away.

Jethro continued to rinse and dab, slowly but tenderly cleaning my smarting back.

"You're strong. Stronger than anyone I've met. But still so naïve, which makes you incredibly dangerous." His touch pulled me deeper into his icy charm.

"What are you trying to do?" I pinched my lips together as a particular sharp lance of pain caught me by surprise. "Why are you saying all of this?"

A minute ticked past.

For the longest moment, I worried he would never reply, just like so many of my questions.

"I don't know." His answer ached with confession, cleaving open my chest.

Memories of what happened at the end of the debt repayment took my mind prisoner. "How could you do that? How could you come after hurting me so much?" I pressed my cheek harder against the bed as agony bonfired down my spine. "To get off on drawing blood makes you sadistic. It makes you twisted."

Jethro paused, letting me go completely to swirl the cloth in the bowl. The brown liquid turned rusty from my blood. "Sadistic?"

I swallowed back a groan as I arched my neck, making eye contact with his turbulent golden gaze. "Yes. You enjoyed seeing me hurt from running in the woods. You like seeing me uncomfortable. Sadistic fits you perfectly."

He sighed, looking at the dripping cloth in his hands. It stained his trousers, not that he seemed to care. "I'm many things but not a sadist."

I scoffed, tearing my gaze away.

He didn't deserve a reply when he blatantly lied.

Silence fell between us as he slowly continued to wash my back.

His hands dropped lower—to where he'd branded me with his orgasm.

I flinched. He sucked in a harsh breath as he reached the

base of my spine. The residue stickiness felt foreign and unwanted. I wanted his pleasure gone. I didn't want to wear evidence of his toxic mind games.

I whispered, "See the evidence? You came in seconds. You were so caught up in needing a release, you couldn't even wait to subdue me to rape me." I sighed. "Who needs to come so badly they'll throw their dignity away and come like a little boy caught looking at *Playboy* for the first time?"

The memory of walking in on Vaughn doing exactly that was seared into my brain. I'd been scarred for life after that. Terrified of what it meant. Unable to understand what my brother was doing hurting himself in such a manner.

I'd bolted the moment I'd seen, and to this day, we'd never discussed it.

"You're right," Jethro whispered. "I disgraced myself. But I had no alternative. I couldn't do what I wanted without hurting you more, and you'd already been hurt enough. It was the only way to see straight—to let the poison out of my system."

"Poison?"

He chuckled sadly. "It's one word for it."

His touch landed on my spine again, wiping away the leftovers of his transgression. "If you want an apology, I won't give it."

"So I'm to accept you smearing your cum into my flayed back?"

I'm to accept that I belong to you, because I have no other choice?

He didn't reply. Tossing the rag into the bowl, he grabbed a tube of cream beside it. Silently, he smeared the lotion onto my cuts.

I hissed as the cream stung before fading to a gentle throb. Every hair on my body bristled with how tenderly he cared for me. My heart raced for an entirely different reason as he meticulously smeared my entire back in balm.

The moment I was covered, he stood.

"Sit up," he ordered.

Sit up? That was asking for the impossible. I couldn't.

When I tried half-heartedly and swallowed a moan of agony, Jethro moved closer. "Let me help."

He hovered, his scent of woods and leather scrambling my heart until I suffered a bad case of arrhythmia.

He didn't touch me, only waited.

He's waiting for your permission—transferring power back to you.

I frowned. What tricks was he playing? Who was this silent attentive man, and what the hell happened to the bastard I wanted to murder?

Jethro continued to watch me, his face tight and unreadable.

I nodded once.

With powerful hands, he helped me sit up and swing my legs over the side of the bed.

Squeezing my eyes, I almost succumbed to pain-induced vertigo as I swayed in his grip.

"Trust me," he murmured, reaching beneath my arms to scoop my weight, helping me stand.

I moaned as a few of the shallower cuts reopened, oozing painfully.

"Can you stand on your own?"

I wanted to berate him. Ridicule his kindness with what he'd done. But something in his eyes implored me to relax—to not fight him on this particular subject.

I blinked, completely lost as to his motives or plans.

Slowly, I nodded.

Leaving me to wobble in place, he pulled free a large bandage from a first-aid kit on the floor.

Between my teeth, I muttered, "You always intended to patch me up…afterwards?"

His eyebrow rose, locking me in his stare. "You still don't understand."

I struggled to suck in a decent breath with the intensity in his gaze. "I understand plenty."

He shook his head. "No, you don't. You think we're going to torture and maim you for the next few years. Yes, your future is set in stone, and yes, it will hang over your head until it's finished. But you have to keep living, keep experiencing. You're part of our family now. You'll be treated as such."

My brain whirled.

"In answer to your question, I always intended to tend to your wounds, just like I will do with every debt. You're mine." His lips twitched. "In sickness and in health."

Temper flared through my blood. "Don't twist the vows of matrimony. This isn't a marriage. This is the worst kind of kidnapping."

His eyes hooded, hiding his thoughts. "A marriage *is* a kidnapping. After all, it's a contract between two people." He came closer, unravelling the end of the bandage and holding it against my side. My arms wrapped around my naked chest hating that even now, even after everything he'd done, my skin still rippled with want.

His face tightened and he grabbed my wrists, placing them forcibly by my sides. "Arms down." His attention turned to holding the bandage against my ribcage. Once in place, he moved in a circle around me, wrapping my torso caringly in gauze. The soft fabric granted needed relief.

I bit the inside of my cheek. How was it that the gentlest of his touches killed me the most? I'd never been this light-headed without the curse of vertigo. Never been this confused by one person.

Jethro kept his eyes down as he waltzed around, slowly binding me with more of the bandage.

On his second rotation, he murmured, "In a way, we *are* married."

I rolled my eyes, cursing my taut nipples. "In no universe would this be called a marriage."

He sighed. "How do you explain the similarities then? The fact we were raised to be a part of each other's lives, groomed by families, governed by dictators, and forced into a binding agreement against our wishes."

The air solidified, turning from unseen substance to heavy bricks of truth. My head snapped up, eyes latching onto Jethro's golden ones. "*What* did you just say?"

The man he kept hidden blazed bright.
Against both our wishes.
That was the second time he'd said it.
Go on. Admit it. Say that all along you've been acting. That this is as repulsive to you as it is to me.

We stood silent, neither of us willing to look away in case it was interpreted as defeat. Slowly, the concern in his eyes shifted to glittering frost—the chill I knew so well giving him somewhere to hide. "You misunderstood me, Ms. Weaver. I meant to say *your* not *our*—slip of the tongue." He continued wrapping the bandage around my middle, covering my breasts with the length of softness, protecting the seeping cuts on my back.

I wanted to yell at him. To find the crack I'd just witnessed and force it to turn from hairline into crevice. But I stood silently, breathing hard as he finished wrapping me like a priceless present, securing the bandage with a small clip.

He stepped back, admiring his handiwork. "You did perfectly, Ms. Weaver. You repaid the First Debt with strength, and you've earned a reward." He moved closer, wrapping his arms around me. His embrace scalded, heating the lash marks to a boil.

I froze in his arms, completely dumbfounded.

To an outsider, it would've looked like an embrace—tender, sweet, the coupling of two people crackling with anger and unwanted lust. To me, it was a torment—a farce.

Pulling back, he whispered, "Do you know we met when we were young? I barely remember, and I'm a few years older than you, so I doubt you will recall."

"What?" My mind flew backward, trying to remember a fiendish little boy with icy winds in his soul. "When?"

He reached up, undoing my ponytail and running his strong fingers through the strands. "Back in London. We met for ten minutes. My grandmother escorted me. They made us sign something—you used a crayon that you'd been drawing a bright pink dress with."

My heart stormed with denial. How could that be?

Jethro bared his teeth, his eyes locking onto my lips. "That was the first document they made us sign—the beginning of our entwined fate. However, soon you'll be signing something else."

Oh, God. My stomach revolted at giving him any more rights over me.

It wouldn't happen. The only thing I'd sign when it came to the Hawks was their death certificates.

His thumb traced my bottom lip. "You can't say no. You promised."

I shook my head. "When?"

"When you ran. We agreed if you didn't make it to the boundary, you would sign another document—one just between us that trumps everything else." The tips of his cool, no longer warm, fingers trailed along my collarbone. He leaned in and placed the slightest of kisses on my cheek. "I've been rather busy, so haven't had time to draw it up, but once I do, that's the one I'll treasure. That's the one that will contain your soul."

I tore from his grip.

I couldn't stand it any longer.

I slapped him.

Hard.

Viciously hard and firm and so full of *anger*. I wanted to smite him into the ground.

He hissed between his teeth as my palm print glowed instantly on his shaven cheek.

I seethed, "You're forgetting that no matter how many contracts you make me sign, none of them will own my soul. I own that. Me! And I'll make you watch, before this is over, while I burn your house to the ground and bury your family."

Jethro turned to a rock.

Grabbing the diamond collar around my neck, I hissed, "And this. I'll find a way to remove it. I'll tear every single diamond from the setting and donate it to victims of bastards like you."

Jethro's anger dissolved, almost as if he shed it in one

swoop. His smile was forced, but the passion in his eyes was fire not frost. "Bastards like me? I don't think there *are* other bastards like me."

Suddenly he lashed out, grabbing the diamond choker and dragging me forward.

My hands flew to cover his, cursing the huge flare of agony down my spine.

His lips hovered over mine, instantly igniting my overwhelming need to be kissed. How many times would he tease me and not deliver? How many times must he jerk me close, whisper his taste across my lips, and renege on following through? "I told you, you can't get it off." His finger trailed to the back of the necklace, tugging gently. "There is no possible way to get this off once it's on. No key. No trick."

I gasped, stumbling a little as vertigo played on the outskirts of my vision. "There has to be a way to undo it."

After all, you took it from my mother's corpse.

Jethro smiled grimly. "Oh yes, it comes undone when it's no longer fastened tightly around something as impeccable as your neck." His beautiful face twisted with something hideously evil. "Think of an old-fashioned handcuff, Ms. Weaver." He forced two fingers down the collar, effectively strangling me. "It has to get tighter and tighter..." He tried to fit a third finger but it wouldn't work. Dark spots danced in front of my eyes.

My heart bucked and collided.

"It has to revolve on itself to open, only then will the latch snap free and be ready to be fastened again."

The horror I'd been locking deep inside took that moment to crest. My knees gave out, hopelessly giving into rage and terror. If I failed in my quest to make the Hawks pay, who would wear it next?

Who?

Vaughn's unborn daughter? The sister Daniel had hinted at in the car but I didn't know was real or fiction?

Jethro caught me, placing me back on the bed.

My life switched. My path, my destiny no longer belonged to creativity, design, or couture.

It had never been that clear-cut.

My fate—the very reason why I'd been put on this earth—was to stop these men. To end them. Once and for all.

There will be no more wearers of the Weaver Wailer collar. No more victims of such a ludicrous, sadistic debt.

The ice that lived in Jethro's soul seeped into mine, and this time...it stayed. There was no Kite to help me soar or hopeful naivety of the girl I used to be. I embraced the chill, letting it permeate and consume.

I will make him care.

My stomach churned with the promise.

I will make him love me.

My conviction wasn't flimsy or half-hearted.

And then I'll destroy him.

My vow was unbinding and unbreakable, just like my diamond imprisonment.

"Kiss me, Jethro."

Jethro froze, eyes wide.

He tried to stand tall after leaning over to plant me safely on the bed. But I lashed out, grabbing his shirt and keeping him folded. "Kiss me."

His eyes flared wider, panic filling their depths. "Let me go."

"If we're effectively married with contracts, carefully designed futures, and interlocking pasts, why are we fighting our attraction? Why not give in to it?" Yanking his shirt, I forced him to stumble closer. "We have years together before the end. Years of fucking and taking and pleasure." Licking my lips, I purred, "Why wait?"

Ripping my fingers from his clothing, he backed away, ferocity and confusion equal bedfellows in his eyes. "Shut up. You're hurt. You need to rest."

I laughed, unable to hide the mania in my tone. "You wanted to take me in the greenhouse. I'm not saying no now." I spread my thighs; apart from the bandage wrapped around my chest, I was naked.

Jethro's gaze dropped to my exposed core, his jaw

twitching.

"Kiss me. Take me. Show me you're a man by being the first Hawk to claim me." My stomach rolled with the filth I spoke.

But I'd made a vow; I intended to see it through.

Dropping my head, I let a curtain of black hair obscure one eye. "Let's draw our battle lines right here, right now. We'll fight. We'll hate each other. But it doesn't mean we have to let family dictate every action we do."

Fire filled my belly. He wanted me. I knew that much. He wouldn't have come all over my back if he didn't. And there was something inside me—some all-knowing part that not everything was as it seemed. Sometimes he was so sure—so resolute and unswerving in the belief of what he said—and other times, it was a lie. A big, fat, obnoxious lie that even he struggled to hide.

"I told you at the coffee shop. If and when I take you, it will be on my terms. Fucking hard and nasty. I won't kiss you, touch you—because I *don't care*. I'll just fucking take, and you'll wish you hadn't taunted me."

"You'll take me against my will?"

Liar—you stopped before.

He froze, a cold veneer creeping over his features. "Exactly. You begged me to take you. Well, keep begging because I'm not ready to grant you my cock just yet."

I tilted my head. "You'll give in. I'll win."

He laughed loudly, the tension dispersing. He looked at me as if I were a feral puppy who he'd been temporarily wary of but now thought was ridiculous. "Back to winning. Always winning with you, Ms. Weaver."

I nodded. "If there is no winner or loser, what else is there?"

Partnership.

The thought appeared from nowhere. Partnership. I tasted the word, wondering just how likely an alliance could be between this law-bound Hawk and me—his victim.

Could I not only seduce him but use him against his

family? I'd thought it before, but it'd been frivolous, something I said to make myself feel powerful...but what if...

The idea was absurd...*but*...

Jethro moved, placing his palm squarely on my bandage-bound chest and pushing me backward onto the bed.

I hissed at the pressure of the mattress on my whipped flesh.

"Stop your silly games, Ms. Weaver. It's time to rest."

His eyes glinted. "You'll need it for tomorrow."

Jethro

DAMN HER.

Fuck her.

She was worse than my fucking father with her manipulation and guile.

I needed a session.

For the first time since I'd turned eighteen, I needed help. I wouldn't be able to fix myself on my own. I hated to do it to her. It was the epitome of cruel.

But the only person who could help me remember why I couldn't let go of the ice in my veins was my sister.

Jasmine.

I'm a Hawk. Remember that fucking fact and own it.

Stalking through the house, I tried to find my father. I didn't want to do this. I hated that we used our own flesh and blood this way. But I had no *choice*.

Not if I wanted to remain strong.

Not if I wanted to remain true.

A child was the product of his upbringing. They had certain obligations to live up to, expectations to obey, and scripts to follow. Elders knew better.

It was time to embrace my life path completely, rather than fight against it.

I was done fighting against it.

It was too fucking hard.
He'd told me it would only bring confusion and pain.
He was right.
Time to stop fighting and become my father's son.
Once and for fucking all.

Nila

TWO WEEKS PASSED.

Fourteen days where I didn't see a hint of Jethro.

Where he'd gone and why was a mystery, and I'd like to say I didn't care.

But...I'd never been a good liar.

No matter the itch of curiosity, I continued to live and didn't let his disappearance undermine my resolve.

I didn't mope in my room. I formulated my attack plan and executed it.

The first three days were hell. My back cracked and bled whenever I moved. I stayed confined to my bed with only the ceiling for entertainment and food delivered by softly smiling maids.

I craved my phone. I missed the freedom of conversing with the outside world.

By the fourth day, I risked a shower and unwound the bandage from my back to twist and stare in the mirror.

As much as the pain crippled me, my skin had knitted together and scabbed nicely. The shallower cuts were nothing more than a pink mark. And the deeper wounds were well on the road to recovery.

I would always bear the scars. A new wardrobe of silver lashes marking me firmly with ancient scandals. However, the body was a miraculous thing—healing itself from crimes of hate and unpayable debts.

I just hope my soul is as curable.

The hot water had killed to begin with, but slowly I grew used to the pain and washed away the whipping and turbulence Jethro had left me with.

On the fifth day, I dressed in a floaty black dress that had no elastic or grabby material that would irritate my back and stepped from my room. I had cabin fever, and as much as I didn't want company, I needed a change of scenery.

Drifting toward the dining room, I jumped whenever I heard the slightest noise. I felt guilty for wandering, even though I'd been told I could. And as much as I wanted to see Jethro, to demand my phone was returned, I didn't have the strength to fight with him yet.

It was well past breakfast, which was fine because I'd had mine in bed, and there were no Black Diamond men around.

Where is everyone?

Hawksridge Hall had an eerie way of hiding people from view. The huge spaces making it seem as if I were all alone. I might not want to suffer through Jethro's company, but his younger brother wasn't blacklisted.

Turning down the corridor leading to Kes's quarters, I found him with four men discussing some sort of strategy at the large table in the saloon.

The moment I entered, Kes's golden eyes lit up. He bounced from his chair and came to offer his hand, tugging me closer to the bikers. "Nila. What a pleasant surprise." His gaze went to my back, spinning me around a little to see. The lash marks were on display, having left the bandage off to help with healing. My dress was a scoop back, permitting my flesh to breathe.

"Ouch. I'd heard he hadn't held back."

"You heard?" I frowned. "He told you what happened?"

Kes swallowed, running a hand nervously through his hair. "Um, not quite. Anyway, that's beside the point. I'm just glad you're well and on the mend." Grabbing my elbow, he carted me closer to the table and beaming men. "You know Flaw."

I nodded briefly at the black-haired man who moved like Vaughn, before inspecting the two other accomplices—one with dirty blond hair, the other with long brown hair in a ponytail down his back. "That's Grade and Colour."

What the hell sort of names are those?

It didn't escape my attention that these were the same men who'd had their tongues on every part of me. But there was no awkwardness—no side glances or intimidation.

I snorted. "Ah, I get it now. I couldn't work out your names before. Flaw, Cut...you name yourselves after diamond properties."

Kes grinned. "Yep. Apart from the Hawk boys, of course. The Black Diamond brothers picked a name based on the gemstone and the properties in which they can be transformed."

Grade—the man with dirty blond hair and a snub nose—grinned. "Happy to meet you, Nila."

I didn't bother saying he'd already met me, or at least his tongue had.

Colour, with his brown ponytail and broad grin, leaned the small distance between us and placed a chaste kiss on my cheek. "Hello, Ms. Weaver. Lovely to see you again."

The other day, Kes had said I was to be treated with kindness and respect, but a part of me hadn't believed him. However, faced with men who had helped strip me of everything, it seemed as if they genuinely liked and wanted me in their company.

I couldn't get my head around it.

Or they're just perfect actors in the pantomime put on by Mr. Hawk.

Waving away the proprietary of my title, I shivered slightly. "Please, call me Nila." I couldn't stomach anyone else calling me by my surname and hated that Jethro continued to use it. I didn't want to be reminded of the man who'd disappeared without a trace.

Kes pulled up an extra chair. "Sit and stay a while. We're just discussing another diamond shipment due in tonight. It will be boring, but we'd be honoured if you'd share your opinions."

I couldn't stop staring at him. How much had Jethro told him of making me pay the First Debt? Did he know the battle that waged between his brother and me?

But most importantly, did he wonder, if he *was* Kite, why I hadn't texted him in so long?

Damn Jethro for taking my phone.

Arsehole.

Flaw disappeared as the men fell back into conversation. He returned a few minutes later with a huge basket overflowing with items.

The bikers laughed, pushing back from the table to give Flaw space to present the basket to me. I strained forward, very aware that my raw back would be on display despite my long, unsecured hair hiding some of the evidence.

"What's this?" I asked, eyeing up the pink concoction of crepe paper, chocolate bars, sweeties, magazines, and a brand new Kindle.

"For you," Kes murmured, moving forward to rummage in the gift basket. "I wanted to come to your room yesterday and give it to you, but…well, Jethro has banned anyone from stepping into your quarters."

Why am I not surprised?

Tentatively, I plucked the Kindle from the basket and turned it on. A stocked library full of romance greeted me.

"Wow," I murmured. Then I looked at the name given to the device in the top right corner. *Weaver Wailer.* That would have to change straight away.

Kes shrugged, standing tall and running a hand through his messy hair. "Figured you must be going stir-crazy in this house. It will keep you occupied."

And, it did.

For the next five days, I spent my mornings relaxing in bed with fresh pastries and fruit salad reading about alpha males and swooning heroines, while my afternoons were spent with Kes and the boys in his quarters.

My strange world settled into routine, and although I

craved my phone and the ability to talk to Kite, I valued the reprieve—the preciousness of a secretive smile from Kes and the gentle touch of a fatherly biker.

They all doted on me.

They all smiled when I walked into the room and listened attentively to anything I had to say.

I felt valued.

I felt *appreciated*.

Which was the oddest thing to admit as I'd never felt cherished, even when delivering fashion-changing designs and bringing the Weaver name to even greater heights. No, that wasn't true. I felt beyond loved and adored by my father and brother, but it'd been the everyday reporters, models, and shop owners that'd made my career a hardship.

Away from the toil of work, I found no drive to return. No urge to create.

It was scary to have that part of my identity taken away but refreshing and almost medicinal, too.

Bizarre to say, the same men who'd licked me had somehow become my...friends. I didn't know how, but I did know I healed faster because of their friendship and found sanctuary for my heart.

Just like Kestrel had said I would.

Just like Cut had said I'd be welcomed into his house. I should've been colder, less easy to win over, but I was tired of overthinking everything and peering around corners for the next trick.

There was only so much fear a person could live with before the brain gave up and accepted.

The days stretched unnervingly...normal. If I wasn't in Kes's saloon, I was wandering down pristine corridors full of priceless artwork and tapestries. I strolled in gardens surrounded by manicured hedges and even took a nap beneath the dappling leaves of an apple tree in the orchard.

Not one person stopped me from entering a room or leaving. Not one person raised their voice or gave me any reason to fear.

If I bumped into a man dressed in leather and stomping in fierce-looking boots, he would smile and ask after my health. If I bumped into Cut heading to a meeting, he would bow and smile cordially, continuing on his way as if I had total right to be sneaking about his home.

The only person I didn't bump into was Jethro.

It was as if he'd disappeared, and with his disappearance went my torment.

I began to wonder if I'd been forgotten.

Not forgotten.

Just *forgiven*…

They'll never forgive.

I had to admit the Hawks were diabolically clever. With their welcome came a relaxation I would never have found if I wasn't permitted to explore on my own. A self-centred acceptance that only came from settling into a new environment with no duress.

I truly felt a part of their household. As sick and as twisted as it seemed.

By the end of fourteen days, with nothing to keep me occupied but reading and exploring, inevitably, my mind turned to what it had always known.

Sewing.

Not designing under pressure or rushing to deliver the next big thing.

Just sewing.

The epicentre of my craft.

I commandeered a writing pad, thanks to interrupting a business meeting. I'd walked in to an office by accident, only to be offered freshly grilled sausages and beer by three Diamond brothers. Their food had been the basics of cuisine, yet they ate it around a fifteenth-century table in a room full of priceless ledgers and power.

The lined paper only lasted me a day before I hunted Kes down and requested a sketchpad with no lines. The moment he'd given me one, I couldn't stop the drive to draw, to pluck the rapidly forming ensembles from my mind and transcribe to paper.

That evening, Kes had four additional sketchpads delivered to my room.

I found the passion I'd lost with overworking and stress. Enjoyment and creativity came back with a vengeance. My hands turned black with lead from sketching well into the night. The pages became littered with rainbows and the barbaric sensuality of diamonds. I embraced a carnal wardrobe of want and inhibitions, creating my most daring collection to date, pulling ideas from my imagination like silver threads, splashing them onto the paper thanks to my trusty pencil.

When my mind was blank of artistic drive, I would turn to the large volume of Weaver history and read my ancestors' scattered thoughts and notations. I wasn't gullible enough to write things of importance—the Hawks would only read it. A diary was the window into someone's soul, and I had no intention of them seeing into mine.

But I did scribble two questions.

Where the hell is Jethro?

What weapons are best used against ice? A chisel or a candle?

It was on the sixteenth night of being Jethro-free that I stumbled upon the official library. Drifting down dark corridors, unable to sleep, I felt as if I'd fallen through a wormhole into ancient literature and knowledge. The ceiling was a dome, painted with a navy sky and glittering yellow stars. The walls were three stories high with swirling ladders leading onto brass walkways to peruse each shelf with ease.

The moment I walked into the hushed world, I knew I'd found home.

That night, I'd spent hours reading by low light, fingering leather-bound limited editions, before curling up in the most comfy of beanbags and falling asleep.

Kes found me the next morning, nudging me awake with an amused grin. "Hi." He threw himself into the chaise lounge that was decorated with bamboo leaves, cranes, and Chinese symbols, not far from my commandeered beanbag.

I sat up, rubbing sleep from my eyes and stretching my

stiff but mostly healed back. "How did you find me?"

Kes pointed upward, smiling. "Cameras."

My heart leapt into my throat. "Of course." *That* was why I was given free reign. Why no one tried to stop me. Everything I did was on show.

I was stupid not to realize it sooner.

I frowned. Was that what Jethro had switched off after he'd whipped me? Did he not wish his family to see him come all over my back—to show he had a *weakness* for me?

And if so...*why* didn't he want his family to see? He was only doing what he was told...wasn't he?

The past two weeks had delivered far too many questions where Jethro was concerned, and I still had no answers.

I did have one scary conclusion, though. As much as I detested Jethro's mind games and sick control...I missed the spark he conjured inside. I missed the clench when he touched me, and I craved the addictive fear of duelling.

As much as I enjoyed Kes's company, and as fond as I'd grown of him, I didn't grow wet at the thought of winning him over or dream of his lips kissing mine.

"Do you like the library?" Kes asked, craning his neck, trying to catch a glimpse at the open sketchpad beside me. The pages depicted a flowing silk cape that would be a mixture of air and thread.

Forcing Jethro from my mind, I nodded. "Yes. I love the silence and smell."

He smiled. "Bet you'll like what Jethro has to show you then."

I very much doubt that.

I stiffened slightly, hearing Kes talk about his brother. I'd picked up on a strange edge in his tone whenever he mentioned him. And I couldn't understand the dynamic between the two. They cared deeply for each other—that was undeniable—but there was something else, too. Something deeper and more complex than just sibling rivalry.

Hang on.

My ears pricked. "What does Jethro have to show me?"

"You mean, he hasn't shown you yet?"

"Shown me what?"

Kes shook his head. "He hasn't come to find you? Hasn't explained?" Dropping his voice, he asked, "How long has it been, since he's come for you?"

My forehead furrowed. Shouldn't he know that? Wasn't he privy to Jethro's convoluted inner thoughts?

Dropping my eyes, I said, "I haven't seen him since the First Debt was repaid."

Kes sucked in a breath. Rubbing a hand over his face, he stood quickly. "Look, forget I said anything. I have to go."

He strode from the library in a rustle of leather and denim, most likely going in search of his wayward brother.

Forget I said anything. Kes's words repeated inside my head.

I would like to forget everything that'd happened since the Hawks had come for me, but that was an impossibility.

Just like obeying Kes was.

From that moment on, I couldn't think of anything else.

What does Jethro have to show me?

And why hasn't he come to torment me?

Jethro

THE NIGHT SKY exploded with a blue and gold firework. It rained through the blackness, dazzling through the skylight of the stable.

Goddammit, they'd started early.

Wings stomped his hoof against the cobblestone at the explosion. He didn't do well with fireworks—almost bucked me off last year when I'd gone for a midnight ride, rather than smile and be merry with my father.

Today was his birthday.

The joyous occasion of Cut being one step closer to a coffin.

Wasn't my fault that I preferred to celebrate for different reasons than his. He would be basking in toasts, counting the obscene amount of wealth gushing in, and patting himself on his back for a lifetime well spent.

Meanwhile, I would be sulking in the shadows just waiting for my turn to reign.

Was it despicable for a son to wish his father to die so he could inherit everything sooner rather than later, or was it merely a coping mechanism at surviving yet more years under his thumb?

Either way, it no longer mattered.

I was thirty next year.

And the fireworks would be bigger, louder, and more extravagant than my father's, because I would be the new owner of Hawksridge and hold all the power. That day had seemed like an eternity away when I was eighteen, but now it was within grasping distance.

I've almost made it.

Wings stomped his metal shoe as another firework detonated. All day the festivities had continued—starting with a hunt for pheasant, which began immediately after breakfast, followed by trout fishing in the fully stocked lake. The staff worked furiously and meticulously, making sure each element of his magical day was better than the one before.

I might secretly enjoy the news that my father inched closer to demise, but I hated celebrating my own birthday. Why rejoice another year passing, another year closer to death? I preferred to pretend I was immortal.

That way, I would never have to pay for my sins or fall from earth to hell.

Another firework boomed over the estate.

Wings huffed, nudging his velvet nose against my tweed jacket.

"You're greedy tonight," I said, fishing out a handful of oats and handing them to the gelding.

In perfect late summer tradition, England had put on a gorgeous day. No wind, no clouds. Endless yellow sunshine drenched Hawksridge Hall, granting perfect conditions for Cut and his Black Diamond brothers to hunt, fish, gamble, and drink all on the front lawn. Gazebos had been erected, and the dinner had been a banquet of roast pheasant, grilled trout, and venison stew.

My mind skipped back to watching Nila. I'd avoided her for two weeks.

Two weeks that I needed to screw my head back on fucking straight and stop allowing my stupid emotions to get the better of me.

Today was the first time I let her see me, but I hadn't gone close enough to talk.

What could I say? Sorry for whipping you? Sorry for coming on you? Sorry for my fucked-up soul that can only be controlled by a regiment of 'fixing myself'?

There was nothing I could say and nothing I wanted to explain.

I sighed.

Jasmine had worked her magic, and I was back. I'd found my way into the cold shell that protected me and spent the last week cold, remote, *unfeeling*.

I was eternally relieved.

The messiness of life no longer affected me, and I trusted myself not to boil over with no provocation. Even *with* provocation, it would take a lot for me to snap. I wasn't just glacial; I was a continent of blizzards and perma-ice.

The moment my brothers, father, and I returned from the pheasant shoot, Nila had been sitting on the front terrace, sketching. She wore a long pale blue skirt with a slight train that rippled over the black tiles of the patio and a cream blouse with a ruffled collar and big buttons.

She'd looked content…centred.

The time apart had given us both much needed space, and the fiery emotion she'd conjured inside was a distant memory.

I didn't even hate her. I didn't have any drive to torment her, fuck her, or fight in any way. All emotions came from the same place.

That was what I'd forgotten.

Hate and love…they were the same thing. I'd tried to harness only one—hate. I tried to be my father's son, full of mistrust for others, while asserting dominance and fear.

And I'd succeeded for a while.

But with hate comes passion—either for those I loathed or circumstances I couldn't stand. Every spike of emotion permitted more awareness to steal my indifference and make me care.

Caring was my problem.

Caring was what got me into messes I couldn't repair.

Caring was what would kill me in the end.

But that was fixed now.

Resting my head on Wings' muscular neck, I breathed in the scent of equine and hay. "Suppose I better get it over with."

Just the thought of confronting Nila made my skin prickle. I'd shown her too much, and now she thought she understood me. She would *never* understand me.

Shit, I didn't understand me.

Then again, there was nothing left to understand. It was all…gone.

Wings huffed, searching my pockets for more oats.

Another boom of a purple and yellow firework shook the stable walls. The dogs howled in the kennels across the courtyard. Seemed everyone was on edge tonight.

Giving the horse one last handful, I left the stables and made my way reluctantly toward the Hall.

Nila's black eyes found mine the moment I joined the milling men and families of Black Diamonds. Women weaved, giggling and tipsy with our own brew and vintage. No children ran around—they weren't allowed on the estate—but the atmosphere of happiness scratched painful nails across my skin.

Nila never looked away as I was congratulated for being the winner at poker this afternoon and for losing the bet that I could catch more trout than my father.

It took ten minutes to cross the lawn with brothers detaining me and gossiping. Kes was in charge of the large bonfire roaring in the corner, burning off boughs and branches that had been trimmed from the forest closest to the house. Daniel—as was typical for my younger, psychotic brother—was nowhere to be seen. And Cut sat like a king on a throne, watching the staff set off dangerous fireworks.

The large box of pinwheels, squealers, and sunbursts waited to die in an extravagance of gunpowder and brilliance.

Stopping a few metres from Nila, I ignored her and watched the swarm of festivities. I hoped she would stay away.

But of course, that wish went unanswered.

"Hello," Nila said, appearing by my side. She still wore the long skirt with blouse and large buttons. Her hair was down, thick and glossy, mirroring the flames from the bonfire. Her cheeks were flushed from being out in the sun all day, but her eyes were clear from intoxication.

"I was beginning to forget what you looked like," she prompted when I didn't move or acknowledge.

Looking at her quickly, I touched my temple in greeting. Taking a sip of the elderberry and thistle beer that had been a trial brew last year, I deliberately refrained from talking. I wouldn't let her sucker me into another fight.

I was done fighting.

I would extract the debts, bide my time until all of this was mine, then get the final requirement out of the way.

Final requirement?

Her death, you mean?

Scowling, I took another sip. The concoction actually wasn't too bad. Standing stiff and remote, I stared at nothing, wishing she'd just leave.

Her presence gave no hint of how she felt about me. I couldn't tell if she hated me, desired me, or nursed vengeance deep in her heart.

I expected all of that and more. I expected to be slapped and told to never go near her again. I tensed for a spark in the tinderbox of emotions we stood in, just waiting for this crumbling truce to annihilate both of us.

What Nila didn't know was, if she struck me, I wouldn't retaliate. I would permit the slap with no spike of heartbeat or temper and walk away. I would stay my distance until the next debt was ready to be paid.

Because I was done.

I'd found peace, and I didn't want to enter the chaos of fighting with her again. It was too fucking dangerous.

"Where have you been?" she asked, moving closer and watching the staff drive a large firework peg into the ground. They fumbled around trying to set the fuse alight.

I didn't say anything. Just took another sip of my beverage.

The hiss and fizzle of the fuse was the only warning before the firework shot into the sky and rained over us with sparks and thunder.

Nila's face lit up with the glowing atoms, dark eyes wide with appreciation.

Once the night sky was no longer polluted by fake sunshine and the cloud of smoke disappeared, Nila frowned in my direction. "Are you going to say something?"

I shrugged. Why? What was there to say? Nothing of importance and I'd done enough talking. Enough fighting. Enough fucking masturbating over the girl I was destined to kill.

Why was she talking to me? Shouldn't she be avoiding me at all costs?

I stilled as Nila placed her hand on my forearm. Her feminine heat seeped through my tweed, reminding me of the last time we'd been together and what I'd done.

I stepped sideways, breaking her hold.

"Jethro—I—" Her voice tugged at the unbeating heart in my chest. I risked a glance at her. Her eyes glowed with onyx intelligence.

"Is this a different kind of torture? You no longer deem me important enough to even talk to?" The hurt in her voice dove under my skin, igniting my blood despite my will.

Locking every muscle, I said, "Don't flatter yourself. I have nothing to say, and you have nothing I wish to hear." Turning my attention back to the fireworks, another explosion wracked the atmosphere, disintegrating into not one but three different sunbursts of colour.

"You are the most confusing man I've ever met." Irritation twisted her voice.

A small smile twitched my lips. "Thank you. That's the second nicest thing you've ever said to me."

"What was the first?"

That you don't understand me.

My secrets were safe as long as I confounded her.

I sipped my beer, deliberately ignoring her.

Masculine laughter suddenly rose as one drunken club member fell face first into the punch bowl. His woman kept slapping him with the ladle as he proceeded to slurp up the spilled alcoholic liquid.

Nila smiled, sighing. "I'd like to say I've missed you, but that would be a lie."

My back stiffened, but I forced myself to relax. Good for her.

I suppose.

"Seriously? What happened to you? Two weeks ago, you would've jumped down my throat and growled like a demented wildebeest. Now…nothing." Nila placed her hands on her hips, glaring.

I drained my beer, placing the empty cup on the food-strewn table to our right.

She huffed, running her fingers through her hair. "Fine. Keep your freaky silence. I'm sure Kes would love to talk to me."

Gathering the front of her skirt, she pranced away.

Kestrel.

Images of her spending so much time with him bombarded me. Despite the success of the conditioning session I'd had with Jasmine, I couldn't seem to stop myself watching the footage of Nila drifting around the Hall and laughing with my brother.

They were close.

She didn't trust him—the look of wariness never fully left her face—but she tolerated and enjoyed his company.

Unlike mine.

She accepted his gifts without suspicion, and never tried to antagonise him to the point of showing his true self.

Why did she accept his friendship yet go out of her way to rip me to shreds?

I gritted my teeth. Stupid question. The answer was plain and simple. I was her tormentor; Kes was her saviour. That was how this was always orchestrated. I should be happy it was working so flawlessly.

Plus, she was drawn to him because of the messages. The ruse of Kite007.

My hands curled. She'd let Kes waltz into her life, because she believed they had history. She might even believe he was ultimately on her side.

Silly, silly Weaver.

She hadn't asked him outright yet. I knew that for a fact. Everything would change when she did.

I stood frozen as Nila traversed the small distance across the lawn toward Kes. He reclined in a deck chair, a cigar dangling from his fingers, his shirt open and showing his muscular stomach. Kes had always been stronger than me—more brawn than brains—but he'd also never used it against me unless it was in play.

Now, though, he played a dangerous game, deliberately drawing Nila away from me.

My teeth clenched as Kes opened his arms and Nila perched on the arm of his deckchair. He said something to her, and she giggled.

My stomach churned; elderberry and thistle flavoured bile crawled up my throat.

Every second I stood and witnessed the friendship that'd blossomed between my captive and brother sent my gut convulsing.

Every moment I watched, my ice steamed until I billowed with smoke.

I didn't give myself permission to stomp across the garden.

I didn't even notice I'd gone from standing to stalking.

And I definitely didn't permit my body to bend and grab her wrist.

But that was what I did.

Somehow, I'd gone from standing to yanking Nila Weaver from my brother's embrace and dragging her like a hunted deer toward the Hall.

"Hey!" Nila dragged her nails over my wrist. It didn't do any good. Pain was another emotion I'd managed to shut off. "Let me go."

"No," I muttered. "There's something I need to show you." The party was left behind, and Kes had the sense of mind to stay where the fuck he was.

No one intervened or glanced our way as I carted her closer to the Hall. Once we entered the huge mansion, I let her wrist go and moved behind her to splay a guiding hand on her lower back. She stiffened but didn't shy away. Silently, I propelled her down the corridor.

What are you doing?

This was important.

You agreed you wouldn't go through with it.

That was before my brother stepped over the line.

Fuck trying to keep myself removed.

Nila was mine, and she would never be permitted to forget it.

At the time, I'd drafted it purely to keep myself busy while staying my distance. But I think I always knew in my heart I would make her sign.

After all, it would ensure Nila would stay mine, even if she fell for my brother. Even if Kes won.

A binding agreement.

Something that trumped even the Debt Inheritance.

An agreement my father would disintegrate if he ever found out.

My study.

My sanctuary.

The one place no one else was permitted to go.

What are you doing bringing her in here?

I hadn't thought this through. But I couldn't turn back now.

Unlocking the thick carved door, I pushed Nila through

the entrance. Once inside, I locked it, letting her drift forward on her own accord. Her eyes moved around the space quickly, expertly going to the exits of bathroom, balcony sash window, and the doorway in which we'd come.

Poor girl.

She'd changed so much already. A true survivalist. A puritan who only wanted to live.

But you'll die. Just like the rest of them.

I searched for the cold smugness drilled into me by my father. I was supposed to enjoy this—to love the hunt and dispatching of Weavers.

It was a family hobby. A trade passed down, linking our forefathers and ensuring our lineage had common ground.

So why did the thought of beheading her twist my gut?

Why did the very notion of watching her fuck my brother churn my heart in a blender?

My entire body rebelled at the thought of an axe detaching her long black hair, slicing through the vulnerable cord of muscle, shutting her dark eyes forever.

My cock twitched as she spun to face me, her hands flying to her hips. She seemed out of place in the rotund room with its six windows, lush Chinese sewn carpet, and treasure trove of small lead figurines from Indian and Cowboy child play-sets.

The wealth of history and monetary value of the things in this room would make a museum weep.

"What are we doing in here?"

I stalked to my desk. Unlocking a secret drawer beneath the jumble of stationery, I pulled forth a drafted document that no one else knew about but me. There were no cameras in this room. No one spying on what I was about to do.

Just us.

Only we would know what we'd done.

"Come here," I said, snapping my fingers.

Nila narrowed her eyes. "You do that often."

"Do what?"

She snapped her fingers. "Summon me like your pet; like your dogs."

I placed both hands flat on the desk. "You *are* my pet. I thought we'd discussed that."

She stomped forward, a conundrum of bright temper in the drab world of my study. Her sandaled feet padded on the thick carpet, planting herself in front of my desk. Her head tilted, long hair cascading over her shoulder, completely free and glossy as the midnight sky. "Funny, I thought we'd established I was something more."

My back stiffened. "Since when?"

Her lips stretched, baring her teeth in an evil little grin. "Since I made you come. Since you showed me you were human. Since you ran from me for the past fortnight, all because you're not dealing with whatever is going on between us."

She moved closer.

I stood ramrod straight, clenching every muscle against her advance.

"Tell me, Jethro Hawk. Would a *pet* be able to suck you? Would a *pet* swallow your cum? Would a pet *pleasure* you?" Her voice dropped to a seduction. "Would a pet admit to missing its owner, because it'd become addicted to the desire it felt in its master's presence?"

My mind exploded.

I swallowed hard, hating the swirl of lust and temper that had no right to build. I'd barricaded emotions from my life, so why did the mere hint of an argument with Nila completely undo everything I'd tried so hard to fix?

I couldn't breathe.

Needing a distraction, I pulled her phone that I'd confiscated from my pocket and held it up.

Instantly, her mouth fell open. Greed and excitement glowed on her face. "You still have it."

"Of course, I still have it." Swiping my finger over the screen, I muttered, "There are some extremely interesting messages on here."

Nila froze. Her cheeks lost all colour. "I told you that I'd been in touch with my brother. I told you he knew."

I nodded. "You did."

She tried to hide her nervousness but didn't succeed. "So what's interesting? I told you the truth."

What was interesting?

How about the fucking messages reeking of smut and combustible need? I'd spent many an evening sorting through the unsent drafts to Kite007. She'd deleted more messages than she'd actually sent, hiding so much.

By reading the messages she didn't want seen, I saw right into her soul. I finally got a clue of who Nila Weaver was. And she was no longer the heartbreakingly timid woman who'd been a plaything for her brother and a slave for her father.

She was so, so much more.

Every draft she'd typed but never sent rested in her phone like a perfect calendar of her growth from naïve daughter to fierce opponent.

Every single message she'd typed to *him*—to the man she knew as Kite—further showed the truth of who she really was.

Her emails had been nothing but work related.

Her brother nothing but demanding and dominant.

Her father nothing but pleading and clinging.

But Kite...

He brought out the best in Nila. And I brought out the fucking worst.

I shook my head, unable to stop the chuckle breaking through my lips. Why hadn't I seen it? Why hadn't I understood it before now? I was a fucking idiot.

Nila crossed her arms, glaring pure death. "Are you done laughing at my personal life?"

I stopped chuckling, embracing vacancy once again. "What makes you think I'm laughing *at* you, Ms. Weaver?"

The moment I spoke her name, the fight, the intoxicating addictive need to battle with her broke free from the prison inside.

Goddammit, it seemed the only time I could be free was to stay away from her. But the only time I was alive was to provoke and drink in her kitten-like wrath like an elixir of life.

Fuck, I'm screwed.

For the first time, I acknowledged it. Not with hatred or fear or frustration—just accepted that Nila Weaver was a force I couldn't control, and as much as I would like to deny it, she had a power over me.

Jasmine had seen it.

That was what my sister meant.

But I'd been too much of an arsehole to listen.

Tomorrow, you're going back to your sister and talking this through.

I needed answers. And she was the only one who I trusted enough to give me unbiased, pure direction. We were the black sheep of the Hawk family, and for that one reason, we'd become close. Kes was my best friend—until recently, of course—but my sister was my rescuer.

Not that my father knew, or even my grandmother, who kept Jasmine far away from us men and our contamination.

No one knew the bond my sister and I shared.

Just like no one knew the bond Nila and I shared.

Both were secret.

And both meant more to me than any other relationship I'd ever had.

Shit.

Running a hand through my hair, I placed her phone on my desk.

Nila never took her gaze from the device. "You seem to laugh at everything I do, so it's only rational to think my messages entertained you to no end."

I had to do what I came in here to do before I lost all focus and allowed Nila to drag forth everything I'd worked so hard to swallow.

I murmured, "You're tempting destruction, Ms. Weaver." My breathing turned shallow as I moved around the desk and captured the ends of her long hair, twirling them around my fingertips.

There was something about her hair. Something that called to the feral part of me that wanted the strands on my cock as she sucked me, or better yet, stuck to my sweaty chest after I'd come deep inside her.

Those fantasies had not helped clear my head. The past fortnight, they'd only gotten worse. And I refused to fucking service myself. However, I couldn't stomach the thought of calling in a substitute.

Just like I had Nila's hair wrapped around my little finger, she had me wrapped around hers.

"Nila. My name is *Nila*. You might as well call me that, seeing as I've had your cock in my mouth and your tongue between my legs. Nothing like tasting each other to be on a first-name basis, huh, *Jethro*?"

I tugged her hair. "Quiet."

"No chance."

My eyes widened. Who was this woman? Taunting me, poking me while her body trembled with anger. It was almost as if she *wanted* me to explode. To hurt her. To retaliate.

Maybe she does?

Perhaps she felt the same way I did—a connection in our arguments, a freedom to give into the overwhelming emotions that didn't need to make sense when in the heat of a fight.

How did I think I could maintain this persona I'd created? This suave sophistication that I'd successfully worn for so many years?

My time was up.

And it would remain up until Nila was gone.

I swallowed hard at the thought of her disappearing.

My eyes fell on the diamond collar. "I could make you, but I think you'd just like it."

As long as the collar remained around her neck, she was alive. As long as the diamonds glinted and drenched her in rainbows, she would be there to torment me.

And day by day, she would make me weaker.

And weaker.

Until one day, I would lose it all.

It can't happen.

But what could I do to prevent it?

Make her hate you. Make her despise you.

Then it would be against my will, even if I suddenly wanted a change of heart.

"Everything you do to me I hate," she hissed.

Crowding her against the desk, I murmured, "Everything?" My eyes fell to her lips. What I wouldn't give to just fucking kiss her. I'd wanted to kiss her for weeks.

Her mouth parted, breath turning soft and quick. "Yes, everything."

Temper swirled in the room, heating the space. "You seem to enjoy the anticipation of me kissing you."

She snorted. "Don't flatter yourself."

Capturing her chin, I dug my fingers into her cheeks. "If I kissed you right now, you'd let me do whatever the hell I wanted."

She struggled, eyes sparkling with black ferocity. "Kiss me and I'll bite you."

I wanted to laugh at the absurdity of our fight, but fuck if it didn't make me feel more alive than I had in two weeks.

I couldn't let it continue, though.

It has to stop.

Letting her chin go, I slapped her.

A puff of surprise and pain escaped her lips.

The ring in my palm reminded me of the man I'd been groomed to be, and I threw myself headfirst into it. The bright flush on her cheek as her face snapped sideways begged me to lick her.

So, I did.

Dragging her close, I lapped my tongue over her hot, punished flesh, whispering, "You would like me too much if I gave into your goading, Ms. Weaver. I warned you before—if you insist on playing this game, you won't win."

She breathed hard. "Funny, I thought the score was pretty even."

I pressed my cold lips against her smarting cheek. "Funny, I thought you lost the day you were born."

She sucked in a breath, her dark eyes swimming with tears.

Strike for me.

I'd won that argument, so why did my stomach feel like fucking lead?

Letting her go, I grabbed the newly drafted contract from the desk and shoved it in her face. "You agreed to this. Sign it."

Her mouth popped wide, taking in the freshly inked document. I'd spent many nights carefully penning it in the way of our custom with quill and ink, rather than computer and printer. It wasn't perfect, but it was binding, and that was all that fucking mattered.

Grabbing the same swan feather I'd used to scratch out the paperwork, I stole Nila's hand and hooked her fingers around the quill.

"What is this?"

"The agreement owed from your disastrous attempt at running." Tapping the page, I said, "Sign it."

"I'm not signing anything until I've read it." Her gaze glowed black, her cheek still pink from my slap.

Taking a step back, I splayed my hands, presenting the contract. "By all means, Ms. Weaver. Read away."

She scowled, her hands shaking as she snatched it from my grip.

Her lips parted as she read.

I didn't need to see it to know what it said. It was ingrained on my soul.

Date: 5th September 2014

Jethro Hawk, firstborn son of Bryan Hawk, and Nila Weaver, firstborn daughter of Emma Weaver, hereby solemnly swear this is a law-abiding and incontestable contract.

Nila Weaver revokes all ownership of her freewill, thoughts, and body and grants them into the sole custody of Jethro Hawk, as per the agreement made the morning of the 19th of August when Nila Weaver took up the offer from Jethro Hawk to run in exchange for her freedom.

The previous incontestable document named the Debt Inheritance falls into second right of claimant and will remain void as long as this new agreement is in effect.

The terms brokered were for Nila's freedom and release of the Debt

Inheritance if she won, and her willing signature revoking everything that she is to Jethro Hawk if she lost.

On the 19th of August, Nila Weaver lost; therefore, this agreement is complete and binding.

Both Nila Weaver and Jethro Hawk promise neither circumstance, nor change of heart will alter this vow.

In sickness and in health.

Two houses.

One contract.

I'd already signed, taking up half the page below.

Nila looked up, completely horrified. "You can't be serious. You—you—"

I tensed. "Careful what you say. Think about how painful it will be for you if you insult my mental health again."

She swallowed back the words dying to spew from her mouth. "I'm not signing this, you bastard."

I tilted my head. "Bastard? Interesting choice of words."

"Don't like that one? How about fuckwit? Murderer? Rapist?"

I slapped her again, revelling in the equal burn we shared.

Pain to deliver pain. Pleasure to deliver pleasure.

Funny how the two were correlated.

"I'll accept 'bastard' and 'fuckwit,' but under no circumstances will I accept 'rapist.' Have I tried to take you? Have I forced you? And, I'm no murderer."

Her eyes glittered, fingers rubbing her cheek. "Are you deliberately blocking out what happened after the First Debt was repaid, or are you that much of a lunatic to remember only the things convenient to you?"

Lunatic.

I ran a hand infinitely slowly through my hair. I had full grounds to punish her. I'd warned her time and time again.

"Tell me, Jethro, you say you're not a murderer—*yet*. But it will be you who delivers the killing blow, won't it? You admitted as much in the past. Unless you're too chicken and make your father do it. Or even maybe poor Kes. Will he kill me? Is he the bigger man than you? To kill off the family pet when it's no longer wanted?"

My jaw ached from clenching so hard. "You really want to know?"

You've already guessed the truth.

The thought blazed bright, almost as bright as her cheek.

"No need, I already know. What will you use? A butchers block? A sharp blade or dull?" The strength and fight in her voice suddenly dissolved into sobs. "How will you live with yourself when my blood pours over your perfect shoes?"

The room shattered with sadness; the walls trampled us with appalling futures.

With a horrified wail, she curled into herself, holding her stomach as if her very soul tried to claw its way out. "Tell me, Jethro, if I only have a limited amount of time left, why go through the charade of making me sign this?!" She shook the parchment in front of my face. "What is this anyway? Does it have a name? 'Weaver Vexation,' perhaps?"

Her sanity quickly unravelled with every syllable.

I stood stiff, frantically clutching at my beloved ice. But in that moment, I felt her pain. I tasted her tears. I lived her grief.

My hands balled. The title I'd given it had been flippant at the time, but now I could see how it could shatter her.

Don't say it.

The air in the office turned stagnant, waiting for me to speak.

Finally, I admitted, "Sacramental Pledge."

She half-cackled, half-giggled, before everything seemed to fold in and crush her. "You made this our vows?! Sacramental, holy matrimony *vows*?"

Before I could answer, she shook her head and collapsed to her knees before me. Rocking, hot tears splashed onto the contract, mixing with ink and staining it with large swirls of black.

She was the one who gave me the idea. After all, we *were* technically married. Groomed for one another, destined to drive each other to insanity. This was our fate. Our motherfucking *destiny*.

Her laughs interspersed with sobs. The sound was utterly heart-crushing. I locked my body from moving as she curled tighter on the floor.

"This is real. This...it's not a nightmare. *This is real!*"

Tears rivered from her eyes, tracking faster and faster as her breath caught and she choked. She choked and sobbed and choked again. "It's not fair. I w—want to go h—home."

I'd never seen anyone come apart so completely.

This wasn't just about the deed. This was about everything she hadn't let herself feel. She hadn't let go of her past. She hadn't faced the reality that this was her future, and there would be no going back—no matter how much she thought it was possible.

Was this how she'd survived—by pretending it wasn't real, that everything would somehow disappear?

Everything crested and breached, shuddering her small frame with grief.

I stood over her, hating to see such weakness. Despising that I'd driven her to break. But at the same time, I stood protective over her vulnerability, standing guard, making sure she had the peace in which to purge.

In a way, I knew exactly how she felt. We were both chained to a future we didn't want, and there was no way out—for either of us.

I didn't touch her. I didn't torment her.

I let her spew her worries and cleanse herself.

I just let her cry.

As each droplet splashed onto the carpet, I found myself growing fucking jealous. I was jealous that finding a release was so easy for her. So easy to come undone, knowing she'd have the power to stitch herself together again.

Half an hour passed, or maybe it was only ten minutes, but slowly Nila's tears stopped, and her wracking frame fell into a deep, eternal silence.

The night was entirely tainted. I had no drive to make her sign anymore or to wage war. And I definitely had no more energy to be cruel.

There was no need. I didn't have to break her—not after she'd broken herself.

I sighed heavily. "Get up."

Slowly, quietly, and obediently, she climbed to her feet. She stood swaying, white as a fucking ghost. In her hands, she still clutched the quill and parchment having drenched it in her tears.

Without a word, she placed the soggy document onto the desk, dipped the swan feather into the ink well, and signed her name.

My stomach swooped in the wrong direction. I should've been happy, but instead my joy was filthy oil, corrupting my insides.

Avoiding eye contact, she whispered, "I want to go back to my room. If you have any soul inside you, Jethro, you will do this one thing for me."

My heart squeezed, cracking its glacier frost, melting drop by drop.

My hands itched to touch her, to grant solace…comfort.

She hates you, you arsehole.

There was no way she would want to be touched. Especially by me.

The least I could do was release her.

With infinitesimal slowness, I turned to the desk and retrieved her phone. "Here." I pressed it into her lax palm.

She didn't even acknowledge me.

With nothing else to say, I guided her back to her room.

Nila

NEEDLE&THREAD: *I wish you'd answer me, Vaughn. Please tell me you're not about to blow something up, charge in here with God knows what, and get yourself arrested or worse... killed. Please...reply. I miss you.*

I swiped at the sticky salt on my cheeks. My heart hung heavy like a charred piece of meat. Last night was a distant memory, rather foggy and blurred. I remembered the fireworks, I recalled the relaxed day of reading and helping the staff set up the garden buffet, but I struggled to remember what happened in Jethro's office.

All I knew was I'd finally snapped.

The cry I'd had in the kennels the day I arrived was nothing to how undone I'd become.

I should care that Jethro had seen me at my absolute weakest, but I couldn't get up the energy. I felt strangely aloof, removed from everything.

He let you cry.

He didn't torment me or make it worse by delivering yet more horror. He'd stood like an ice statue, completely unyielding and not melting at all, towering over me while I wept into his carpet.

But in that arctic silence, there'd been something...something different.

His silence had throbbed with regret…of understanding and even mutual anguish.

The moon and stars had given way to another stunning day, miraculously cancelling the horrible ending to a nice party. The best thing? I'd slept like the dead after Jethro had left me alone. The cry had drained me of everything, leaving me with a thick headache that sent me slamming into unconsciousness.

My phone buzzed.

Shaking my head, I dispelled last night and looked at the glowing screen. I wanted a reply from my twin. But what I got was better.

My heart soared as I read the first message from Kite007 in two weeks.

Kite007: *Don't know why I keep hoping you'll reply, seeing as you've been quiet for two weeks, but I had a shit of a night and need to talk to someone who won't judge.*

He'd been trying to message me?

I quickly scrolled through the inbox but found nothing. My stomach rolled at the thought of Jethro deleting Kite's messages. What an arsehole.

I'd gone from a secluded seamstress, whose only contact was her father and brother, to being torn in three directions. As much as I wanted to deny it, I had feelings for Kite. He'd been a bastard to me, but he'd granted me the strength to stand up to him, which then led me to develop feelings for Kestrel. *Because he's the same person; I know it.*

I still hadn't gotten up the guts to ask him, but sometimes I'd catch him watching me with secrets in his eyes.

I didn't care that it might all be a ruse to get inside my head. I didn't care I was nothing more than a marionette being told what to think and who to trust. I had to forget about all that and follow my heart—because, ultimately, that was the only thing that might save me.

Then, of course, there was Jethro. He confused me, perplexed me, and completely befuddled me. One minute I would gladly pour gasoline over his wintry shell and see if I could burn him into the person I saw rare glimpses of, the next he did things like last night and ruined all the softness I had for him.

How could I understand someone who didn't even understand himself?

You can't talk. One second you're trying to seduce him, the next you're trying to make him bleed.

We were as bad as each other.

Looking at the text again, I clicked reply. Biting my lip, I wondered why Kes/Kite had had a bad night. What had happened when Jethro tugged me away? And why hadn't Kes tried to talk to me when he realised I wasn't replying to his messages?

We saw each other every day. All he had to do was whisper something in my ear. Something that would confirm this labyrinthine mystery once and for all.

Perhaps Jethro showed the new contract to Kes—rubbed it in his face that no matter how Kes felt about me, he could never have me?

Ugh. The headache from last night came back with a heavy cloud.

Needle&Thread: *I'm here now. And you're right, I won't judge. What happened last night?*

It was odd to have nothing sexual included in the message, but our 'friendship' had more depth now.

I settled deeper into the pillows. The diamond collar bruised my neck, throbbing with heat; it wasn't exactly comfortable to sleep in.

Kite007: *I stooped to an all-new low. Remember when I said we're all products of our upbringing? Well, I keep blaming everything wrong inside me on that. I use it as an excuse, but what if it isn't good enough anymore?*

Oh, my God.

I'd never heard Kite sound so melancholy. My heartbeat increased as my fingers flew over the keyboard.

Needle&Thread: *There's nothing wrong inside you.*

I paused before pressing send. If I did this, he would

know I suspected. If he read between the lines and didn't see it as a blasé comment, the truth would be out and the choice of how to proceed would be in his court. Did I want him to have that power?

Gritting my teeth, I pressed send.

Immediately, I got a reply.

Kite007: *You don't know anything about me.*

Needle&Thread: *We can keep pretending if you'd like, but it's just another excuse. It sounds like you're ready to face the truth. So...it's your call if you want to or not.*

Minutes ticked past.

My mind skipped back to the day I'd arrived. The welcome luncheon, the night in the kennels, and the strange degrading encounters with Jethro. How was it the Hawks had everything, yet everyone seemed to be hiding the truth? Jethro was hiding. Kes was hiding. Daniel had disappeared—the little creep—and Cut walked around with an air of mystique.

There was so much beneath the surface that no one dared discuss.

And, if I was honest, they'd transformed me into the same kind of creature. Someone who had evolved from a single dimension and now lived with so many avenues of personalities.

I was still the quiet, vertigo-stricken girl from London, but I was also the woman who *liked* being tormented, who thrived on a fight, and who thirsted for sex.

And that stupefied me even more, because I wanted sex with *Jethro*, not Kestrel.

What does that mean?

Jethro had made me come totally and spectacularly in front of witnesses. He'd manipulated me—given me a reward. It was both sick and...sweet.

No, never sweet, Nila.

Yes, sweet.

Beneath the mask, he was so many things, and sweet *was* one of them.

Kite007: *My call? You're so sure I'll be honest?*

Needle&Thread: *Why wouldn't you be? You know who I am. I want to know who you are. I'm trustworthy.*

Kite007: *You're wrong. I don't know who you are. Every day I think I do, but then you do something that changes my perception. You're a complexity.*

My heart exploded.

Finally. Confirmation.

Every day you do…

Not say, or text, or imply. Do—as in action—*physical.*

My hands shook as I replied.

Needle&Thread: *Perhaps you need to drop your guard, in order to see in to others. You're just as complex, just as confounding.*

The second I pressed send, I panicked. He'd admitted we knew each other. I'd admitted it, too. This anonymous freedom was now a knowledgeable cage.

Kite007: *Tell me one thing you've lied about. Tell me the truth. Let me see what you're hiding.*

My brain smarted. There were so many secrets, too many puzzles. I'd changed so much; I no longer knew what I should hide. The little kitten who didn't have claws would've curled into a ball at such a revealing question, but that was no longer an option, and I didn't want it to be.

I was no longer afraid of diving deep and finding out who I truly was.

Needle&Thread: *You want something real? I've only come once in my life, and it was just a few days ago.*

It seemed like a small confession, but it was huge after all my fibbing of releases and kinky messages.

Kite007: *How is that even possible? What was with all the other fucking releases you had? I thought you were a master at self-pleasure.*

Needle&Thread: *You're asking questions that will lead to finding out who I am. Are you ready for that, Kite? Truly? No turning back once you do.*

Radio silence.

Typical.

He'd run again.

My fingers hovered over the keys, determined not to end

this. Not when we were so close to admitting this charade.

Needle&Thread: *I could continue pretending I'm the masturbating minx you think I am or be honest with you. Again, your choice.*

I rolled my eyes. *He's a Hawk.* Maybe he already knew everything about me? They'd probably had my family under surveillance for years. Maybe that was the whole reason why Kes messaged me on a wrong number—to drip-feed Jethro information on how pathetic and hopeless I was.

I slumped against my pillows. It made sense. And hurt far too much.

Kite007: *Masturbating minx? I like that title.*

My eyes flared; my stomach twisted with eagerness.

Kite007: *I need to know more. Stick to the subject and give me the truth. Nothing more. Nothing less. What were you doing when you said you came?*

My heart raced.

Needle&Thread: *Releases for me were found either on my treadmill or from working until my brain was numb.*

Five minutes passed.

Kite007: *And the only time you came? How did that happen?*

As if you don't know.

Suddenly, I was over it all. Over the fibs, the half-truths, the veiled secrets. He knew how it happened. He'd watched his damn brother stick his tongue between my legs and make me combust.

Needle&Thread: *I came with the tongue of my enemy between my legs. He drove me so damn high and hard that I gave him a piece of myself no one else ever had, and he used it as a weapon against me. There, you happy?*

My chest rose and fell. Arguing via faceless messages wasn't enough. I wanted to strike and hurt and scream.

Kite007: *If you were here with me, I'd give you your second release. I'd finger you until you were soaking, then I'd do what I've wanted to fucking do since I set eyes on you.*

My mouth went terribly dry.

Needle&Thread: *What have you wanted to do?*

Kite007: *I want to feel how tight you are. I want to experience your* wet heat as I fill you. I want to give you my cock, Needle. Would you let me?

Oh, my God. My body turned boneless with desire.

Another message from a different sender arrived.

Textile: *Nila? I understand why you haven't replied to me, but I thought you should know that V and I are closer to figuring a way to end this ridiculous nightmare. Don't lose hope, sweetheart. I love you so much.*

Oh, bad timing, father. *Seriously* bad timing.

My lust turned to smouldering rage.

Ridiculous? He thought this was *ridiculous*? This debt that killed my mother and all the firstborn women in my family tree was ridiculous?

I laughed at his choice of words. This wasn't ridiculous; it was insane.

Needle&Thread: *Father, you let them take me. You knew all along they were coming, yet you did nothing to protect me. You handed me over like a fattened calf with no tears or violence. How can you say you're coming for me? How can you say you love me? I'm not losing hope. I'm building my own brand of hope, and for the first time in my life, it doesn't hinge on you. Leave me the hell alone.*

I shook hard when I pressed send. I'd never spoken to my father that way before. Never been so disrespectful. It made me feel sick but also free. Free from the fear of disappointing him.

Because he'd disappointed me first.

Kite007: *Would you let me fuck you? Would you break the rules and give me what I need so fucking much?*

My mind swarmed with images of sleeping with Kestrel, but try as I might, all I could see was Jethro. All I could feel was Jethro. All I wanted was Jethro.

Shit.

I wanted to throw my damn phone against the wall.

Needle&Thread: *Answer me one question before I give you an answer.*

Kite007: *What?*

Taking a deep breath, I typed:

Needle&Thread: *Would you kiss me first? Or is that against the rules?*

A minute. Then two.

Kite007: *I wouldn't just kiss you. I would hold your cheeks and worship your mouth. I would devour your lips and make drunken love to your tongue. I would fucking inhale you, so you would live forever in my lungs.*

I couldn't move.

Yet another difference between the Hawk brothers. One would kiss me, and one went out of his way to avoid it. One would adore me until the day of my death, and one would probably dance upon my grave because it meant his obligations were complete.

My heart crumbled into dust.

I couldn't—I couldn't do this anymore.

Turning my phone around, I undid the case, tore the battery out, and dumped the dismantled device into the drawer of the bedside table.

I didn't care about replying.

I didn't care if my silence hurt his feelings.

All I cared about was nursing the cyclonic pain inside me.

And trying to forget all about Jethro fucking Hawk.

The next morning, I was showered and clothed in a black maxi dress with a sequined orchid on the chest and purple ballet slippers.

I needed some space and planned to go for a walk around the estate. I still hadn't turned my phone on and had no desire to do so. It was still in pieces in the drawer. For now, I didn't care about the outside world or even Kite's reply.

I didn't *care*.

It was liberating.

Sitting on the end of my bed, I quickly plaited my hair and draped the long rope over my shoulder.

My head wrenched up as the door to my room slammed open.

"What the—"

Jethro stood breathing hard in the doorway. My cold-hearted nemesis wore black jeans and a grey t-shirt—seriously, didn't he own any other colours?

"Where do you think you're going?" His voice was gravel and granite and ice.

I stood up, planting my hands on my hips. "Good morning to you, too. If you must know, *master*, it's time for my walk. I'm a good little pet, you see. Making sure I have my daily exercise."

I knew I played with fire, or ice as the case might be, but I really didn't give a damn.

The previous night in his office had broken something inside me and Kes/Kite had finished me off with talks of wanting me.

I couldn't decipher my panic last night when Kite said he would kiss me—my sudden terror hadn't made sense. But now it did.

If I let myself fall into Kes's/Kite's trap of kindness, I would lose everything I'd fought to gain. And I wasn't willing to give that up. I was selfish and liked this new Nila. And if that meant I had to keep my distance from kind-hearted people and only surround myself with bastards, then so be it.

Jethro would be the only one permitted to spike my heart and draw reluctant wetness. No one else.

"Careful, Ms. Weaver," Jethro murmured. Stalking into the room, he kicked the door closed behind him.

His presence was a challenge, and I was prepared to meet it. Crossing the small distance between us, we met in the middle of the carpet; every muscle tense and ready to fight.

His nostrils flared, golden eyes delving deeply into mine. "I thought you'd be hiding under your bed after your debacle in my office."

I shrugged. "Everyone has a limit, and I crossed mine. Unluckily for you, my limit has now increased, so don't expect me to break again anytime soon." I smiled, thinking of my reply to my father. I'd finally had the balls to tell him to leave me alone. Jethro would be no different.

I was prepared to unplug him, just like I'd unplugged my phone.

Taking another step, my fingertips landed on his chest, dipping coyly to his belt. His eyes flared, but he held his ground. "Thank you for pushing me, Jethro. Without you, I would still be terrified. But now I feel surprisingly...calm."

A calm where I'd stopped fretting over the future. A calm where I was just as volatile and just as unhinged as they were.

"I can't keep up with you." His voice was dark with a trace of anger. He cocked his head, his salt-and-pepper hair catching the morning sun glinting through the window. "You've surprised me again, Ms. Weaver, and once again, I don't like it." He leaned forward, his lips so close to mine. "I'm beginning to wonder if everything I know about you is a lie."

I stood firm. "You don't know a thing about me."

Why does this conversation sound like the one I had yesterday by phone?

He chuckled. "We Hawks have our ways. I know more than you think."

His cryptic comment didn't derail me. He'd read Kite's messages. He knew everything about me that I'd meant for a perfect stranger.

I stared harder, trying to uncover his many, many layers. But it was pointless—like staring into a black lake with no reflection other than myself.

"Come. It's time for Gemstone and breakfast." He smiled coldly. "I have no doubt you'll be starving after your...what was that? Would you prefer the word *breakdown* or *hysterics*?"

I straightened my shoulders. "Neither."

"You have to pick one."

"No, I don't. If you want me to define it, I'll call it my way of saying goodbye."

He jerked. "Goodbye?" His knuckles went white as his hands clenched into fists. "To whom?"

My eyes tightened, trying to read him. He played the perfect part. If he knew Kestrel messaged me, he hid his deception so well—too well. The perfect liar.

"To my past, to who I used to be, to a friend called Kite."

The reaction was subtle.

The small intake of breath. The slight whitening of his face. The indiscernible flinch of his muscles.

Then it was gone, hidden beneath the snowy exterior he held so well. "Ah yes, the James Bond idiot, 007. The same idiot who just can't seem to stop messaging you." Moving quickly, he grabbed my elbow, dragging me toward the door. "Well, I'm glad you said your goodbyes. Nothing worse than dying with unfinished business." His smile sent gale-force winds howling through my suddenly torn-open chest.

I slammed to a halt. "You can't help yourself, can you?"

He paused, forehead furrowed.

"You just have to be so damn cruel."

He sighed dramatically, backing me away from the door and toward the centre of the room again. "I'm not cruel."

I laughed. "Says the heartless human who probably doesn't have a reflection when he stares in the mirror."

He took another threatening step. I took one, too. Backing away from him, waltzing slowly around the room as hunter and prey.

"You're saying I'm soulless?"

I nodded. "Completely soulless."

He smirked. "Okay, try me. Ask me to do something. Make me prove to you that I have a soul."

I frowned. "Like what?"

He took another step, pressing me closer to the bed. The anger throbbing around him switched to sexual interest. My breathing picked up as his golden eyes darkened. "You're the one who needs proof, Ms. Weaver. You make the choice."

What could I make him do?

What would prove he had a heart and my resolution to seduce him would actually work?

I know.

The one thing that seemed to be the epicentre of whatever I was trying to do.

I stopped retreating, locking my knees to prevent myself

from losing confidence and running. "I have something. A test. It will prove you're not the monster I think you are."

He came closer, a slow smile spreading his lips. "Go on."

I balled my hands, taking a deep breath. The precipice opened wide. I took a leap of faith and leapt. "Kiss me."

The oxygen in the room disappeared. My heart erupted into flurries.

Jethro froze. "Excuse me?"

Standing tall, I said, "You've come so close to kissing me. By the stables, in the forest, when you made me pay the First Debt, even in your office. I'm done with your teasing, Jethro. I'm done with you pulling away whenever things get interesting. I want to know why."

Jethro's hands clenched by his sides. "And you think a stupid kiss will prove—what will it prove?"

I narrowed my eyes. "That you're not as cold as you think you are. That you do care—care enough to be affected by kissing your arch enemy."

Jethro laughed, but it was laced with uncertainty and…was that fear? "I'm not kissing you to prove such a ridiculous point."

I splayed my hands, mocking him. "You said you'd do anything I asked."

He chuckled softly. "I said something worthwhile."

"Kissing me isn't worthwhile?"

His gaze latched onto mine. A second ticked past. Another.

Then he lost his icy shell. "What the fuck do you want from me, Nila?"

My heart stopped.

Nila.

He'd called me *Nila*.

I'd won. I'd somehow made him say my name.

My heart winged just as surely as my core flickered with desire.

Say it again.
Let me hear the bliss of winning.

Jethro's eyes widened, noticing his slip, then furious temper etched his face. He stormed forward, threading his fingers around my throat. The smooth edges of his control were now jagged with temper.

I backed up until the bed stopped my escape. Jethro followed, his fingers tightening around my neck. "Tell me, goddammit. What the fuck are you trying to do?"

My heart hurt at the indecipherable expression in his gaze. He hid himself so well. The brief flashes of truth I'd gleaned didn't add up. I was fishing for something that didn't exist.

It does exist. Keep pushing.

My eyes were heavy, body pulsing with rapidly building lust. "I just want...."

There was no point to this argument. It was over before it began.

"I need..."

To know you are capable of caring, just a little.

For you to want me, just a little.

For you to find something inside me that prevents you from killing me.

It was like wishing for Pegasus to fly in and whisk me away. I wouldn't get anything I wished for. Whatever I felt for Jethro was misplaced, ill-advised, and false. I'd seen him hunt me. I'd seen his cold enjoyment of talking about taking my life. Everything else that I thought I'd seen had been a lie.

He breathed hard, his scent of woods and leather surrounding me.

My hands flew up to hold his, trying to pry his fingers off. "Just...forget it. Let me go. Forget I was stupid enough to say anything."

Jethro dropped his hands, pacing away. "Forget it? You're the one bringing it up. Time and time again, you bring it up. I'm fucking sick of you asking me to kiss you." Dragging a hand through his hair, he added, "*You're* the one ruining the agreement between us."

"What agreement?"

"The debts, Ms. Weaver! That's all we're meant to do. I

don't care about your wellbeing or emotional satisfaction. Sex between us is meant to be a punishment, yet you keep making it seem like a reward. A fucking delicious reward."

His jaw clenched at another slip, his features blackening. "You ruined a straight-forward obligation by trying to fucking kiss me in that coffee shop! This is all your fault. If you'd just been fucking petrified of me, then this would've been easy!"

My head shot up. Jethro was close to losing it. His eloquence became littered with curses.

"*Easy?* You think this would've been *easy?* None of this would've been easy, Jethro—for either of us. Even if I'd been crying in the corner every time you came to harass me, it wouldn't have been better. It would've just been *different.*"

Jethro exploded. "It would've been better than me fighting a fucking battle every damn day with how much I want to fuck you!"

My heart swooped, nipples pebbling with the tormented need in his voice.

"Don't you think I have the same problem? How can I live with the knowledge that I hate you, that you're my future killer, yet I can't stop my body from craving you? Don't you think I hate the fact that you make me wet against my wishes?"

Shit, I shouldn't have said that.

Jethro froze, panting hard.

The silence was deafening.

Sighing, I tugged my plait. "Look, I tried to kiss you that night in the coffee shop because for the first time in my life, my father gave me freedom. Can I help it I found you attractive? We're suffering the same pain. Our bodies want what the mind knows it shouldn't. It's the law of chemistry, and I refuse to let you put this disaster on me. *You're* the one who stole me. *You're* the one in control of my fate. If this is anyone's fault—it's yours!"

The atmosphere changed, shedding its brittle battle for heavy heat and intoxication.

His lips twitched. "You found me attractive?"

God, he was so obtuse.

I couldn't stop the insane laugh bubbling from my mouth. "Do you honestly think I would've sucked you in the forest? Do you think I would've writhed on someone else's fingers the way I did yours? I'm sexually starving but I'm not so desperate to allow someone to touch me unless I want them to!"

I clamped a hand over my lips. Shit. Another thing I hadn't meant to say. That was a lie I was hiding unsuccessfully, even from myself. Sex with Jethro was supposed to be a weapon. Whenever I thought of him touching me, it was to win—not to give in to my overpowering urges.

I wanted to *take* from him. Not enjoy what he'd give me.

Jethro prowled closer, pinning me against the pole of the four-poster bed. His body heat sparked hot and dangerously close to mine. His hands opened and closed at his side. So close. So temptingly close.

"This is getting interesting, Ms. Weaver. You mean to tell me you want my cock? You want me to…fuck you?"

My stomach twisted. Wetness built in my core as the argument switched from exposing his weaknesses to exposing mine.

I bit my lip, refusing to answer.

He smirked, his eyes dropping to my mouth. His lips parted as his breathing turned heavy and ragged. "Tell me what you want from me. You have my undivided attention."

All the frustration from dealing with Kite came back. Despite the crudeness of our sexting, I missed messaging. Talking dirty fanned the need inside, amplifying the sexual burn. I had no reprieve from living an endless torture with a man who meant to kill me. A man my body wanted more than anything. A man who gave me the gift of pleasure—who would always be wrapped up in some twisted way in my soul.

I embraced the heat of anger, glaring into Jethro's golden eyes.

Don't do this.
You'll get hurt. Terribly hurt.

I couldn't stop myself.

"I told you what I want. Kiss me." My arms swooped up,

looping around his neck.

He reared back, breaking my hold. His chest rose and fell as he breathed hard. His eyes were almost black with need. Need I was sure reflected in mine. "Stop asking that, damn you." He snapped, "Why would I stoop to kissing you? A kiss is emotion. A kiss is a weakness." Placing his hands on either side of me, he grabbed the post and murmured, "I've told you time and time again; a kiss is not something you'll get from me."

I moved forward, pressing my chest against his until he broke away. He stepped backward; it was my turn to stalk him for a change. "A kiss is nothing. What are you so afraid of?"

What am I doing?

What were *we* doing?

Rules were being broken. Houses were being betrayed.

Consequences would come. Pain would be endured. But in that moment, I didn't care.

All I cared about was Jethro's lips on mine.

He dodged my grasp, then forced himself to stand tall and unmovable. I pressed myself against him, looking up into his gaze. His lips were so close. My heart fluttered like a dying hummingbird, my stomach twisted. So…close.

I couldn't move.

Jethro didn't shift back, he stood there, his hips flush against mine. Suddenly, his hands came up, grabbing my waist, holding me in place.

We didn't speak, only breathed. The truth crackled around us. We knew how dangerous this fight was, how frayed our self-control had become.

We'd been dancing this tango for weeks, and the electricity between us was a lightning storm threatening to incinerate everything in its path.

"Stop. Stop playing me. What did you hope to achieve? That I'd kiss you? Fuck you? Come to care for you? That I'd fall in *love* with you." Jethro dropped his voice to a whisper. "That I wouldn't kill you?" He shook his head. "You're still as clueless and naïve as the day I stole you."

You don't believe that.
"Prove it."
His nostrils flared. "I will not."
Cocking my chin, I anchored myself in as much courage as possible. "Prove it, Jethro. Prove how cold you are by giving me something I desperately need."
I need to see there is hope. Just a small shred of hope.
"What makes you think I can be manipulated? I don't care about your needs or desires."
"Liar," I whispered. "You *do* care. Otherwise, you wouldn't still be here. You wouldn't be fighting this." I rested my hands on his chest, digging my fingernails into his t-shirt. "You would've struck me and left if you were anything like you portray."
I stood on my tiptoes, reaching for his mouth. "I told you, you're a hypocrite."
He paused, calculation dark in his eyes. "One kiss?"
I nodded. "One kiss."
Jethro's control broke. "Just one fucking kiss? Don't you know what you're asking from me? I don't want to fucking kiss you!"
My heart broke. Was I so repulsive he didn't want his lips anywhere on mine?
I withered in his gaze, falling back to my position of Weaver Whore. But then, I stopped. This was the only time I might get him this undone, this close to snapping. It might be my only hope.
Glaring, I snarled, "Kiss me. Give me one fracture of human company, and I'll never say another word to you again. I'll be whatever you want. Just kiss me!"
His eyes narrowed. "You're an idiot."
"So you keep telling me."
"You're wasting your time."
"So you keep telling me."
"I don't want to kiss you!"
I lashed out. My arms came up. I opened my palm. And I slapped the self-righteous, egotistical arsehole on the cheek.

The moment went from lust-heavy to stagnant with violence. We stared, caught dead centre in war.

"You're a fucking nightmare," he snapped.

"Kiss me."

"You're ruining my life."

"Kiss me."

"You're—"

"Kiss me, Jethro. Kiss me. Just fucking kiss me and give me—"

His body crashed against mine. His hands flew up, grabbing my cheeks and holding me firm. His lips, oh his lips, they bruised mine as his head tilted, and with pure anger, he gave me what I'd wanted for weeks.

He kissed me.

My lungs were empty—he'd stolen all my air, but I no longer survived on oxygen. I survived on his mouth, his taste, his unbridled energy pouring down my throat.

His tongue tore past my lips, taking me savage and hungry. There was nothing sweet or gentle. This was a punishment. A reminder that I hadn't won. He wasn't kissing me. He was fighting me in every underhanded way.

His hands dropped from my cheeks, cupping my breasts. The violence in his touch throbbed instantly. I arched my back, opening my mouth wider to scream, but he swallowed my cries, kissing me deeper, harder, stealing every inch of sanity I had left.

I thought a kiss would put me on even ground—show him that he did care. That he was human—just like me. I hadn't gambled on being detonated into a billion tiny pieces that had no notion of who I'd been before he'd stolen my soul.

He backed me up, faster and faster to the bed. His breath saturated my lungs. His touch skated from my cheeks, to my breasts, to my waist, to my arse. Jerking me hard against the huge length of arousal in his jeans.

The bed stopped our motion, tumbling us onto the sheets, but nothing, absolutely nothing could unweld our lips.

We were joined, kissing, frantic, *desperate*.

He groaned as I slid my hands beneath his t-shirt, needing to feel his skin against mine.

He was blood and fire and heat.

So different to the glacier he pretended to be.

"Fuck," he grunted as my fingers drifted to his buckle. I thanked my past of making countless pairs of trousers as I ripped through the barrier and dived into his boxer-briefs with eager fingers.

His teeth clamped around my bottom lip as I stroked him. The faint taste of metallic smeared between us as our kiss turned into pure violence.

My vision went black, seeing only white sparks and sensation.

Jethro's hands suddenly went to my waist, rolling off me to shove up my dress and tear my knickers from my hips. He shoved them desperately down my legs.

The world spun faster and faster as we discarded every item in our way and left the rest. Our lips never unglued; our heads twisted and turned as our tongues slipped and glided.

Moans and groans echoed in my ears, but I didn't know who made them. Fingers bruised my skin, nails scratched my flesh, and our souls grew teeth—snapping and tearing, trying to consume the other before it was too late.

We were furious.

We were wild.

We were completely delirious with lust.

Jethro grabbed my hip, planting me hard against the mattress. My inner thighs tickled with wetness of all-consuming desire. I'd never been so wet. Never been so slick and dying to be taken.

His hand disappeared between my legs, wedging his naked hips between them. The moment he found how much I wanted him, he groaned. "You—fuck—I—"

My heart winged at his incoherency. I loved that he'd given up, given in. Stabbing my fingernails into his lower back, I panted, "Don't stop. I don't want you to stop."

His head flopped forward, his lips capturing mine again in

a soul-searing kiss. His five o'clock shadow razored across my sensitive skin, but I loved the burning, loved the assault.

My back arched as one long finger entered me.

"Yes—God..."

His tongue slipped between my open lips, forcing me to kiss him back. I struggled to pay attention to the exhilarating taste of him and the eye-popping sensation of his finger rubbing my inner walls.

The tingly precipice he'd shown me that first day returned; I latched onto it hungrily.

I wiggled closer, needing more...needing something bigger, broader...I needed his cock.

He grunted as he forced a second finger inside me. The garbled noise might've had words strung together, but they poured unheard down my throat.

"Don't stop." I arched my hips, welcoming, imploring him to thrust harder.

I didn't care I wasn't on birth control. I didn't care about anything but driving us out of his nightmarish world and into a new dimension.

"I can't—you don't—" Jethro groaned between kisses.

"Yes, you can. You can't stop. Not now."

His fingers froze.

I refused to let him overthink this. It was my turn to bite his lip. Hard.

He bellowed...then...he went rogue. The final barrier he'd always stayed behind shattered, and he poured his broken soul into my being.

His fingers hooked inside me, making me unbelievably wetter. His lips nibbled and ravaged, leaving me hollow of thoughts and humanity.

His free hand shot to my chest, twisting my nipple beneath the fabric of my dress while his fingers plunged harder, faster inside me.

The invasion blew my mind.

It was too much. *It's not enough.*

I arched in his hold, spreading my legs wider. All thoughts

were gone. All worries were dead.

I didn't care how I looked or what would become of me afterward.

I just wanted him.

"Take me. Please."

He stopped kissing me. His lips swollen, red. His eyes frantic with passion and affliction. His jaw tightened, and for a horrible second, I thought he'd refuse. He knew my sexual history; there was no reason to fear taking me bare. I didn't know his, but he was impeccable in all facets of his life. Somehow, I couldn't see him sleeping around. I couldn't see him putting himself in such a vulnerable position.

His lips crashed against mine again, his tongue tearing past my lips. I grabbed the back of his neck, forcing our mouths harder together.

His fingers disappeared from inside me, smearing my wetness onto my thigh as he pushed me ever wider. I let my legs spread shamelessly. I was beyond decency or concern. My body was flushed, acutely sensitive, and entirely feverish.

In a seamless male move, Jethro clamped my hip and pulled himself higher. The relief at *finally* feeling the broad head of his cock against my entrance sent me spiralling into madness.

"Shit, you feel..." His voice was a decadent purr. "You feel like..."

"Like freedom," I breathed, taut and trembling, just waiting for him to enter me.

His eyes flared wide, dazzling me with bronze need. "Yes, exactly."

The moment stretched for far too long, somehow turning this from fucking to something unbearably precious.

With our gazes still locked, he pushed inside me.

A breathless cry escaped me as discomfort blazed. I squirmed beneath him, trying to find relief from the pinching, consuming pressure of him filling me.

I'd been terrified once of taking him. Horrified at his huge size, so sure he would never fit, but inch-by-inch he stretched me, changing my whole perception.

My core rippled around him, welcoming and rebelling against his invasion.

He was perfect.

Utterly perfect.

Our foreheads crashed together as he sank deeper and *deeper*. Only once he was completely sheathed did he close his eyes and kiss me again. Pleasure seeped from the one place where we were joined—the only place we were naked.

It was carnal, lewd, and fit my salacious need better than any position.

I reached up to kiss him back, diving my fingers into his sweat-misted hair. His body radiated heat, trembling above me as I sucked his tongue into my mouth.

He didn't stop me. He didn't try to control me. He gave that part of himself, so gently and sweetly, my heart cracked with unknown joy.

I rocked my hips, grinding myself on his thick cock, seeking the solace from the overbearing need to explode. My mind scrambled with the primitive instinct to fuck, to claim, to drive each other until we burst and this intolerable hunger would be sated.

The rawness of being laid bare, of being full to the brink and taken so thoroughly, pushed me to the edge of an orgasm.

My knuckles turned white as I anchored myself on his waist. My mind swirled with vertigo as the first scrumptious rock annihilated my world.

There was no shame or shyness.

This was beyond that.

This was the first true thing that'd happened to me in my entire life.

My gaze locked with his, unable to look away.

In that moment, he owned me. I'd do anything he wanted. And he knew it.

He rocked again, sending spindles of fireworks in my blood. The smell of our desire laced the room, a seductive mix of wrongness and right.

My nipples pebbled as he drove into me again; my breasts throbbed, heavier than they'd ever been.

This was what I'd wanted, what I'd fought for. Every time we'd duelled, I'd wanted to possess him, to climb on top of him, and impale myself on his aristocratic cock.

"Fuck," Jethro groaned, driving hard, rocking his hips to an uneven rhythm.

His back was granite beneath his t-shirt, his skin a rippling volcano of heat.

I gasped, flexing around him as he thrust once, twice.

"More. Please, more."

Somehow this had turned from war to intimacy. We'd both stepped over the line, and I had no clue how to go back.

His gaze was turbulent as he drove again. I knew he struggled with what I did—sensed he was just as ruined and destroyed as me. We'd been fighting against each other, but ultimately, we'd won and lost.

Eye-to-eye, skin-to-skin, there was no room for bullshit or lies.

And it was perfectly petrifying.

I opened wider, taking more of him.

He sucked in a loud breath, stretching me exquisitely.

There was no way any other man could ever compete with the elegant chilliness of Jethro. He was exactly like the iceberg he favoured, only in different lights, more truth shone. Some bright and light and blinding, others black and deep and terrifying.

But it didn't matter, because in that moment, I was in the heart of the iceberg, and all I found was passion.

Our rhythm lost its sedateness, straining toward a frenzy to mate. To dominate.

His pace picked up, bruising me in all new ways. "Fuck, I want to come."

My neck arched, rising off the mattress. "Then come." Searing pleasure split me in two as he drove explicitly hard.

A gleam of masculine smugness filled his eyes, knowing he had me completely in his control, completely submitting.

He groaned as my core rippled around his cock.

Then, he lost it.

His lips descended fast and hard on mine as his hips surged upward, driving my spine deeper into the mattress.

My mouth popped open as every nerve-ending zeroed to my womb, to the melting liquid coating Jethro as he claimed me.

Then, pain.

Glorious, furious, mind-numbing pain as he thrust harder and harder, faster and faster.

Every inch I screamed with agony. He was too big, too long, too damn much. Even with the slow acclimatization and gentle welcome, I wasn't wide enough, long enough, prepared enough.

I cried out as he drove never-endingly into me.

There were no more walls, no more locks or secrets. This was him. Caught up in lust—both sexual and savage. He gave me what I wanted. He gave me himself with nothing hidden.

His lips opened beneath mine as he thrust again, hitting the entrance of my womb. I couldn't breathe. I couldn't think. His incessant need to take never ceased, his kisses never stopped.

Sweat sprinkled my skin as he drugged me body and soul. The room fogged with the sounds of skin slapping against skin and heavy breathing.

But then, the pain disappeared, switching into exquisite pleasure.

My body deliquesced, adjusting to his huge invasion.

My hips arched to meet his.

His heart thundered against mine.

We drove again and again and again, our grunts and moans and groans plaiting into one angry battle.

I scraped my fingernails down his back, grabbing his behind, driving him harder still.

I didn't think I'd survive it. I worried we'd end up killing each other before we finished.

The pleasure was too much!

The dark promise of finding a satisfying ending seemed an impossible task.

A curling, unfolding orgasm barrelled from nowhere. I tensed, moaning beneath his invasion.

My legs stiffened as he took me ruthlessly, never stopping his angry thrusting.

I couldn't control my body. I didn't want to.

With a scream, I came so fucking hard I almost passed out with vertigo. Ecstatic spasms of bliss undid my world as surely as threads from gossamer. My mind fluttered like a flimsy ghost, deprived of its old home—decimated by euphoria.

The room swam. I felt sick and overjoyed and ruined.

Jethro cupped my throat, linking his fingers through my diamond collar as his eyes shot black. His jaw locked as he witnessed me falling apart. I held his gaze, even though I wanted to look away and hide just how shattered I was.

I was possessed, enraptured.

Another wave of paradise shuddered through my core, making me jerk with spent muscles.

Jethro didn't stop. The minute my pussy stopped clenching around him, he gave himself permission to follow. I moaned as his hips pounded unforgivingly into mine, punishing me with heavenly corruption.

The tip of his cock hit the top of me with every lunge, bruising me, ensuring I would feel the ache of his possession for days afterward.

With every thrust, he grew in size, throbbing hotter, thicker, harder, driving toward the finish he craved. His face etched with danger, his eyes positively beastly. His self-control was non-existent as he hurled himself over the edge.

He orgasmed with a primitive snarl of feral ecstasy, his release splintering him into pieces.

"Shit, shit, shit!" His voice echoed with ferocity and vulnerability at coming completely undone. Pulling out, he grabbed the base of his cock and fisted himself as ribbons of white liquid shot through the air and splattered against my pubic hair and lower belly.

His stomach rippled as spurt after spurt drained him, marking me with musky threads of semen.

Breathing hard, he looked down at the mess he'd made—the evidence of our betrayal to hatred, family, and debts.

We couldn't deny what'd just happened.

It wasn't just sex. It wasn't just lust.

It was something *more*.

I expected him to leave. To hate me.

But he folded over me, planting his slippery cock against my belly, smearing the now translucent mess until we stuck uncomfortably together.

My core cramped and trembled from such abuse, but I'd never felt so languid or tranquil.

Slowly, hesitantly, I brushed my lips across his, comforting him.

He didn't say a word, nor did he kiss me back. His head fell forward, nuzzling his damp face into the curve of my neck.

I froze as his strong arms wrapped around me, crushing me against him.

Tears raced into being as my heart twisted and pulverised. I couldn't handle him holding me like that—especially after what'd happened. I needed him to be cool and aloof if I had any chance at keeping my soul in one piece.

Liar.

It was already shredded, like shards in a breeze.

Jethro's heart hammered against mine, beating hard, slowing its drumming the longer he held me.

We stayed like that for a long time. Too long. Both of us acknowledging wordlessly what we would never be able to do with conversation.

We were stripped. Naked. Exposed.

Woefully defenceless against each other.

With every second that passed, I tried to repair the damage he'd done. I felt him trying to do the same, gathering the pieces of his façade, gluing them unsuccessfully back into place.

Moment by moment, our connection drifted, slipping us further and further away.

My skin turned to goosebumps, exchanging sweaty lust for aftermath regret.

Finally, Jethro pulled away, climbing off me, tainting any illusion of togetherness. Not making eye contact, he whispered, "What just happened can never happen again. If it does, they'll see the truth, and I won't have any power to keep you."

His powerful neck convulsed as he swallowed. "We're fucked, Nila Weaver. Well and truly fucked."

Jethro

GODDAMMIT.

I needed to get out of there.

I needed to fix myself, find my ice.

I need to destroy the camera footage.

No one must know. *No one.*

Not looking at Nila, I grabbed my jeans off the floor and jerked them on. I couldn't get a grip on my breathing. Everything inside me had switched upside down, and just the thought of walking away from her, after something so life changing, brought me to my fucking knees.

But I had no *choice.*

My mind replayed sinking inside her—hearing her moans, feeling her clench around me as she shattered.

Fuck.

Go.

Before it's too late.

Before she sees.

Before he sees.

Before everyone sees the goddamn truth.

Dragging a hand through my hair, I glanced at her once out of the corner of my eye. She sat dishevelled and used. Her dress bunched around her waist, her broken knickers discarded on the floor, and her lips swollen and red.

I refused to look between her legs and see the sticky evidence of the best orgasm of my life. I thought blowing down her throat was amazing, but it'd been nothing compared to thrusting inside her.

I'd held back at the start, knowing I would be too big for her.

But like everything about Nila, she'd surprised me. She'd been able to take my entire length, and the moment I'd felt her body give and welcome, that was it for me.

I'd fucking lost it.

"Jethro—"

I held up my hand, cursing the tremble in my muscles. "Don't. Stay here for the rest of the day. Do. Not. Tell. Anyone. You hear me?" My eyes narrowed, and I hoped I looked vicious and crazed, rather than unguarded and scared shitless about the consequences of what we'd done.

I knew what they'd do to her if they found out.

She didn't.

It was best to keep it that way.

When Nila didn't respond, I growled, "Promise me. This is our fucking secret. Don't tell anyone. Got it?"

Wrapping her arms around her knees, she looked five years younger than she actually was. Her legs were coltish and long, her grace almost balletic. She was the perfect willowy female, but with soft curves and fragility came danger.

Danger in the form of being so fucking breakable.

"I won't tell anyone, Jethro."

"Good." Stomping to the door, my mind was already on the things I'd have to take care of in order to hide this catastrophe.

Twisting the key, Nila's voice stopped me. "When—when will I see you again? Are you disappearing?" The sheets rustled as she shifted on the bed.

I refused to turn and look at her. I couldn't. I didn't trust myself not to grab her and sink inside her wet, tempting heat again.

"Stop asking questions, Ms. Weaver."

She sighed angrily. "So, we're back to Ms. Weaver again? Stop it. Just stop it. Don't run from me, and call me Nila, for God's sake."

Looking over my shoulder, I tried to ignore her flushed skin, her sated sigh, but most of all, I pretended I didn't see the connection blazing in her eyes. The understanding.

It pissed me off just as much as it made me crave a simpler existence.

"I meant what I said, Ms. Weaver. We're well and truly fucked. So keep that pretty little mouth closed and forget what happened."

Opening the door, I added low so she wouldn't hear, "You've destroyed me, Nila. And now it's my job to make sure they don't destroy you, too."

Nila

THE MOMENT JETHRO left, I knew I wouldn't be seeing him again for a while.

Sure enough, a week passed where my life fell into a routine of sketching, reading, and hanging out with Kes and the Black Diamond brothers.

On the seventh day of missing Jethro—of having erotic dreams that made me wake on the echoes of orgasms and of living with a heart tied into so many knots it'd forgotten how to beat properly—I gave up trying to hide my confused sadness and spent the afternoon outside.

The summer had finally given way to autumn, and the air was crisp. The leaves hadn't started to turn yet, but they bristled in the breeze, just waiting for that certain magic to turn them from green to orange.

My latest sketchbook was almost full, and my fingers were chilly as I put last-minute details onto a matching sable coat that would go with my Rainbow Diamond compilation. Over the past few days, I'd created my favourite collection yet. Turned out, I wasn't one of the lucky people who thrived on stress to meet deadlines. I preferred lazy afternoons with birds chirping and insects humming in the shrubbery.

A shadow fell across the paper.

Shielding my eyes with my hand covered in pencil

smudges, I looked up into the golden eyes of Kestrel.

"Been looking for you." He smiled. His face was open and scruffy with a five o'clock shadow. He wore blue denim jeans, a black shirt, and a leather jacket.

"I'm hardly hiding." I spanned my arm, encompassing the pretty lounger, lace umbrella, and side table complete with a carafe of tart cranberry juice and sugar crystals.

"No, you're not hiding." His smile fell as he shoved his hands into his pockets. "Have I done something to upset you?"

My heart dropped to hear the distress in his voice. "What? No, of course not."

I waited to see if he would ask why I never messaged him back after his text of wanting to kiss me, but the questions lurking in his eyes suddenly disappeared. "Okay, just checking."

Ever since telling my father off and hearing the passion in Kite's latest text, I hadn't been strong enough to turn my phone on. My past scared me, and I preferred to keep my head in the sand for a little while longer. Not to mention, I'd been distracted with repeating replays of Jethro thrusting between my thighs and an orgasm that seemed to live in my every heartbeat.

Tilting my head, I asked, "Why do you ask?"

Come on. Be honest, so we can get this out in the open once and for all.

Kes cleared his throat. "Well, to be honest, you've seemed...distant the past few days. Even when you're hanging with me in the saloon, your mind is elsewhere."

Yep, it's reliving the best sexual experience of my life. With your brother, no less.

It'd taken a miracle for me to walk normally and not show the world that Jethro had bruised me deeply. I hadn't stopped cramping for hours afterward. But I wouldn't trade the pain for anything. As much as the discomfort drained me, I wouldn't change a thing. Every movement—every clench of muscles shot my mind back to the pure bliss I'd found in his arms.

It wasn't just sex.

I'd repeated that over and over again.

It wasn't just sex, but I had yet to determine what exactly *had* happened between us. Debtee and Debtor were no longer relevant.

"Just had a lot on my mind. I've been worried about the Second Debt."

Not entirely a lie, as the days ticked past, I freaked out wondering how and when I'd be summoned to pay the next one.

Kes sighed, looking chastised. "Shit, yeah of course. Sorry." Running a hand through his hair, he perched on the end of my lounger. The watery sun dappled his face as he hesitantly reached out and touched my knee.

His touch warmed me through the comfy pair of jeans I had on. The grey hoody I usually wore when working at the Weaver headquarters was marked and torn in places, making me look totally underdressed.

"Do you need anything? Want to talk?" he asked. His face was earnest, young—entirely confide-able.

Suddenly, I wanted to tell him everything. About my crazy feelings for Jethro, for my regret over not replying to him as Kite. I wanted to purge and get it out of my heart.

What are you thinking?
You can never do that.

I could never confide. Not because I'd slept with his brother. Not because I had no words to confess how much I'd unravelled when Jethro drove deep and dangerous inside me. Not because of the traitorous truth—that in the moment when I'd come around his cock, I'd never felt so alive or so dead.

I could never confide, because my emotions for Kes were simple—I *liked* him. I appreciated his friendship and enjoyed his company. But that wasn't enough for him. He might have gone out of his way to make me feel welcome because of some warped instruction from Cut, but he genuinely liked having me around.

I wasn't inexperienced enough not to understand when another was attracted to me. The tingles of awareness when he looked at me made me blush and glance away.

No matter how much I liked him, though, it wasn't close to what I felt for his brother. Which gave me yet more strength as Kes was the lethal one—to me at least. He had the power to undermine my newfound courage—the snake just waiting to coil around me and asphyxiate me in a hug.

I didn't think he knew how nervous he made me—how anxious I was of his kindness.

"You sure nothing happened? You're completely in your head." Kes nudged my knee again, capturing my attention.

I smiled quickly. "Yes, I'm positive. Nothing's happened, apart from leaving my old life and entering this new Hawk world." I hoped the minor zing would stop him from prying.

Jethro said not to tell a soul about what we did.

I intended to obey him.

And I couldn't do that if Kes kept asking me in his tender voice.

I shifted my knee away from his warm fingers. Sitting cross-legged, I said, "Thanks for the concern, but I'm good. Truly."

He scowled, not believing me. But he let it go.

We sat in silence for a moment as his eyes fell to my sketches. "They're really good."

I stroked the page, thinking how much I'd love to start creating. I missed my studio back home. I never thought I'd admit it, but it was true.

"If you want to start making them, you can place the order for the material and whatever else you need. Bonnie will make sure it gets to you."

"Bonnie?"

He smiled, showing perfect teeth. "My grandmother. She's in charge of expenses for the business and family. If you want something, just tell me, and I'll make sure she orders it."

My mind raced with thoughts of demanding all types of things. How about a compass or a helicopter to find my way to freedom?

"Do you think she'd give me a one-way ticket out of here?" I laughed softly, knowing I could get away with such a joke around Kes. Jethro—never. But Kes...he understood that my captivity was fucked up and was pretty open with what he thought about the Debt Inheritance.

Was that a cleverly played ploy or the truth?

"Believe me, if there was a way, I would."

I froze at his confession.

Awkwardness fell, and I hunted for a different subject before we treaded deeper into forbidden waters.

"Did you need me for something? Is that why you were looking for me?"

My body flushed with panic at the thought of paying another debt so soon. For some reason, I felt at ease, knowing the Hawks meant to keep me for years. Unless they had thousands of debts for me to repay, I had some holiday time between repayments.

Kes looked into the distance, drinking in the view of Hawksridge Hall. No matter how long I resided at this estate, I would never get over the impressive turrets, gleaming windows, or dripping wealth.

"I came as a favour." He narrowed his eyes. "Jethro is looking for you."

I blanched. My heart consumed with both happiness and fear.

What did he want? To punish me for what happened between us? Did he hate me so much that he'd blame the incredibleness of what'd happened completely on me?

That wouldn't be fair.

But nothing about Jethro was fair.

He was certifiably crazy.

But...thawing.

"Do you know what he wanted?" I murmured, flicking the cover of my sketchpad closed.

Kes shook his head, spreading his long legs in front of him. "Nope. Where did you guys end up the night of the fireworks, by the way? You missed the grand finale."

I fought to keep a natural smile on my lips and not relive the pang of breaking in his office. "Nowhere. He just wanted to make sure I'd behaved while he'd ignored me for two weeks."

That was another thing I couldn't tell Kes. The Sacramental Pledge Jethro had made me sign was our secret. Another one. *Seems he's dragging you deeper into his secretive world.*

Inch by inch, he was drowning me in his icy existence, making me an accomplice rather than a hostage.

I shifted, sitting higher. Even a week later, I still winced from internal bruising of Jethro's passion.

"You okay?" Kes caressed my arm in concern. My skin warmed beneath his fingertips, but it was nothing like the sharp sting whenever Jethro touched me.

I patted his hand. "Yes, I'm fine. Thanks."

Kes was everything I wanted in a man. Warm, dependable, sweet with a kinky side he only showed in messages. *If that's true, of course.*

God, it hurt my head trying to figure out these men.

Jethro was everything I *never* wanted in a man. Temper, complexities, secrets, and a dominating side that terrified. *Yet I feel safer with him than I do with Kes.* Was that stupid, or was there something instinctual inside that understood more than I did?

Why was I drawn to Jethro? *Why* did I have no hope in hell of ever forgetting about him, even while his younger brother was so much nicer? And *why* did I prefer the man who admitted he would kill me?

You can't be serious?

I sighed. I was deadly serious. I wasn't in love with Jethro. I didn't think I could ever fall in love with someone who I could never understand, but I couldn't deny I was desperately in lust with him.

So much so, my mouth watered at the barest thought of having him inside me again. My core grew wet at the slightest memory of what we'd done. And my heart fluttered at the very idea of conquering him.

Kes cupped my cheek. "Nila…talk to me. You okay? He didn't hurt you again, did he? I know the First Debt needed to be paid, so I can't get angry about that payment, but anything else outside what is owed is completely uncalled for." Temper made his golden eyes boil with fire. "Tell me—what did he do?"

He made me doubt everything.
He owned me the second he kissed me.
He made me grow claws, and I like it.

"Nothing." I smiled, laughing away the uncomfortableness. It wasn't right to have Kes care so genuinely about my welfare, not when I didn't know if it was true or fake.

If it wasn't real, he was a fabulous actor. My heart raced at the concern in his face, reacting to the compassion in his eyes. It'd been a long time since anyone looked at me with...pity. V and Tex used it more than any other expression, keeping me in my place of uncertain, fumbling daughter.

Now, it just made me angry. So damn angry.

"Hey..." Kes leaned forward, gathering me in a hug. "It's okay. Whatever he's done, we can fix it."

I stiffened in his embrace. Rage bubbled in my blood.

I felt...played.

What is he doing?

The longer he held me, the more my anger boiled, morphing into recklessness. Words tingled my tongue—words I shouldn't say out loud.

What's your purpose?
What do you get if I fall for your tricks?

Then guilt smothered my lividity. What if I had it all wrong and Kite/Kes was the one true person in this slithering cesspool of lies?

Perhaps Kes was right, and I should fear Jethro more.

Maybe I was totally wrong about everything.

I slouched in his arms, giving in to the pounding headache and questions.

Once again, Kes had the uncanny ability to make me doubt. Jethro gave me power, but with one hug, Kes took it all away.

I transformed into Nila—dutiful daughter and fumbling twin sister, not the fierce fighter I was when Jethro called me out to fight.

Even fucking each other had been a fight.

A delicious, incredible, insidious fight.

Kes's arms tensed as he pulled back, holding me firm. My eyes widened as he leaned forward, pressing his dry lips against mine.

Whoa—what?

I locked in place as Kes closed his eyes, licking the seam of my mouth with a questing tongue.

What should I do?

I couldn't move.

His taste slipped through my lips, bringing the richness of coffee and chocolate. His heat was nice but not consuming. His touch was gentle but not devouring. There were no fireworks, no detonation, just sweet...

I whimpered as his tongue speared into my mouth against my approval.

"Kestrel."

My heart galloped at the barely muttered word.

We jumped apart.

Guilt saturated my lungs, even though I had nothing to be guilty about. After all, I'd been told I was to be passed around the Hawks.

So why did Jethro stand rigid and furious above us with his hands fisted by his side? "I see you did as I asked and found her but went against my orders and decided to keep her for yourself."

Oh, shit.

Kes stood up, his body tensing against his brother's wrath. "I could say the same thing about you the other night."

My eyes whipped between the two men. How much did Kes know?

Jethro's eyes flashed, looking over Kes's shoulder directly into mine.

I saw a question and an answer.

Did you fucking tell him?

Because I didn't.

My heart bucked against my ribcage. Subtly, I shook my head, giving him my oath that our secret was still safe.

Jethro relaxed just a little. His gaze landed back on his brother—the man he now saw as a rival.

"You can't monopolise her all the time, Jet." Kes spoke quietly, keeping his temper in check. I didn't want to come between family, even if it was the worst family on earth who meant to exterminate mine.

Jethro balled his hands. "You're forgetting I'm the firstborn son. She's mine until I tire of her. Only then can she be chased. But until then..." He prowled forward, closing the distance. "She's fucking off limits. Got it?"

Kes stood taller, his arms locked by his sides. He didn't look like he would back down. Seconds ticked past, the late summer sky filling with throbbing testosterone.

I waited for the kindling of a fight to erupt, but Kes rolled his shoulders admitting defeat. "Fine. But I'm not waiting until you tire. Fair's fair, brother. I'll catch you around." Prowling away, he turned to wave goodbye. "See you soon, Nila. Remember, my quarters are always open to you."

The moment he'd disappeared, Jethro rounded on me.

I huddled on my lounger, wishing he wasn't towering above and blotting out the sunshine like the devil incarnate.

If he wanted to berate me for what happened the other night, then so be it, but I wouldn't take his temper without drawing blood of my own.

But just like Kes had shed his animosity, Jethro managed the same.

His face settled from rage into normalcy. Bowing, he held out his hand. "Come. There's something I've been meaning to show you."

My jaw dropped to the floor.

I'd never seen anything so spectacular and perfect and inviting in my entire life.

Is this real? Or am I in a dream?

"What—what is this place?"

Is this what Kestrel meant when he said Jethro had something to show me?

Jethro placed his hand on the small of my back, pushing me forward. The double doors behind him closed. Leaning against them, he never took his eyes from my wonder-filled face.

"It's yours. Your quarters. Your *real* quarters."

"I—I don't understand."

He chuckled softly. "The buzzard room was a stupid idea I had to keep you in line. I've grown up a little since then."

I had so much to ask, but all I could do was drift forward in awe.

The room was huge, completely open plan with arched walkways leading to a sitting room, dressing room, bathroom complete with huge shower and claw-foot bathtub, and a bedroom that looked straight from a Persian souk. Acres of divine beaded material hung in heavy swathes from the teak four-poster bed.

But it was the room we stood in that fascinated me.

It was better than any haberdashery I'd been in.

Far exceeding any priceless material market I'd travelled to with my father and brother on expeditions to find exclusive textiles.

The walls were decorated with floor-to-ceiling racks. Bolts and bolts of every colour fabric imaginable hung enticing and new. Ribbon spools, lace sheaves, threads of every style and width rested on huge tables groaning with scissors, needles, chalk pens, and tape measures.

In the centre of the room stood three sizable busts, two full-size models to design the perfect dress on, and a skylight above, which drenched the space in natural light.

Comfy couches, love-seats, and velour stylish chairs were scattered beside bookcases full of histories of fashion; there was even a fish tank in the corner with tropical fish glowing in pristine turquoise water.

My fingers ached to touch everything at once.

Then my eyes dropped to the carpet.

Deep emerald richness glowed with elegance and the repeating design of W.

"This is the Weaver quarters. They're only shown and offered when the current Weaver fully understands her place."

I couldn't stop my smirk, turning to stare at him. "I haven't learned my place."

His face remained locked of emotion. "No, you haven't. And my father won't be happy that I'm giving you this so soon, but...things changed."

My heart sprung into an irregular beat, waiting for him to continue.

But he didn't.

Moving through the room, he stood out in his black shirt and grey slacks like a spot of ink or a stain on such pretty fabric. He didn't belong.

I followed him. Finally seeing what I should've seen all along.

He doesn't belong in these rooms.
He doesn't belong in this house.
He doesn't belong with this family.

Everything I knew about Jethro was wrong. And despite his task and our fates that were horribly entwined and shadowed with death, I wanted to *know* him.

Following him through the space, I slammed to a stop as he spun to face me.

His face twisted. "I don't want to talk. I don't want to discuss what's happening or even try to fucking understand it."

My stomach flipped over at the lust glowing in his gaze. "Okay..."

Closing the distance between us in one large stride, he captured my cheeks, holding me firm. "I want to fuck you again. So fucking much."

I couldn't breathe.

"You're asking my permission?" I whispered.

His face contorted. "No, I'm not asking for your damn

permission."

"Then...just do it."

The air solidified and for a second, I thought he'd throw me away and storm off.

But then his fingers dug into my cheeks and his mouth crashed against mine.

Jethro

WHAT THE FUCK am I doing?

I'd spent the past week working for my father, having sessions with my sister, and running the latest diamond shipment—not to mention the frantic hour I'd had after fucking her and sneaking into the security room to destroy the camera footage.

I was playing with fucking fire. And instead of getting burned and becoming a puddle of melted ice water, I was stronger, better, firmer in my convictions than I'd been in...well, forever.

I didn't understand how the direct contradiction to my world could improve me rather than destroy me.

I knew I should question it—find answers rather than keep going down a path I didn't understand, but how could I stop when Nila was at the end, beckoning with a corrupting smile, spreading her legs in wanton invitation?

I wasn't a monster, but I wasn't a fucking saint either.

My willpower to stay away had snapped this morning when I'd seen her disappear into the gardens with a hungry haunt in her eyes.

I liked to think that look was for me.

But then she'd kissed my fucking brother.

Nila's hands flew up, her fingers slipping through my hair.

She moaned, sucking on my tongue, driving me mad.

My stomach swooped as my cock instantly thickened.

If she was hungry, then I was fucking ravenous.

Her cheeks were pliant beneath my fingertips. Our tongues meshed and parried. Her soft moan echoed in my chest, and I couldn't stop myself from walking her backward to the bed.

Countless evenings Cut had told me how I was to fuck her the first time. A game plan of pain, torture, and no pleasure permitted for her. That was part of the Third Debt—amongst other things.

But here I was again. Disobeying.

Fucking disobeying everything I was, just for one little taste.

My cock wasn't supposed to go anywhere near her for months. How did this happen? How was I so weak when it came to her?

Nila cried out as the back of her legs crashed against the bed. She tumbled from my grip, her cheeks pinpricked with red from where my fingertips had dug into her flesh.

My dick had never been so hard as she clambered onto her knees and looped her arms around my neck, jerking me close.

I should stop this. I should walk out the fucking door and lock it. Better yet, I should strike her and make her cry—instil a healthy dose of fear into the woman who was supposed to be my toy. Not my master.

"Jethro—please…stop thinking. I can hear your thoughts; they're so loud."

I reared back. "What?"

If she could hear my thoughts, why the hell wasn't she running? Couldn't she see the danger? Didn't she understand the nightmare this could turn into?

I not only played with my life but hers, too. Death wouldn't be given lightly if Cut found out. He'd make her beg for it. He'd tear her apart piece by piece for every delicious feeling she invoked in his firstborn son.

Every kiss, every touch—I was sentencing her to worse

than any debt she could repay. And all for what? Because I was fucking weak. Weak. *Weak.*

You can have today.

I'd premeditated this—that was how addicted I'd become.

'Someone' had spilled something sticky onto the security hard drive; a new part had to be ordered before the cameras in the Weaver quarters would be operational.

I calculated two days, possibly three, before it was replaced.

Two or three days to fuck her as much as I could, before going cold-turkey and forgetting that this ever happened.

"Kiss me," she murmured, her black eyes glittering with lust.

A smile tugged the corner of my mouth. "Aren't those the two words that got us into this mess?"

She grabbed the front of my shirt, her expert fingers undoing the buttons in record time.

My head fell back as her tiny hands splayed on my chest and tickled their way around to my spine.

She pulled me close, sealing her lips over mine.

The second her taste entered my mouth, I snapped again.

I couldn't help it.

She was a fucking drug.

Grabbing the diamond collar, I shoved her hard. Toppling from her knees, her nails scraped my ribcage as she fell backward on the bed. The moment her ballerina legs spread, I pounced.

I couldn't resist anymore—it was futile.

Ripping my shirt off my shoulders, I kneeled on the bed and grabbed her hips to drag her body beneath mine. Pressing myself over her, we both shuddered in delight.

Her belly fluttered like a dying creature; while her heart pounded so hard, it rearranged my own beat.

I'd never enjoyed kissing anyone as much as I enjoyed kissing Nila. I felt her tongue in my mouth but felt it stronger on my cock. I'd never been high on the taste of another person. It wasn't just chemistry sparking between us or the battle of willpowers or even the knowledge of how this would all end.

It was *different,* and I had no urge to put a description on it. The moment I knew what it was, was the moment I would have to run from it.

Her tongue stroked slow and inviting with mine, dancing like liquid silk.

My hand fell between her legs. The jeans she wore were my worst enemy as I attacked the button and zipper.

She giggled against my mouth, shoving my fumbling fingers away to release it with one twist of a single hand. "Now you can get rid of them."

My stomach clenched at the need in her voice. "Thank fuck for that." Rolling off her, I yanked the offending material away and bent my head over her hip to tear at the black lace knickers she wore. Ripping them off, a groan echoed in my chest.

"Hey! You keep doing that and I won't have any underwear left."

My cock lurched at the thought of her spending the rest of her days walking around with nothing on beneath her fancy skirts and dresses. I liked the idea way too much.

An image of her dressed in that gorgeous black and feather gown when I'd stolen her from Milan filled my mind. I wished I'd brought it with us, instead of leaving it on the sidewalk, tattered and dirty. Nila was the type of beauty who deserved to wear decadence every day.

I couldn't deny I liked seeing her in shorts and regular clothing, but there was something overwhelmingly sexy about a woman in corsets and garters.

Fuck, stop thinking about that.

I was hard enough to kill someone with the weapon in my trousers; I didn't want to come before I'd even filled her.

Her hands landed on my belt buckle. I blinked as she magically undid both my belt and jeans. With feisty hands, she shoved them, along with my boxer-briefs, down my thighs.

I groaned as her fingers latched around my cock.

The fire she conjured in me was too fucking strong. My

psyche did what it had been trained to do and retreated instantly, protecting itself, hiding the truth.

I went frigid.

Nila paused, panting. "What—what's wrong?"

Everything.

"Nothing." I pulled back, sitting up and swinging my legs over the edge of the bed.

This is so bloody dangerous. You have to stop it.

I sucked in a breath as Nila's graceful arms wrapped around my neck, pressing her now naked breasts against my back. The swell of soft flesh and pinpricks of hard nipples almost undid me.

I curled my hands, drawing blood as I bit hard on my lower lip. "Let me go."

"No."

A small flare of anger shot through my blood. "Christ, woman."

"Nila. My name is Nila." She pressed a kiss on my shoulder. "Try it…it won't kill you."

You're wrong. You're already killing me.

"Jethro—if you're pulling away, then you should know if you walk out that door and leave me for days on end…we're done."

The very word implying I would never be allowed back inside her welcoming body was blasphemy. My anger increased, thickening my blood. "You're forgetting that you're mine to do with as I see fit."

"I'm yours to torment, I agree. But somehow I think your father wouldn't be pleased with us doing this." Her lips grazed my shoulders again. "You can't lie about that. That's why you told me to keep it a secret."

I slumped forward, trying to dislodge her hold.

Silence fell awkwardly between us. I battled with doing the right thing by leaving and the wrong thing by spinning around and thrusting my aching cock inside her.

Nila murmured against my skin. "Sex is meant to strip us back. It's meant to show the truth of what we keep hidden.

Don't be afraid of something that could ultimately save you."

My heart froze at the thought of revealing my innermost secrets.

I laughed coldly. "I don't want saving, Ms. Weaver. And sex is the opposite. It's a projection of nothing more than animalistic need."

"You don't believe that. Not what we have."

"What we have is so far out of my comfort range, I'm hanging on by a fucking thread."

What. The. Fuck?

I snapped my lips closed at the awful confession.

Nila stiffened, her heartbeat tapping against my back. "See, you can be honest when you don't censor yourself."

I sighed. "You want honesty? Fine. I'm used to living my life with an iron fist of control. You undermine that control. I can't let that happen. I don't handle things well when I'm not..."

"Cold."

I nodded. "I'll admit that you've gotten under my skin in a way I didn't think was possible. I'm feeling things I've never—" I cut myself off. What the hell was I saying? I sounded like a fucking pussy. "I won't deny, now that I've had you, that I want you again and again and fuck, I doubt I'll ever want to stop, but it *has* to stop."

It has to stop before I do something worse.

Nila pulled away, moving to sit beside me. "Something this good shouldn't have to end, Jethro. Screw family. Screw the debts. We want each other. Let's just give in to that and forget about tomorrow."

If only it was that easy. If only we had unlimited tomorrows.

But we don't.

"What—what do you want from me, Jethro? You've taken everything—either by force or by allowing me small glimpses of who you are. What are you so afraid of?" Her voice lowered to a curse. "What do you *want?*"

I want...I want...

Fuck, I don't know what I want.
My body ached with frustration, confusion, and need. How did this go from sex to revelations?

Everything I'd ever wanted in my life had turned me into this…mess.

Everything I'd ever let myself crave was used against me and taught me to hate rather than love.

It was easier to run from compassion and empathy when they were the very things that had the power to steal everything I'd worked so hard for.

I would continue to fuck Nila, because I was done depriving myself of everything *good*. But I wouldn't let her get inside my head, and I definitely wouldn't let her climb inside my heart.

Bracing myself, I snapped, "I want you to understand that you will never know me. You'll never have any power over me, nor will you have any hold on my loyalties. No matter what goes on between us, I will never release you, never take your side against my family, never bow to any demands you make. Nothing has changed in that respect."

Breathing hard, I finished, "If you can handle that, then I'll fuck you and grant us both some happiness. But if you can't, then I'm walking out that door and won't be back until it's time for the Second Debt."

She cupped my cheek. Her hand was steady; her eyes clear from vertigo or stress. It seemed the truth from me didn't upset her nearly as much as when I locked myself in ice. "I want to keep feeling this. So I'll agree…for now." Her gaze dropped to my lips, anxiousness and passion pinking her cheeks. "Enough talking. Kiss me."

I groaned. I'd never hear the command 'kiss me' again without wanting to devour her.

This was a steep learning curve for both of us. We just had to make sure we didn't fall off the edge and plummet to our deaths.

She fell backward on the bed. My body took over, intolerable need ordering my limbs to follow. Kicking off my jeans from still around my thighs, I planted my elbows by her ears on the mattress and settled between her legs.

My cock twitched, dying to enter her.

Lowering my head, I bit the soft vulnerability of her neck.

My mind ran riot with everything I wanted to do. Resting between her legs was enjoyable…but it wasn't what I wanted. It wasn't what would keep me sane.

If I let myself fuck her again, the next time I took her—it would be very different. It would have to be. I had no choice.

She gasped, writhing beneath me, pushing her hips upward.

She was eager—ridiculously so. And I was damn near desperate to fuck her again. I wanted to pour inside her. I wanted to look into her eyes as I let loose and filled her.

Nila's hands grabbed the back of my neck, guiding my face to hers. Licking my bottom lip, her warm tongue was searing torture.

My stomach clenched.

Kissing her deeply, I stiffened. Pulling back, I drank my fill of her naked body. I'd seen most parts of her—either running, hiding in a tree, or spread-eagled on a table—but her bruised skin and elongated muscles seemed to control my cock completely.

My brain scattered as I followed the hollow path of her belly to her sharp hipbones over silky skin. There wasn't an ounce of fat anywhere on her delicate frame. She had abs that were impressive but cute and a pussy that was tight and hidden demurely by perfect pink lips.

She was pure female—the embodiment of fragility and tenacity that I coveted and fantasised about.

The things I wanted to do to her. The things I'd always locked away bubbled beneath the surface.

I hadn't noticed before, but she had a singular subtle scent of freshness—a comforting perfume that was both an aphrodisiac and intoxicant, making me fall deeper into hell.

I wanted to tell her she was beautiful.

I wanted to tell her what she was doing to me.

But I couldn't.

Grabbing her breast, I pinched her nipple, before bowing my head and sucking it into my mouth.

She moaned, clamping my head to her chest. Every lash of my tongue made my cock ripple with need.

Her hands were insatiable as they slid over my burning shoulders, kneading, stroking, seeming to both calm and drive me wild.

I crawled back up her body.

Her eyes latched onto mine, glowing with things that were too intense and painful. My heart cleaved and lurched, exceeding my realm of ability to function.

Frantically clawing at a small hint of ice, I kissed her deeply.

It should've just been a kiss, but her mouth had a sorcery against my control. Her silent plea for more whispered around us; her body shifted and begged beneath mine, driving me closer to throwing myself into the pit that I'd climbed from and not give a flying fuck about anything anymore.

"I want you inside me, Jethro," she whispered, her breath misting over my skin.

My hand went to her throat, tensing around the tender column. "I've never wanted to fuck someone as badly as I want to fuck you."

She moaned, "Then stop delaying."

"No, I like watching you squirm." I dropped my nose to where I cupped her throat. "After all, you won again, Ms. Weaver—"

"Nila. Please...you can call me Ms. Weaver when we aren't millimetres from claiming each other."

I shook my head. "As I was saying, before you rudely interrupted." I bit her bottom lip, sucking it into my mouth. "You won because I fucked you."

"I think you won on that account, too."

I licked her, tracing the tip of my tongue along her jaw, making her tremble. "You didn't beg though, did you?"

She stiffened, a small moan echoing in her chest.

"Don't... don't make me."

A small smile played on my mouth. "Oh, I'll make you, Ms. Weaver." Nuzzling into her throat, I kissed a cold diamond on her collar. "Let's begin, shall we?"

She growled, "Just put it in me, Jethro."

I chuckled. "Just put it in me? That's hardly romantic."

"This isn't romantic. If it was, we'd have candles and rose petals and soft music. This is a means to an end."

I reared up on my elbows. "A means to an end?" I shouldn't be hurt, but goddammit I was.

Nila clenched her stomach, reaching for me. "I want to come. You want to come. Stop prolonging it."

My cock wept at her distress—she'd passed the edge of common sense. I wanted to give in—fuck, how I wanted to—but I also wanted to win just once. She'd somehow become the victor in all our battles. This one I intended to walk away the vanquisher.

Slamming my hand on her sternum, I pressed her against the mattress and scooted down her body. Every inch I travelled, I nipped and sucked—her nipple, every rib to her naval.

"Jethro..." she panted, her hands once again diving into my hair. My heart did weird things when she held me like that—her fingernails digging into my scalp, her barely restrained lust causing pinpricks of pain that felt better than any pleasure.

"Tell me what I want to hear, Ms. Weaver. Then I'll give you what you want."

"I won't. I won't beg. You'll break before me."

I laughed softly, rimming her belly button with the tip of my tongue. "Are you so sure about that?"

She's right.

My cock hadn't stopped throbbing, and the sticky wetness at the top told me I'd been unsuccessful in stopping my need.

She yanked on my hair, trying to pull me up. Biting her flat stomach, I caught her wrists and pinned them against the mattress. "No more touching, Ms. Weaver. Remember that control I mentioned? Well, I need it." Blowing air on her pussy, which was mouth level and glistening, I murmured, "You have the tightest, wettest, greediest cunt I've ever had the pleasure to taste. And I plan on dining again. Take your time and decide if it's beneath you to beg."

"Bastard," she growled, fighting my hold on her wrists.

"I'm the bastard?" I positioned myself, swiping my wet tongue along her slit. Her back bowed as her breath caught. "I'm the bastard for wanting to give you pleasure instead of pain?"

Stop that.

I hadn't meant to say that. Another slip. Another fucking dangerous slip.

Nila didn't notice as I tongued her again, diving below and dipping quickly and intrusively inside her.

"Ah!"

A violent shiver of lust commandeered my muscles. My ears roared with the need to forget about taunting her and fuck her dirty and wrong.

"Jethro…please…"

"Almost a beg, Ms. Weaver." Without pause, I buried my face in her pussy.

She tried to move, but I kept my fingers locked around her wrists and gave her no room to move as I fucked her with my tongue.

I looked up, following the delicious contours of her stomach. She glared down at me, her eyes full of black flames.

I smiled, licking her harder.

"I won't do it."

I didn't reply, only sucked her clit into my mouth.

She spasmed, shuddering uncontrollably.

"It all ends with one little word, Ms. Weaver."

"I won't. Not until you call me Nila."

My tongue drove into her tight pussy; her muscles clenched viciously around me.

"How about a tr—truce?" Her voice strained as her legs stiffened, toes curling.

"A truce?"

"Two winners."

I breathed hot, drenching her inner thighs with everything boiling inside me. "Fine."

"You go first."

I chuckled, so turned on with need, I rapidly lost the skill for conversation. "No chance. Beg." I pressed my mouth and nose hard against her, inhaling deeply until my lungs were soaked with her smell.

"Jethro!"

My heart raced. My breathing made every word clipped and breathless. "Say it—put us both out of our misery."

Her head twisted to the side, pressing her cheek against the sheets.

"Do it and I'll do what you want. I'll use your name. I'll climb on top of you. I'll spread your legs and drive my cock so deep and fast inside, you won't be able to walk for a week."

We both groaned at the mental image. Fuck, she better beg. Otherwise, she would win another round. I was two seconds away from taking her.

My impressive self-control—the same restraint that had protected me all my life—had disappeared.

Her hips churned as I dragged my tongue through her quivering pussy. "Beg, Ms. Weaver. *Beg.*" Her velvet skin against my tongue sent all thoughts of family and consequences far into the stratosphere.

I sucked her clit again, my ears straining for her to give in to me, but *still* she resisted.

I stuck my tongue deep, driving her toward an orgasm. Her cunt convulsed, milking my shallow penetration.

I groaned. Sweat ran down my temples, and my back ached from tension. My hips rocked against the mattress, driving my cock into the surface, seeking relief from the quaking pleasure-pain.

"Beg, damn you!" I hissed against her clit. I couldn't take it anymore.

"Use my name and I will."

Fuck, we wouldn't get anywhere. We were both too strong. Too damn stubborn.

Panting hard, I looked up into her blazing eyes, glassy and intoxicated with desire. "Together." It was the first time I'd conceded a truce. I didn't like it, but if it got me inside her, so be it.

Nila froze, her mouth falling wide. Finally, she nodded. "Together."

Pressing a kiss onto her pussy, I climbed her body and settled between her legs. Locking my fingers in her hair, I held her firm with nowhere to go. My cock twitched, resting against her entrance, imploring to slide inside.

Our hearts matched with racing beats, our breathing just as threadbare and frayed.

Her lips moved; sound spilled. "I'm begging you to fuck me, Jethro Hawk."

My eyes snapped shut as a full body shudder took me hostage. "Again." I swallowed hard. "More, Nila. *Beg.*"

The moment her name fell from my mouth, she let go of everything she'd been holding back. Her hands fell to my arse, digging her nails and drawing her knees up. With a fierce burst of power, she jerked me forward, forcing my tip inside her.

We both moaned. Loudly.

"Fuck me, please. I'm begging. I need it. I need you. I've never needed anything as much as you filling me." She tried to reach up to kiss me, but my hands in her hair kept her open and honest and stripped bare.

"Jethro, I'll die if you don't fuck me this very minute. I'm hungry. I'm starving. I don't know what's wrong with me. I just know I'm itchy and achy and weepy and so damn angry that you won't give me what I want."

"And what do you want...Nila?"

She shivered. "I want your cock. Now."

And you can have it.

I thrust.

There was no gentle easing like last time. My self-control was done. Over. Finite. I sank inside with a barbarous impale.

She screamed.

I groaned.

We both collapsed into one another.

Falling. Falling. Swirling. Swirling. We took each other prisoner. Punishing our bodies, focused on one blistering goal.

"Oh, God, no...stop," she cried. Her hips tried to dislodge my size.

"I can't stop."

"It hurts." Her breath was cool against my fevered flesh.

"Let me in." I thrust again, gritting my teeth as a wash of pleasure shot into my balls.

Her mouth opened to scream again, but I clamped a hand over her lips, silencing her. Her cheekbones were stark, skin stretched with lust. Her eyes were so dark they mirrored my reflection, showing a man I didn't recognise. A man who'd well and truly passed the boundary of right and wrong.

Then a drawn out keen of welcome vibrated in her chest.

My eyes snapped shut as her body gave in to me, stretching, inviting.

Fuck.

My hands fisted harder in her hair. The foreplay had drained us of everything. This would be hard, fast—bloodthirsty.

"I'm going to fuck you now, Nila."

"Yes." Her fingernails sliced deeper into my lower back as I thrust into her. I rammed inside over and over, balls-deep and buried. I wasn't just fucking her body but her mind and soul, too.

She let me in everywhere.

She dropped everything, letting me bulldoze through her defences.

My heart bucked at the preciousness of what I held—the gift in which she gave. It fucking tore my innards out and turned me hollow.

The connection was too acute. Physically, spiritually. I'd never wanted to belong...always been an outcast and outsider, but between the legs of my Weaver Whore, I found....redemption, salvation.

She clamped around me, dragging a ragged groan from my chest. I ground my hips harder, deeper, faster.

We locked eyes.

I shouted at her silently.

Cursed her wordlessly.

You feel me inside you?

You feel me claiming you?

You feel me destroying you?

My muscles went rigid as her eyes recognised my message and shot one of their own.

You feel me around you?

You feel me undermining you?

You feel me making you care?

I slammed forward, drawing a primitive sound from her.

"God, you—you feel..."

"What? What do you feel?" I growled.

"Good. Too good. I need—I need to come."

You and me both.

I couldn't do this anymore. I needed it over, so I could run and hide. So I could fix everything that was wrong with me. So I could find the man I'd been for fifteen fucking long years.

She made a helpless sound of need, grinding herself on my cock. We dripped with sweat, our skin slipping and slicking against each other, our lungs desperate for air.

Tightening my hold on her hair, I increased my rhythm. Nailing her to the bed, I fucked with wild savagery.

Her orgasm came from nowhere and with no warning. One second she rode me as hard as I rode her, the next she went stiff and taut. Her mouth fell wide. A moan that twisted my heart fell around us as her pussy fisted my cock with strength that tore me into pieces.

My own release percolated like a typhoon inside, howling and buffeting my every cell.

"Fuck." Grabbing her hip, I tilted her body so she was angled for even deeper punishment.

Tears of delirium trickled from her eyes as I drove my

cock further inside her. Her face squeezed tight as I hit the spot where I could go no further. Her body halted any deeper claiming.

The moment she finished coming, I couldn't stop.

Pleasure surged through me with every thrust. I turned to stone as fiery release exploded from my balls and splashed inside her.

Fuck, pull out. Pull out.

Lurching upright, I wrapped my fingers around the base of my dick and fucked my own hand as I shot thread after thread of release onto her belly.

The second it was over, the guilt came back.

The fear.

The anger.

We were now doubly fucked, and I had no clue how to fix it.

Nila looked at her stomach, and in the boldest, sexiest move, ran her fingertip through my release and sucked it into her mouth.

Fuck. Me.

My entire body tingled.

"If sex with you is like that every time, I have a horrible feeling we'll end up fucking each other into an early grave."

An icy gust skittered down my spine. If only she knew how true that sentence was.

She had no clue what I would do to her the next time. She'd had me twice with only skin between us. The next time...shit, I couldn't think about what I'd do without getting hard again.

The joy at what I planned trickled into my double-crossing heart, and I knew this was the beginning of the end.

We would keep on ruining each other.

We would keep on desecrating debts and vows.

And we would keep on fucking up our future until nothing but horror remained.

Nila

LIFE HAD TURNED from manic to surreal.

I still lived in a den of beasts, with fear around every corner and dread in my future, but my present had never felt so right.

I had obligations to talk to my father and brother before they appeared with guns blazing.

I had messages to reply to Kite.

I had bridges to mend with Kestrel.

But for some reason, I couldn't bear to leave the insanely comfortable mattress of the Weaver quarters.

The ceiling above was obscured by the bolts of Persian material, and the scent of freshly spun fabric was the best air freshener I'd ever smelled.

I stretched, basking in the echoing pain of being used by Jethro once again.

He'd shown me how much passion was hidden beneath his wintry shell, and I knew he'd only just started to thaw. The thought of more sex, better sex, deeper, soul-blistering sex made me shiver in both excitement and nervousness. I meant what I said about killing ourselves with pleasure. I didn't think I could stand much more. But nothing on earth would stop me from willingly walking to my demise if it meant I could take Jethro with me.

Don't forget the plan.
I froze.
My goal of seducing him had worked. He'd changed and for some reason, had let me worm my way into his affections. But by letting me inside him, he'd stripped me of my defences. The moment when my body stretched around him, letting him take me fully, I'd felt something give inside. More than just an invitation or coy come-hither to destroy him—it had been real, and I'd had no willpower to stop him from invading.

You're playing such a dangerous game.
My heart crawled up my throat at the thought of losing.
What can truly happen, though?
I already lived with a death sentence. So what if I died with a broken heart as well? It wouldn't change my fate. It would only grant fullness to a life while it was still mine to enjoy.

Common sense didn't like my conclusions, but I switched off my thoughts.

I rolled over, inhaling the scent of his woodland leather from the pillow he'd rested upon.

After we'd crashed back to earth, he'd spent an hour just lying there. Regrouping or thinking or just being himself...once he'd gathered his façade, he'd wordlessly disappeared and not come back.

All my belongings had already been transferred, and I noticed my phone, recharged and no longer in pieces, blinking with incoming mail on the duck-egg-blue bedside table.

Not only had Jethro given me my phone, but he'd left it on and waiting for me to use.

Why did Jethro want me to use it? Wasn't he jealous that I had an affinity with Kes/Kite? *You have to put a stop to that.* It wasn't fair to confuse Kestrel by flirting with him via messages only to pull away in person.

I had too much to juggle with dealing with Jethro; I couldn't enter into another masquerade with his brother.

Grabbing the device, I skimmed through my emails and opened text messages.

There were a few from Vaughn, a couple from my father,

and one only an hour old from Kite.

    My heart skipped a beat as I read.

    Kite007: *I dreamed of kissing you last night.*

    I reclined against the pillows. Ordinarily, I would've loved to respond and tease. Now, I felt as if I was cheating on Jethro.

    Needle&Thread: *Sorry I haven't been in touch. I—I think...it's time to end this. Don't you? We both know who each other is. It's too complicated to keep pretending.*

    I chewed on the inside of my cheek. My heart ached at pushing him away, especially as I'd relied on Kite to be neutral. Giving him up, even though I knew the truth, seemed like I'd pulled away from the last remaining part of my past.

    Kite007: *End it? As in the thought of sleeping with me was so abhorrent, you're done?*

    Needle&Thread: *I just...I'm sorry.*

    Kite007: *Fine.*

    Needle&Thread: *We'll still be friends. I'll still see you every day.*

    Kite007: *Sometimes, having a relationship entirely based on seeing each other stops us from learning the truth. Sometimes, the only way to see that truth is to block off all other senses but the mind. Goodbye, Needle. Guess you weren't ready to see the truth after all.*

    Four hours had passed since Kite's text, and I still hadn't shed the pain inside my soul. What had he meant? And why wouldn't he reply to any of my messages?

    I'd frantically sent text after text, asking for forgiveness and an explanation.

    But nothing.

    It was only hunger that drove me from my room in search of lunch.

    I hadn't seen Jethro again, and the burn between my legs was the only reminder that something irreversible had happened between us last night.

    Irreversible and responsible for me hurting Kes and ruining any chance of having another Hawk on my side.

Goosebumps scattered along my arms at the thought of bumping into him and the awkwardness that would follow.

I might've lost Kestrel, but I'd somehow chipped into Jethro's arctic shell. No matter what Cut or the debts did to me, no one would be able to ruin what I'd found with one of their own.

I had no clue what it all meant, but Jethro Hawk was no longer Cut's little plaything. He was mine. And despite the guilt I felt at potentially using Jethro to save my life, I knew I would do it. Eventually, I hoped to bring Jethro deeper into my spell. I would make him protect me. I would somehow survive this Debt Disaster.

We'd started as enemies and still were, but now…now we were enemies with a common goal. A driving need to fuck and devour.

A strange combination of delivering pain and pleasure.

It wasn't ideal. It probably wasn't healthy.

But it was the best damn relationship I'd ever had.

Deciding to make my way to the kitchens, rather than have staff wait on me, I entered the realm of baking and home, inhaling deep the delicious smells of rosemary and garlic.

One of the maids, who I recognised with curly blonde hair, looked up. Her pretty button nose and brown eyes were open and honest. "Hungry, miss?"

I nodded, drifting forward and running a fingertip through the dusting of flour on the countertop. Hawksridge Hall had been updated with every modern convenience imaginable but still managed to retain its heritage. The kitchen was no exception, with a brilliant blend of old world and new. Stainless countertops rested on rickety handmade cupboards. Ancient flues, stained black from coal smoke, loomed over top-of-the-line stovetops and ovens. The massive rotisserie was still used over a large open fire, and a huge black pot dangled on a tripod in the corner. Mortar and pestles lined the windowsill with herbs and flowers drying above.

The maid kindly wrapped up a fresh baguette with a dollop of fresh cream and strawberry jam, and shoved a packet of salt and vinegar crisps into my hand.

A random meal, but I took it with gratitude. "Thank you."

She smiled. "Don't be outside too long today. A storm is coming, according to BBC. The fine weather is over."

Is that a metaphor for my life? That my summer is past and now I have to survive the winter?

Nodding my assurances, I climbed the steps to the main part of the house and exited Hawksridge by the front door.

The maid was right. On the horizon rested heavy clouds, black and ominous. Regardless, I wanted to stretch my legs; fresh air never failed to bring clarity to my world.

And I needed clarity after Kite's message. Every time I thought about it, my heart squeezed in regret.

My jewelled flip-flops, cut-off shorts, and turquoise t-shirt were hardly suitable clothing, especially as small raindrops splashed from above, but I refused to go back inside.

"Nila!" Kes appeared from the side of the house, his boots crunching on the gravel as he jogged closer.

Shit.

As much as I wanted to confront him, I had no clue what to say. Breathing shallowly, I hoped the faint bruises Jethro had left on my upper arms didn't show.

Kes came to a stop, his eyes drifting over me. "Where are you going?"

I frowned, drinking in his face, seeking the hurt that had been in his message. His gaze was blank, locked against any cypher or clues.

How is he hiding what happened between us?

Unable to understand, I shrugged. "Nowhere in particular. Just getting some air."

"Mind if I join you?"

I shrugged again. It was best to clear the air sooner rather than later. "Sure."

Kes fell in step beside me, his gaze rising to the black clouds on the horizon. His silence was heavy, judging.

"Where were you going?" I asked. *Were you running after me?*

His golden eyes landed on mine. My stomach twisted,

thinking how fiery Jethro's had been last night as he pushed himself inside me.

"I was just going to the stables. There's a polo match next week—wanted to make sure my horse is shipshape." Kicking a pebble, he added, "Bloody Jet always wins at polo. This time, I'm going to kick his arse." His voice was sharp, completely unlike his usual ease.

I wanted to bring up the message but had no idea how.

Instead, I took a bite of my baguette. Once I swallowed, I mumbled, "I've never watched a polo game. Do you think I'll be allowed to come?"

Please tell me I haven't ruined our friendship. That you'll let me hang out with you still.

If I didn't have Kes's company, I would go bonkers when Jethro disappeared.

God, I was selfish.

Selfish and greedy to try and keep both men, while using them for my gain.

Kes grinned, but it didn't reach his eyes. "Of course. All the staff are given the afternoon off to come and watch." He joked, "Even prisoners are allowed to go."

Before Jethro had shown any signs of caring for me, that would've stabbed me in the heart and fortified my need to run.

Now…it only gave me courage to continue with my plan. And gave me strength to ignore the hurt I felt at pushing Kes away.

Yes, I enjoyed sleeping with Jethro. Yes, I could even admit to developing confusing emotions toward him. But my end game was the same.

I wanted him to fall in love with me.

Only then would he stand up to his family. Only then would he be so blindsided by affection, he wouldn't see the knife when it went into his heart.

Gratefulness filled me. Kes had just reminded me of my goals. I had no time for bruised feelings or misunderstandings. I had to be as manipulative as they were and never waver.

You're just as bad as them.

Good.

I never admitted I would die for them. I would eat their food, play with their toys, and fuck their oldest son, but I wouldn't die. If the Weaver Wailer collar couldn't come off until my death, I planned to wear it until I died in my sleep at a very old age.

Kes and I walked in awkward silence, neither of us willing to go too deep. The Hall grew smaller behind us as we traversed the lawn, heading into the woods.

Silently, I offered him my packet of crisps. With a sideways glance, he took it.

A bird of prey swooped from a tree as we moved further into the forest.

Kes paused. "See that?" Slowly, so as not to spook the animal, he pointed to his bare forearm and the bird tattoo inked into his flesh. "See how similar they are?"

My heart beat faster. I peered into the foliage. The plumage of the bird glistened like fine auburn.

"That's a kite—see him?"

Something twisted inside at the mention of Kite.

I narrowed my eyes. The raptor spread its wings, soaring away. Glancing at Kes's tattoo, I said, "It didn't match the bird on your arm."

He nodded. "That's because mine's a kestrel. They're from the same family, though."

Everything went very still.

Was this it? The admission.

Nerves scattered over my spine as Kes looked at me with tension etching his jaw. "Same family, same genes, just a different name."

I stopped breathing.

He stepped away, popping another crisp into his mouth.

Dammit.

Why didn't he just come out and admit it? I didn't want to have to prompt him, but I was done waiting for the truth.

Wiping my crumb-riddled fingers on my shorts, I asked, "Same family just a different name. Tell me, Kes, do you have another name, or was that a riddle I'm supposed to never figure out?"

He stopped, sucking in a breath. "If you're asking if I have another name, I do."

My knees wobbled, waiting.

Go on...

I waited. And waited. Tension thickened. *Come on. Admit it. Admit that you're Kite.*

Admit that, until recently, you were the man I spoke to every night. The man I relied on for my sanity, even while you were cruel and unpredictable.

My heart bucked in sadness.

I'd been kidding myself. I would miss Kes. I would miss our affinity and dirty conversations. I would miss the strength he gave me and the sexual power that came from talking like a masturbating minx.

Suddenly, I didn't want to give him up.

He was the missing link—the brother so different from Jethro. Maybe I could have them both—have a balance of nasty and sweet.

My eagerness to uncover the truth waned.

Taking a step back, I whispered half-heartedly, "What is it? Your other name?"

Kes shook his head. "I don't want to tell. It sucks."

Kite doesn't suck.

It was rather...sexy. Not Falcon or Eagle or Vulture. Kite.

A sharp bite of a name. Violent and dangerous, but also whimsical, with its fellow paper-bow-flying counterpart.

I shifted closer, placing my hand over his. "Tell me."

He froze, his eyes filling with uncertainty.

"You can say it," I whispered. "I know I ruined it, but it's best if you tell me."

His forehead furrowed. "Ruined what?"

Before I could reply, he licked his lips and asked, "Promise you'll still like me after I tell you?"

My heart skipped, fluttering faster at the thought of *finally* knowing. I couldn't hide the ugly truth anymore. The lies I'd spun disintegrated. It didn't matter I was Jethro's plaything; I wasn't prepared to give Kes up. Not when faced with all my future held.

I wanted to keep him. I would play two games. One twisting Jethro around my finger and another evolving Kite's and my conversations to something deeper.

I could have both.

I nodded. "Yes."

He sighed, his large shoulders rising and falling. "Fine. It's Angus."

My world screeched to a halt. "What?"

He shifted, his body wary. "I know it's not the greatest name in the world, but it's my given name. People called me Gus as a kid, which I hated. Luckily as a Hawk, we're given nicknames. I demanded everyone use mine from my eighth birthday onward."

My mind wheeled.

Pieces slowly realigned, slotting unwillingly into place.

No. It couldn't be.

Horror filled my heart.

Could Kestrel be using another name or could it be worse...

Could Kite be Daniel? That psychopathic fiend who would die at my hand the moment I had the opportunity.

Holding my chest, I demanded, "What's—what's Daniel's nickname?"

Kes smiled. "He hates it. That's why he sticks to his true name." He ran a hand through his hair. "Can't say I blame him, though."

Stop stalling!

"What is it?" I croaked.

His eyes tightened, staring at my shivering frame. "Buzzard. His nickname is Buzzard."

I couldn't breathe.

It's not him.

Then...

Oh, my God.

The betrayal. The unfairness.

Please, no.

I swayed on my feet as a black gust of vertigo took me prisoner. I fell forward, crashing into Kes's arms. "And Jethro's?" My voice was just a whisper. "What's his nickname?"

My heart roared. I felt sick. I felt suicidal.

Kestrel held me tight, his fingers digging into the bruises his brother left last night. The brother I'd believed was falling for my games.

But all along...was I falling for his?

Alarm at my sudden change of mood widened his eyes. "Nila, it's okay. Sit down and breathe." He tried to gather me close, but I flinched away. Blinking back the nausea and urge to topple, I breathed, "Tell me, Kes. What's Jethro's nickname?"

I waited with bated breath.

I cursed my flying heart.

I overheated with terror.

My sanity hinged on the answer Kestrel gave, but it was too late.

I already knew.

Of course, I knew.

Of course, it was true.

Why did I think otherwise?

My instincts blared an answer I didn't want to believe.

The name reverberated with every panicked breath.

Kes placed his large, warm hands—so unlike his older brother's icy ones—on my shoulders. "Jethro? He never goes by it. Never has."

I don't care. Tell me!

I swallowed back my scream. Impatience roared in my blood.

Kes sensed my unravelling. He narrowed his eyes, anger flushing his skin. "It's Kite."

I couldn't do it.

I collapsed, landing in his arms.

He huddled me close, pressing a kiss against my forehead.

"His nickname is Kite...but I think—I think you've known that all along."

I wanted to cry, but no tears came.

I wanted to rage, but no sound remained.

Him.

He'd not only stolen my body but my mind and fantasies, too.

He'd infiltrated me when I still believed in princes and fairy tales. He'd corrupted me before he'd come to steal me.

Kite.

Jethro.

Kite is Jethro.

A wail clawed up my throat.

Not only had I given my body to my mortal enemy, but I'd unlocked my heart for him, too.

He'd gotten under my skin. He'd heard my innermost desires.

He was playing me like a master of duplicity.

My ridiculous game at making him fall in love with me pulverised.

I had no chance at winning.

Not when faced with the proficient firstborn Hawk.

My salvation was now my damnation.

Jethro is Kite...

...

And he'd successfully trapped me in an aviary of deceit.

To be continued in…

Second Debt

Releasing Early 2015
Updates, Teasers, and Exclusive News will be released on
www.pepperwinters.com

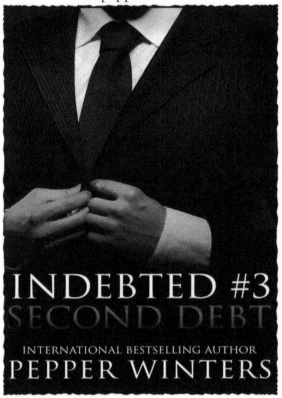

"I tried to play a game. I tried to wield deceit as perfectly as the Hawks. But when I thought I was winning, I wasn't. Jethro isn't what he seems—he's the master of duplicity. However, I refuse to let him annihilate me further."

Nila Weaver has grown from naïve seamstress to full-blown fighter. Every humdrum object is her arsenal, and sex…sex is her greatest weapon of all.
She's paid the First Debt. She'll probably pay more.
But she has no intention of letting the Hawks win.

Jethro Hawk has found more than a worthy adversary in Nila—he's found the woman who could destroy him. There's a fine line between hatred and love, and an even finer path between fear and respect.
The fate of his house rests on his shoulders, but no matter how much ice lives inside his heart, Nila flames too bright to be extinguished.

Add to **Goodreads**

About the Author

Pepper Winters is a NYT and USA Today International Bestseller. She wears many roles. Some of them include writer, reader, sometimes wife. She loves dark, taboo stories that twist with your head. The more tortured the hero, the better, and she constantly thinks up ways to break and fix her characters. Oh, and sex... her books have sex.

She loves to travel and has an amazing, fabulous hubby who puts up with her love affair with her book boyfriends. She's also honoured to wear the IndieReader Badge for being a Top 10 Indie Bestsellers, best BDSM series voted by the SmutClub, and recently signed a two book deal with Grand Central. Her books are currently being translated into numerous languages and will be in bookstores in the near future.

Her Dark Romance books include:
Tears of Tess (Monsters in the Dark #1)
Quintessentially Q (Monsters in the Dark #2)
Twisted Together (Monsters in the Dark #3)
Debt Inheritance (Indebted #1)
First Debt (Indebted Series #2)

Her Grey Romance books include:
Destroyed

Upcoming releases are
Ruin & Rule (Motorcycle romance)
Je Suis a Toi (Monsters in the Dark Novella)
Forbidden Flaws

To be the first to know of upcoming releases, please join Pepper's Newsletter (she promises never to spam or annoy you.)

http://eepurl.com/120b5

Or follow her on her website

www.pepperwinters.com

You can stalk her here:

Pinterest
Facebook Pepper Winters
Twitter
Website
Facebook Group
Goodreads

She loves mail of any kind: pepperwinters@gmail.com

Other Books by Pepper

Published Books
Tears of Tess (Monsters in the Dark #1)
Quintessentially Q (Monsters in the Dark #2)
Twisted Together (Monsters in the Dark #3)
Debt Inheritance (Indebted #1)
Destroyed (Grey Romance, Standalone)

Coming soon
Je suis a toi (Monsters in the Dark Novella) Coming End 2014
Ruin & Rule (Grand Central Published Motorcycle Book) Coming 2015
First Debt (Indebted #2) Coming End of 2014
Last Shadow
Forbidden Flaws Coming 2015
Ribbon (Date Unassigned)

All other titles and updates can be found on her **Goodreads Page.**

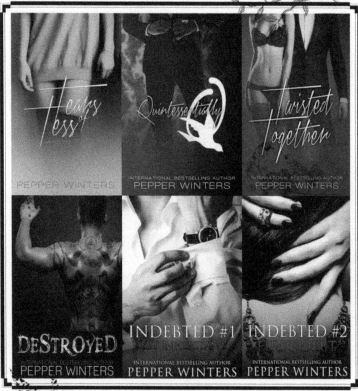

Animals by Maroon Five
Fight for my Love by Jack White
Dark Horse by Katie Perry
The Lonely by Christina Perri
Titanium by David Guetta
Bittersweet Symphony by The Verve
Warriors by Imagine Dragons
I know what you did in the dark by Fallout Boys
Budapest by George Ezra
Moth by Hellyeah
Desire by Meg Meyers
Time is Running Out by Muse
Roar by Katie Perry
Human by Christina Perri

Acknowledgements

This will be short and sweet. And I know I've forgotten a bunch of people, so I'm sending you extra hugs for that faux pas.

Thank you to Ari from Cover it! Designs for my amazing covers. I'm so in love.

Thank you to Aussie Lisa and Nina for being so amazingly supportive and awesome friends.

Thank you to Katrina, Tamicka, Kiki, Mandi, Melissa, Yaya, Cerian, Vicki, Vickie, Amy, Ellen, Michelle, and Natasha for reading the first copy of First Debt, typos and all. (I'm sure I missed someone in that line up. I'm SO sorry—forgive me?)

Thanks to Jenny from Editing4Indies and Erica Russikoff at Erica Edits for the amazing proofreading job. I recommend you ladies to anyone.

Thank you to Skye Callahan for being my writing partner extraordinaire. I think I talk to you more than I talk to my poor hubby.

Thanks so much to Aleatha Romig for always believing in me and being such a huge supporter.

Thanks to Nadine for running my street team and the amazing girls who help spread the word.

Thank you for my Pepper Pimpettes who do a fabulous job sharing and reviewing.

Thank you to The Rock Stars of Romance for hosting the review and blog tour.

Thank you to my readers who just make me feel so loved and appreciated in all things that I write.

Thank you to hubby for cooking me dinner, keeping me alive, and overlooking the fact I now work entirely in pyjamas.

And finally, thank you universe for making my dreams come true.

Other Book Blurbs & Reviews

Destroyed

This book enticed & enthralled me completely. Pepper's stories are like a fine piece of art. They are profound, unique, raw and beautiful—**Kristina, Amazon Review**

Pepper Winters has a ridiculous level of talent, and I'm in awe of how deeply she delves into her characters. There are not enough stars, seriously—**K Dawn, Amazon Reviewer**

If you like a bit of grey in your romance then you need to get this book because it's one of the best books I've read this year—**Bookfreak**

*

USA Today, #1 Erotica and Romantic Suspense Bestseller.

She has a secret.
I'm complicated. Not broken or ruined or running from a past I can't face. Just complicated.

I thought my life couldn't get any more tangled in deceit and confusion. But I hadn't met him. I hadn't realized how far I could fall or what I'd have to do to get free.

He has a secret.
I've never pretended to be good or deserving. I chase who I want, do what I want, act how I want.
I didn't have time to lust after a woman I had no right to lust after. I told myself to shut up and stay hidden. But then she tried to run. I'd tasted what she could offer me and damned if I would let her go.

Secrets destroy them.

Buy on all online retails & coming soon to bookstores

***

Tears of Tess (Book one of Monsters in the Dark) Book two: Quintessentially Q, and Book Three: Twisted Together, are available now

6 Holy Wow This Author Took Me On A Ride I Never Saw Coming and Left Me Speechless Stars. I've never rated a book 6 stars before so this gives you an idea of just how good I believe this book to be. This story will take you by the hand and show you how both darkness and light exist within all of us. It will ultimately take you by the heart and you will be so glad that you read it—***Hook Me Up Book Blog***

DARK AND HAUNTINGLY BEAUTIFUL....IT WILL LEAVE YOU BREATHLESS!!!!
Pepper Winters is a standout! An absolutely stunning debut!—***Lorie, Goodreads***

*

A New Adult Dark Contemporary Romance, not suitable for people sensitive to grief, slavery, and nonconsensual sex. A story about finding love in the strangest of places, a will of iron that grows from necessity, and forgiveness that may not be enough.

> *"My life was complete. Happy, content, everything neat and perfect. Then it all changed.*
> *I was sold."*

Tess Snow has everything she ever wanted: one more semester before a career in property development, a loving boyfriend, and a future dazzling bright with possibility.

For their two year anniversary, Brax surprises Tess with a romantic trip to Mexico. Sandy beaches, delicious cocktails, and soul-connecting sex set the mood for a wonderful holiday. With a full heart, and looking forward to a passion filled week, Tess is on top of the world.

But lusty paradise is shattered.

Kidnapped. Drugged. Stolen. Tess is forced into a world full of darkness and terror.

Captive and alone with no savior, no lover, no faith, no future, Tess evolves from terrified girl to fierce fighter. But no matter her strength, it can't save her from the horror of being sold.

Can Brax find Tess before she's broken and ruined, or will Tess's new owner change her life forever?

Forbidden Flaws, coming 2015

She's forbidden.
Saffron Carlton is the darling of the big screen, starlet on the red carpet, and wife of mega producer Felix Carlton. Her life seems perfect with her overflowing bank balance, adoring fans, and luxury homes around the world. Everyone thinks they know her. But no one truly does.
The silver limelight is tainted the day the couple announce their divorce.

He's flawed.
Raised in squalor, fed on violence and poverty, Cas Smith knows the underbelly of the world. He's not looking for fame or fortune. He's looking for a job to get him the hell away from the danger of illegal fighting, and comes face to face with the woman who ran all those years ago.
Unable to turn down her job offer, he agrees to be her bodyguard and personal trainer, all while she hides her secrets.

He had no intention of letting her back into his heart.
But neither of them were prepared for what happens when forbidden and flawed collide —fracturing the world they know, changing the rules forever.

Thank you so much for Reading

xxx

CPSIA information can be obtained
at www.ICGtesting.com
Printed in the USA
LVHW04s0219040918
589090LV00001B/223/P